"*Ten* is a book for people interested in finding a better way to live. I love the Ten Words and this fresh look at the ancient biblical text of the Ten Commandments. But mostly, I love Sean's perspective. It reminds me of something I tend to forget: Whether we worship in a meeting room with a *Big Book* or in a congregation that studies the Bible, we humans are more alike than we are different. We are at our best when we are encouraging one another to live well. I give it a ten."

Teresa McBean, executive director, National Association for Christian Recovery

"Sean Gladding reveals to us a grand biblical narrative refracted through ordinary people's stories. Like light reflected in broken shards of glass, the purity of God's vision for a peaceful, generous, restful, faithful world is described through the struggles and anxieties of everyday folk. You've never heard the Ten Commandments taught quite like this."

Michael Frost, author of *The Shaping of Things to Come* and *Exiles*

"Sean Gladding has done it again. In this immensely readable book, the goodness of God and the relevance of Scripture shine through. Sean draws us into a community of honest conversation by masterfully weaving together believable characters, biblical stories, theology and cultural reflection. As the story of Pastor John's Monday-morning coffee-shop group unfolds, the reader is helped to see that the Ten Commandments are an invitation to live in true freedom. I hope this book will be read and discussed widely, both inside and outside the church."

Lindsay Olesberg, author of *The Bible Study Handbook*

TEN

WORDS OF LIFE

FOR AN ADDICTED,

Compulsive,

CYNICAL, DIVIDED

AND WORN-OUT

Culture

SEAN GLADDING

IVP Books

An imprint of InterVarsity Press
Downers Grove, Illinois

InterVarsity Press
P.O. Box 1400, Downers Grove, IL 60515-1426
World Wide Web: www.ivpress.com
Email: email@ivpress.com

InterVarsity Press® is the book-publishing division of InterVarsity Christian Fellowship/USA®, a movement of students and faculty active on campus at hundreds of universities, colleges and schools of nursing in the United States of America, and a member movement of the International Fellowship of Evangelical Students. For information about local and regional activities, write Public Relations Dept., InterVarsity Christian Fellowship/USA, 6400 Schroeder Rd., P.O. Box 7895, Madison, WI 53707-7895, or visit the IVCF website at www.intervarsity.org.

All Scripture quotations, unless otherwise indicated, are taken from the New American Standard Bible®, copyright 1960, 1962, 1963, 1968, 1971, 1972, 1973, 1975, 1977, 1995 by The Lockman Foundation. Used by permission.

Cover design: Cindy Kiple
Interior design: Beth Hagenberg
Images: Diner sign: Alan Copson ©/Getty Images; neon cup: © Valerie Loiseleux /iStockphoto; blue sky: © PLAINVIEW/iStockphoto

ISBN 978-0-8308-3656-7 (print)
ISBN 978-0-8308-6486-7 (digital)

Printed in the United States of America ∞

Library of Congress Cataloging-in-Publication Data
A catalog record for this book is available from the Library of Congress.

P	21	20	19	18	17	16	15	14	13	12	11	10	9	8	7	6	5	4	3	2	1
Y	31	30	29	28	27	26	25	24	23	22	21	20	19	18	17	16	15	14			

To all those who read the paper

or watch the news and think,

There has to be a better way to live than this.

And to those who take personal inventory of their

own lives and respond in similar fashion.

Contents

Acknowledgments

This book has its origins in a series of sermons that I preached with Matt Russell and some friends at Mercy Street, the community in Houston, Texas, that I had the privilege of copastoring for seven years. Mercy Street is made up of all kinds of people, many of whom have been wounded in some way by a church or its members, or who are simply tired of church as they know it. Many members of the community are in recovery from some form of addiction—or they're trying. As the series unfolded, our community began to lean into these Ten Words as we discovered their liberating power, and as they confronted all the things we live in bondage to as human beings. They became words of hope for us as individuals and as a community. May they do the same for you.

My gratitude list for this book:

The members of the Wednesday night r:evolution group at Mercy Street who provided much of the fertile soil for both the sermon series and this book.

The members of Mercy Street, for telling me your stories with courage and vulnerability during the series and over the seven years my family shared life with you.

Matt Russell, for fostering communities where these kinds of conversations can happen, and for constant encouragement for the book from day one.

Rebecca Gladding, for changing everything by saying, "Stop trying to write a book and just tell a story."

Brad Flowers, for helpful advice on character development and dialogue in the early stages of writing.

Leslie Downing, for encouraging feedback when I really needed it.

Leslie Leyland Fields, for some very helpful input during the latter stages of writing.

Clay E., for your experience, strength and hope, which are found throughout these pages.

Pat Gerhard, Hendrick Floyd and Gretchen Lee Collins, for making Third Street Stuff such a great neighborhood space for conversation and writing. And, of course, for the coffee.

Carolyn and Dale Martin, for constant support and encouragement throughout the two years this book took to write.

Andrew Bronson and Adrianna Wright at IVP, for all the support, guidance and laughter.

Dave Zimmerman, for being such a patient editor and valued friend.

The One who calls us into freedom, and who gives us both power to choose it and grace when we don't.

The Ten Commandments—Who Cares?

Cause I need freedom now . . .

MUMFORD & SONS, "THE CAVE"

"Can you believe these idiots?"

The loud exclamation rose above the murmur of early morning conversation in the coffee shop. John, a regular and pastor of a church in the neighborhood, sighed as the serenity of the day's first sip of aromatic coffee was shattered. Looking up, he caught the eye of the man. "OK, Steve, I'll bite. Which particular idiots are we talking about this morning?"

The source of the exclamation, a local business owner, held up the newspaper he had been reading and jabbed a finger at the headline: "Ten Commandments Fight Is Costly,"[1] he recited, practically spitting the words out. Some of the other early morning regulars turned their attention toward Steve, anticipating one of his customary rants. He obliged.

"Seems like some good Christian council members in a couple of counties south of here decided the best use of taxpayers' money was to fight the ACLU so they could post copies of the Ten Commandments in their courthouses. They argued all the way up to the Supreme Court and lost, and now they owe the ACLU close to $500,000 in attorney fees." Steve turned back to the paper, "And I quote, 'Officials from the counties admit they do not know how they are going to pay the bill.'" With a snort of disgust he threw the paper down on the table. "What do you think about that, preacher?"

As the attention shifted from Steve to John, he took a long swig of coffee, wondering what it would be like to be able to simply drink a cup of coffee in his neighborhood café without being the resident expert on religion. "Well, why *would* they do that? As a matter of principle?"

"Pretty expensive principle," interjected Steve.

"Indeed. Maybe it was the belief that posting them will keep people on the straight and narrow?"

"But if the first time someone sees them is in a courthouse, don't you think it's a little too late by then?" That got a big laugh from the morning crowd. Steve stood and took a bow. John smiled.

"That's not exactly news, is it?" said someone at the bar. "People are always trying to post the Ten Commandments in public spaces." "Yeah," said her companion. "How many millions of dollars have been wasted arguing *that*?"

Jenny, a popular figure in the neighborhood who ran a nonprofit organization working with at-risk youth, jumped in. "Seriously. Those things are thousands of years old. Why does anyone care? It's not like people still go to church—no offense, John."

"None taken, Jenny."

Sam, long-time resident and a deacon in the local Baptist church, piped up from his stool at the bar. "But they're not just a religious symbol, are they? They're a pretty weighty cultural symbol—if you'll excuse my pun."

One of the baristas leaned around an espresso machine. "I read recently that whenever opinion polls are conducted about the Ten Commandments, 70 to 80 percent of Americans oppose removing them from public display. Yet at the same time only 40 percent of us can name more than four of them."

The other barista snorted. "Ha! Sounds like we know what they look like, but not what they are. How many could *you* name?" His friend shrugged.

Jenny chimed in again, "If it makes you feel better, I remember watching Stephen Colbert interview some House Representative who was sponsoring a bill to display the Ten Commandments in public buildings. When Colbert asked him to name them, he managed three."[2]

"You see," said Steve. "That's what I'm talking about. Another bunch of do-gooders posturing for their constituents."

Will, a retired law professor, spoke up. "Let's get back to your headline, Steve. To begin with, I wonder if spending $500,000 of taxpayers' money on this breaks the commandment 'Thou shalt not steal.'"

Steve laughed. "Too right!"

"But there has to be a reason for their choice to pursue this for so

long at such cost," Will responded. "It's easy to dismiss these officials as misguided religious zealots or do-gooders, but that may be
unfair. Perhaps they *are* motivated by religious beliefs, but I don't
think that's true for everyone who's in favor of posting them in
courtrooms. I wonder if these kinds of lawsuits originate with
people who have a deep sense that we've lost our way as a society."

A few people indicated their agreement with this sentiment.

"For all our talk of personal freedoms in the land of the free, there
seems to be a savage irony at work. We no longer feel free to walk
the streets after dark without fear, or to let our kids play in the street
during the day, or to let them do research for homework on the
Internet for fear of what they will stumble across. We are in bondage
to all manner of addictions. We are in debt up to our eyeballs in our
free market economy. We have freedom of speech, but we are not
free from increasingly—if not pervasively—being lied to, abused
verbally, or mocked."

Steve shifted in his seat. "OK, sure. So?"

"I wonder if the headline on the front page of the paper that has
you all riled up has its roots in what lies on the pages inside. Why
don't you read us a few of *those* headlines."

Steve started to flick through the paper, his words punctuated by
the rustling of the turning pages. "Copper Theft Set Stage for Blast";
"Teacher Accused of Sexual Contact with Student"; "Arsons Appear
Linked"; "Deputy Allegedly Traded Rent for Sex"; "Politician Center
of Attack Ads on Eve of Primary"; "Boyfriend Admits Abusing Baby";
"Meth Lab in Car." A grim silence followed this litany of woe.

"That's why some of us stopped reading the paper, right?" Will
continued. "And I wonder if that's what motivates some of the drive
to post the Ten Commandments in public spaces. This need to have
something concrete to point to in the light of such headlines and say,
'No—*this* is how we should treat each other.' Because it's hard to
believe that we're capable of doing those other things to each other."

"It wasn't like that in my day," Sam piped up. "When we were kids we played in the street all day. The only thing we were afraid of was getting in late for supper and getting a clip round the ear from our father. We knew right from wrong. I don't know about posting the Ten Commandments in courthouses—maybe we should tattoo 'em on people's foreheads."

This drew another round of laughter. Sam leaned forward. "Ah, but it's not the knowing, is it? It's the doing. When I was young, we all knew 'em—and did our best to keep 'em. So I'm all for getting back to the Ten Commandments—maybe those headlines would look a lot different if we did."

"That makes me think of a poem my mother taught me." The attention shifted back to Jenny. "It's by a British poet—I liked him because his poems were often short and easy to remember. This was always one of my favorites:

These are the good old days.
Just wait and see."[3]

Sam laughed.

Jenny gestured earnestly. "For all our belief in progress, don't we all sense that our common life is heading in the other direction? I love the kids I work with—they're good kids. But you all know the kind of realities they live with, how hard it is for them to make the choices we wish they would make. I don't think posting the Ten Commandments in courthouses—or even in schools for that matter—is going to change any of that."

"Truth be told," said Sam, "I doubt if most of the people in my church could tell you all ten of the commandments. Even those who say they ought to play an important role in society."

"Why do you think that is?"

"I don't know. Because what they represent is more important to us than their actual content?" Sam paused. "Or maybe because most of us don't have neighbors with asses to covet." There was a moment of silence before Steve roared with laughter. When Sam caught on, his cheeks colored. He turned to John and said gruffly, "What do you think, pastor?"

John, trying to hide a smile, turned the coffee mug in his hands as he thought. "I wonder if it's because deep down, if we're really honest, none of us likes to be told what to do. We really are quite fond of our personal freedom. Based on what I have observed of some of your driving habits, you consider the posted speed limit to be a suggestion rather than a rule. That is, until a police officer gives you an expensive lesson in hermeneutics."[4]

Sam laughed.

"That must be a preacher joke," observed Steve.

"So," continued John, "while we may agree in principle that we should have rules, that there should be sets of laws to help us all get along together in society, those rules are really for other people. Sure, we may have lost our way as a society—but that's because of *those* people, right? People like *us* are not the problem. So I don't need to be told what to do. As long as I'm not hurting anyone else, I should be free to do what I want. How many times have you heard people say something along those lines?"

Jenny wondered aloud, "But aren't these particular rules—the Ten Commandments—just a little out of date? Irrelevant, even? Take the one about the sabbath day. This idea of taking one day in seven to rest. What place does that have in a 24/7 culture? We can pretty much buy whatever we want, whenever we want."

"What about 'Thou shalt not bear false witness'?" Steve chimed in. "That's practically a national pastime when we're filing our taxes. Although I prefer to call it 'being creative with my accounting.'"

"Then there's 'Honor thy father and mother,'" called out a high school senior listening at a nearby table with some friends. "How are you supposed to do that when they treat you like you're still in diapers?" Another student said, "Yeah. Or when they're total hypocrites."

"Or when they do something to you that is unforgiveable." The conversation abruptly halted as Jenny said these words, a distant look on her face. Color rose in her cheeks as she realized she had spoken her thoughts out loud.

Sam spoke into the awkward silence, "'Thou shalt not kill'? Given that the last century was the bloodiest in human history, we've clearly given up on that one."

Steve leaped to his feet and walked over to the chalkboard. "Perhaps we should just scrap the Big Ten and come up with a new set of commandments that are a little more realistic." He erased a few poems and a rather impressive caricature of one of the baristas. "I'll get us started." He looked at the teenagers and wrote, "Thou shalt not text while driving."

"Thou shalt not take up two parking spots with your big-ass pickup," came the retort. Sam did a spit-take.

One of the students looked at another across the table. "Thou shalt not end a relationship by text message."

The early morning crowd proceeded to fire off more suggestions, which Steve furiously scribbled up.

A barista called out, "Thou shalt not abuse chalkboard privileges."

"And," said John, "thou shalt not give someone the bird in the parking lot after church."

More laughter.

John continued, "So we're able to come up with some new commandments—a new list of rules. Because isn't that how the majority of us have experienced the Ten Commandments? As a set of rules? Either rules that *those* people should keep, or rules that *those* people are trying to force on us. But rules, nonetheless. And as we've already noted, most of us don't like being told what to do. I wonder if the way the church has tended to talk about the Ten Commandments has left many of us with the impression that God is just the cosmic killjoy."

Jenny said, "And when our entire economy is fueled by advertising designed to make us dissatisfied with what we have, when the most popular show on TV is *American Idol*, when adultery is still an essential plot line for the few remaining daytime soaps, when our home offices are filled with supplies stolen from our actual offices, what place *do* those words carved in stone millennia ago have today?"

"Sounds like you can name more than the average person, Jenny!" said Will, with an admiring smile, which Jenny returned.

"But John," Sam chimed in, "didn't Jesus come to do away with the law anyway? 'For the law was given through Moses; grace and truth came through Jesus Christ.'"[5]

John rubbed his chin. "Yes. And no." Digging in his backpack for a moment, he pulled out a Bible and found the passage he was thinking about. "Jesus had this to say about that:

Don't suppose for a minute that I have come to demolish the Scriptures—either God's Law, or the Prophets. I'm not here to demolish but to complete. I am going to put it all together, pull it all together in a vast panorama. God's Law is more real and lasting than the stars in the sky and the ground at your feet. Long after stars burn out and earth wears out, God's Law will be alive and working.

Trivialize even the smallest item in God's Law and you will only have trivialized yourself. But take it seriously, show the way for others, and you will find honor in the kingdom. Unless you do far better than the Pharisees in the matters of right living, you won't know the first thing about entering the kingdom."[6]

John added, "For those Christians who claim to take the Ten Commandments seriously, as Jesus calls us to, I wonder if the truth is we don't take them seriously enough. I wonder if we're more like the Pharisees—the religious experts of Jesus' day—when it comes to living them out. And to those of us who think they're no longer important, Jesus says, 'I'm not here to demolish the law but to complete it. Long after stars burn out and the earth wears out, God's law will be alive and working.' So apparently, even if we think they're culturally irrelevant, we're stuck with them. God has given us a bunch of rules to follow, and the bad news is most of us don't even know what they are."

The scraping of chair legs signaled the departure of the students for school. One of them paused to say, "So they *are* just a bunch of rules then." John smiled and shook his head. "No, I don't think they're just a bunch of rules. But speaking of rules, you'd better head across the street if you don't want to start your week with a tardy."

As the teenagers left, Jenny leaned in. "Well if they're not rules, what are they?" Sam indicated he was very interested in hearing John's answer. John turned to Steve. "I don't mean to hijack your rant."

Steve laughed. "It's all good." He bowed and handed John the chalk. "I yield the chalkboard to you."

"I'm not sure I'll need it. But I *do* need another cup of coffee—why don't we all do any necessary refilling or emptying, and then let's see if we can't approach these Ten Words from another angle."

Coffee cups refilled, they took their seats again. John said, "How about we leave today's troubles behind for a while and go back a few millennia in time? To the story of the exodus, which is one of my favorite stories. You've seen the old Charlton Heston movie, right?"

Most of those listening in nodded.

"Picture this scene. You're part of a crowd of people standing at the foot of Mount Sinai. Your leader, Moses, goes up to talk to this God who has just set you free from slavery in Egypt, which has been your life's story to this point. From first light to nightfall, life has been one of toil, of tedious, back-breaking labor, building the pyramids and the great cities of Egypt, building these stone tributes to the power and wealth of the Pharaohs. But then in the not-too-distant past, everything suddenly changed. The land of Egypt is swept with ten plagues, which pollute water, devastate crops, kill livestock and turn Egypt into a stinking cesspool. Then you're told to gather in your homes and kill a lamb, splash its blood over the doorway so that the angel of death might pass over your family.

Then in the middle of the night, you grab a cloak and some food and you leave the only home you've ever known to head out into the desert." John took a swig of coffee before continuing.

"You arrive at the Red Sea and turn to see the dust clouds thrown up by the wheels of Pharaoh's chariots that are pursuing you to carry you back into slavery once more. Suddenly, there's Moses raising his staff over the waters, and in amazement you watch as the water piles up on two sides, leaving a path for you to walk across to safety. But as you walk through on dry land, Pharaoh's army follows you into the watery tunnel. As you reach the far side and turn to look, you watch God bring the sea down upon them and destroy the people who have oppressed you your whole life. Then you turn to follow Moses into the desert to who-knows-where, to find who-knows-what."

Steve interjected. "Hey, you're pretty good at this stuff." He grinned. "You should think about doing it professionally."

John laughed. "Thanks, Steve. I'll bear that in mind."

"Now you're standing at the base of the mountain and you hear the rumble of thunder; you know that this liberating God is speaking. You're free, but in many ways you're still a slave, because that's been your identity since birth. You've been told what to do your whole life. Every minute of every day has been dictated to you by the Egyptians. And now suddenly you're free—no one to tell you what to do. But you have absolutely no idea how to begin this brand new life that you have been given. As you look around, you realize that pretty much everyone else in the crowd is thinking the same thing that you are: *Now what do we do?* You never thought you'd be in this place. You have no idea where this place even is! You're completely lost, you're out in the desert, at the foot of some mountain, just a bunch of slaves who have seen this God do some amazing things, but now . . . What comes next?

"You look up at the mountain. You hear the thunder and see the flashes of lightning among the black clouds, and you think to yourself, *Moses is up there getting some new rules for us to live by. God's telling Moses what we're supposed to do—and judging by all that storming, we're not going to like it very much.* But when Moses finally comes down the mountain, this is what you hear:

> *You have seen what I did to Egypt and how I carried you on eagles' wings and brought you to me. If you will listen obediently to what I say and keep my covenant, out of all peoples you'll be my special treasure. The whole Earth is mine to choose from, but you're special: a kingdom of priests, a holy nation.*[7]

"Do you get what you expected, a bunch of rules? No, you get *chosen.* By God. The God who told Moses,

> *I've taken a good, long look at the affliction of my people in Egypt. I've heard their cries for deliverance from their slave masters; I know all about their pain. And now I have come down to help them, pry them loose from the grip of Egypt, get them out of that country and bring them to a good land with wide-open spaces, a land lush with milk and honey.*[8]

"Instead of rules, God offers you a relationship, a covenant relationship. A marriage proposal, if you like. You hear words that make little if any sense to you at this stage in your life. 'You'll be a kingdom, you'll be priests, you'll be a holy nation.' But you look around and all you see are slaves. There aren't any kings here; there aren't any priests here. And don't you need land to be a nation? But you're just somewhere in the desert. Then God's words begin to sink in, and you hear them for what they truly are: the promise of an utterly different future than you could have dreamed of while enslaved in Egypt. You begin to realize that God is offering to adopt you, to make of you a brand new family, to look out over all the peoples of the earth and say, 'I choose *you* to be my people. I choose *you* to make covenant with.'"

John looked each of them in the eye. "And that covenant, I believe, is not a set of rules, even if that is how the church may have characterized the Ten Commandments. I believe the covenant is more like a set of practices that God invites the people to place at the very center of their lives. Practices given for the purpose of shaping the identity of God's people when they're lost in the desert and don't know who they are. Practices that, if embraced, will transform them from slaves into human beings. Humans created in the image of God, the God who is now inviting them into God's family. Humans who will experience the freedom we were created for."

Taking a swig of coffee, John looked at the thoughtful expressions on the others' faces. Jenny asked the first question. "OK, let's say you're right, and these aren't just a bunch of rules to live by. They're a covenant."

"An invitation to a relationship," Sam added.

"Right, a relationship. A marriage proposal, didn't you say?"

John nodded.

"Well," Jenny continued, "I'm not married, but I've been to a bunch of weddings. And what I heard you say sounds very different than the wedding vows my friends made. This 'proposal' sounds very conditional: '*If* you keep my covenant, you will be my people.' Doesn't sound very 'til death us do part.'"

Sam said, "That's right—that is what it sounds like. But why wouldn't it sound like that? Just about every relationship I've ever had has been conditional. Starting way back in kindergarten. 'If you let me play with your toys, I'll be your friend.' And then it just continues throughout our lives."

Steve said, "Like those kids over there earlier. I've overheard one say, 'I'll date you exclusively if you have sex with me.'" He shook his head.

"If you only drink on the weekends, then I won't leave you." They looked at Jenny. "That's what Mom told my dad, or some variant on that theme, like, a hundred times. Or Dad, to me, 'If you go to that college, I'll pay your tuition.' We call it love, but it's really just selfishness. It's about giving something to get something. It's about control. How are the Ten Commandments any different than that?

'Keep this covenant and you'll be mine.'" She paused. "But let me down and it's all over." Her eyes dropped to her coffee mug.

John waited until she looked up again. "I know that's what this sounds like. And maybe that *is* what's going on in the desert—the offer of a conditional relationship. The threat to end it if they don't keep their end of the deal. But what if it's not a threat? What if it *is* a promise?"

Jenny frowned. "What do you mean?"

"What if God is saying, 'If you keep covenant with me, if you do these things, then you *will* be my people. You'll be a people that reflect who I am to those around you.' I wonder if it's not so much God who reveals to us the Ten Commandments, but the Ten Commandments that reveal God to us.[9] 'If you keep these practices, then you will see in yourselves—and each other—the image of God that was almost wiped out through years of slavery. And you won't be slaves to anything again. Not even to yourselves. You will be truly free. If you keep my covenant, you *will* be my people.'"

"I think I get what you're saying," Jenny observed. "But the commandments themselves—Thou shalt not—that still sounds like a rule to me."

Will spoke up, "Here's something I find interesting, Jenny. In the Bible, what we call the Ten Commandments are only referred to as 'commandments' once.[10] Every other time they're talked about, they're referred to as 'the Ten Words,' the Ten Words that God spoke to God's people. That's why we sometimes call them 'the Decalogue'—from the Greek words for 'ten' and 'word,' *deka* and *logos*. They're not commandments in the usual sense, as there's no punishment listed for breaking them."

"Right," said John. "That's another reason why I believe these words are not a list of rules but are instead practices that God invites us to take up in our lives. Practices God has given us to shape our lives and to shape our communities. Practices given to protect us from ourselves, to save us from our darkest impulses. The impulses that got shaped in us when we were slaves, just like those folks standing in the desert. The impulses that lead to the headlines Steve read aloud from today's paper."

"I wonder if we're not much different from that crowd gathered there thousands of years ago," John went on. "In many ways we're just a bunch of slaves. Our identity has been shaped by the things we've become enslaved to, whether voluntarily or not. Things like our addictions and compulsions. Our need to consume, to acquire, to know how we stack up against everyone else. Our perfectionism. Our need to be right.

"Even our religion, which instead of setting us free, has made us slaves to all the hoops we're required to jump through in order to be acceptable to God—even as we're told that God loves us unconditionally. All these things have power over us. They control us, whether we like it or not, and whether we're willing to admit it or not. We need to be set free." John paused. "I know that's true for me."

"That's my conviction," said John. "The Ten Commandments really are Ten Words. Ten Words that can bring life, that can breathe life into us as we adopt them together. I used to see them as coming from a God with a hand raised, just waiting to give me the back of it when I messed up. But today I believe they come from a God who extends a hand of friendship to us and says, 'Will you receive these Ten Words as my gift to you, that you might learn how to live together as I always intended?' A God who says, 'Do these things and they will set you free. They aren't a bunch of rules; they are the path to freedom. Adopt these practices and you will discover how to love yourself, how to love others and how to love me.'"

Sam interjected, "Which sounds a lot like how Jesus summed up the Ten Commandments: 'Love God, and love your neighbor as yourself.'"[11]

"Exactly!" responded John. "The Ten Words begin with, 'I am the Lord your God' and they end with 'your neighbor.' Between these two words lies the description of what it means to love God and neighbor. 'Do these and you will be my people: adopt these practices and I will be your God. Adopt these practices, these Ten Words, and they will guide you toward relationships that are built on trust and not on fear; trust of God and trust of each other.' Maybe they're not only a word of hope for us as individuals or for the church, but also for a society that has profoundly lost its way."

Steve picked up his paper. "So you think these Ten Words can somehow magically stop all the stuff we read about in here? That I can stop worrying about someone ruining my A/C unit to get the copper, or that I don't have to jump every time a car backfires because I think another person is getting shot in my neighborhood?"

John responded, "No, Steve, I'm not saying that. The Ten Words won't somehow magically protect us *from* evil. But the Ten Words may protect us from *committing* evil. If my friends in Alcoholics Anonymous have taught me one thing, it's this: we can only take care of our side of the street. We cannot control what other people do.

"Like I said, the Ten Words check our darker impulses, our slave impulses. They warn us that if we choose to nurture those impulses they might bring about terrible consequences. Because the painful truth is this: no matter what we do, we cannot control life. We cannot save ourselves from the very things we find in these Ten Words: betrayal, theft, envy, greed, deception, even murder. We can't save ourselves from those things happening to us. Nor can we save ourselves from the very impulses that might cause us to violate these Ten Words and commit acts that wound people deeply. I really believe all of us are capable of such violations. Some of us have done so in the past. I certainly have."

John looked around the circle of faces. "Some of us might be doing so right now. And those violations leave deep, lifelong wounds. You and I know that they tear the heart out of friendships, out of marriages, out of communities, out of churches. My guess is that most of us have been wounded profoundly in at least one of these ways, and we continue to feel the pain of them deeply."

John looked up to see that several others had been listening in on the conversation. There was a palpable heaviness in their corner of the coffee shop. "Saint Augustine said, 'Love God and then do what you like.' We say, 'Do what you like.'"

Steve looked at John. "And then spend the rest of our lives wondering, *Why don't I like what I do?*"

John clapped his hands together. "I've got an idea. I've been thinking about the next sermon series I want to preach for my community. I've never preached on the Ten Commandments." He looked at Steve. "Mostly because I'm not sure how people would react, for all the reasons we've been talking about this morning. But why not? After all, I've obviously got some pretty strong opinions about them—mostly because of the less-than-helpful ways we tend to approach them."

"That's great, preacher," said Steve. "Just don't expect to see me front and center on Sunday mornings." Steve's declaration lifted the mood, and John joined in the laughter.

"I wouldn't expect to, Steve." John picked up the paper and waved it around. "I imagine you'll be preaching to your own congregation right here!" Jenny groaned loudly, and the whole group broke out laughing. Steve took it in stride, tipping his hat to Jenny and standing for another bow.

"But that's not my idea," continued John. "I'm not asking you to come and *listen* to the sermons. I'm asking you to help me *prepare* them. To ask questions. To tell me where these Ten Words intersect with your life, regardless of what you think about them or what other people say about them. Because even though the Ten Words were spoken to the crowd gathered at Mount Sinai, they were addressed in the second person singular: *You.* The God who has set them free and wants them to live in freedom, speaks to each person gathered there directly. These are words that meet me right where I live, telling me what to do with my stuff, with my relationships, with my genitals."

"Awk-ward," said Jenny.

John laughed. "Yet while the crowd is addressed as individuals, it is not as individuals that they will practice—or not—these Ten Words. It is only as the community adopts them that we will understand what they mean. Because left to my own devices, I am fully capable of understanding them in ways that make little or no demand on my life, leaving me like a Pharisee, feeling confident about my own righteousness while condemning others. Which I think is what really gets your goat, right, Steve?"

"Absolutely. It's like you said, spending $500,000 of taxpayers' money for the right to post 'Thou shall not steal' in your courthouse seems pretty hypocritical to me."

"Right. So, what do you say? Most of us are here when the door opens on Monday mornings—how about we spend an hour or so talking through one of the Ten Words every week." John looked each of them in the eye. "I'm serious—you would really help me."

"Sounds good to me," said Sam.

"And me," said Jenny.

They looked at Steve. "Are you sure you want my opinionated self in the mix?"

John punched him on the shoulder. "Of course. Who else is going to keep me on the straight and narrow?"

"OK, I'm in. But I reserve the right to do some research ahead of time. So what's the first word?"

John picked up his Bible.

I am GOD, your God,
who brought you out of the land of Egypt,
out of a life of slavery.[12]

"Well, if you start there," observed Steve, "you're going to lose me from the get-go. Seeing as how I'm not convinced there is a God."

"I'll tell you what, Steve. Are you convinced that people are dissatisfied with what they have?"

Steve snorted. "Convinced? Our whole economy is fueled by people dissatisfied with what they have!"

"Well why don't we start there then, with the Tenth Word, and then work our way back to the First Word.[13] I imagine you might have something to say about 'coveting your neighbor's ass.'"

This time Sam joined in the laughter.

Steve said, "All right, preacher. It's a deal. Next Monday at 7. And how about you find some of your church folk to bring too—I'd be interested in what the amateurs have to say, as well as your professional self."

"That's an interesting way of putting it, Steve. You're on. I know a few folk who will show up for anything if there's coffee involved. And regardless of how the sermons turn out, it will probably do me good to start the week with a little intellectual conversation . . . and some soul searching. Feel free to invite anyone else you think might be up for a little of that!"

Sam stretched and asked for a cup to go. Jenny opened her laptop and returned to the grant proposal she had barely enough time to write. Today's conversation had been interesting, but she wondered if she had time for ten weeks of conversation about something that had little bearing on her life. And why had she said that stuff about her family? Steve returned to the paper, clearly satisfied with the morning's conversation and eager to mix it up in the weeks to come. John was already second-guessing himself. But he recognized he also felt invigorated in a way he hadn't for quite some time. As John walked out, Will said, "Should be an interesting few weeks, my friend."

"We'll see," said John. "We'll see."

1

From Envy to Contentment

The Tenth Word

> *The best minds of my generation are thinking*
> *about how to make people click on ads.*
>
> JEFF HAMMERBACHER

> *If I hadn't seen such riches*
> *I could live with being poor.*
>
> JAMES, "SIT DOWN"

> *You shall not covet your neighbor's house;*
> *you shall not covet your neighbor's wife or his*
> *male servant or female servant or his ox*
> *or his donkey or anything that*
> *belongs to your neighbor.*
>
> EXODUS 20:17

John removed his motorcycle helmet, a grin stretching from ear to ear. It had been a brisk if short ride to the coffee shop. As he walked across the parking lot, he saw Steve sitting across from Will at one of the tables outside, smoking a cigarette and reading the paper.

"Morning, Steve. Morning, Will."

Steve looked up. "Morning, preacher! You're looking mighty pleased with yourself."

Will laughed. "Of course he does. He's got beautiful weather for his day off."

Steve looked from one to the other. "So you guys know each other, then?"

Will replied, "Oh, John and I go way back. I could tell you all kinds of stories about the preacher here."

Steve looked back at John. "I'm all ears!"

"I'm sure you are, Steve," said John. "But how about you let me get a cup of coffee first."

"We'll be coming in right behind you—but only after I've heard at least one story." Steve turned back to Will, who looked at John and shrugged. John smiled, then noticed a familiar car pulling into the parking lot. He walked across to greet the occupants as they got out.

"Hi, Rick. Hey, Carlos. Thanks for coming. Ready for that first cup of coffee of the day?"

The driver, a stout figure with a salt-and-pepper beard, snorted. "Hardly! I've already seen off a pot at home." He looked at the young man beside him, who was yawning and running his fingers through matted hair. "Although I imagine mister bedhead here could use a cup."

Carlos gave him a mock scowl. "Especially if you're buying, old man."

"Hey, I gave you a ride. You're the one buying the coffee." Throwing an arm around the young man's shoulders, Rick steered him toward the door. "I'll even let you buy me a bagel!"

John started to walk over with them, but then spotted Jenny riding up on her bicycle. As he walked across to greet her, a car pulled in and the driver honked. John looked up, and when he saw the loud print of the occupant's dress, he smiled.

"Morning, Jenny. If Sam's seated at the bar, I think the gang's all here."

Jenny pulled her bag out of a pannier, and then locked her bike. Swinging the bag over her shoulder, she said, "Well, let's go find a table."

The last arrival walked across to them, and John said to her, "Did you choose the dress to match your hair color, or dye your hair to match the dress?"

The woman twirled around. "I don't recall which came first. But don't I look fabulous?"

Jenny laughed, as did John. "As fabulous as always, Sarah. Glad you could join us."

Sarah looked at Jenny. "And who is this beautiful young lady?"

"I'm Jenny."

"And I'm Sarah. Delighted to meet you."

John grabbed his helmet off the table as they made their way to the door, and held the door open for them before entering with a spring in his step.

Sam was seated on his usual stool at the bar. He had pulled a couple of tables together next to him. John, steaming cup of coffee in hand, walked up to the group now seated there, and seven faces turned to greet him. Sam said, "We've all introduced ourselves, so now it's over to you, John."

"Thanks so much for coming." He took the seat that Steve held out for him. "I must confess, I've really been looking forward to this morning, and I'm so glad you all came. I know most of you have jobs to get to, so I'll try to keep our conversation to an hour or thereabouts. How about we jump right in, and I'll read the Tenth

Word to remind us where we're starting out?" He pulled his Bible out of an inside jacket pocket.

No lusting after your neighbor's house—or wife or servant or maid or ox or donkey. Don't set your heart on anything that is your neighbor's.[1]

As he put the Bible down on the table, the group looked at him expectantly. "Do you remember the London riots in the summer of 2011?"

"Of course," said Steve, "it was all over the news here."

John continued, "I was making breakfast for my family one morning that week and listening to the BBC World Service's *Newshour*. For several nights the riots had struck different parts of London and other major cities in the United Kingdom. I was wondering if the violence affected any of my friends who live there. As I listened, the newscaster described the violence, property destruction and looting. With sirens wailing in the background, a reporter interviewed a young girl. The conversation went something like this.

'Why are you out here doing this?'
'To show the police and the rich that we can do what we like.'
'Who are the rich?'
'You know, people with money. People who own businesses.'
'That's why you're stealing from them?'
'Yeah, to show them we can do what we like.'

"At the time commentators seemed at a loss to explain why this was happening. Unlike the Occupy Wall Street movement that started a little later here in the United States, these riots didn't appear to be rooted in political protest or social unrest. There were no marches, no banners or placards with slogans. No one was giving speeches. It was just mobs of mostly young people looting, smashing windows and burning cars. People were destroying property and taking what they wanted, 'to show them we can do what we like.'"

Sam snorted, "And what they liked, apparently, was other people's stuff."

"Either as something to take for themselves," added Steve, "or to destroy so that other people no longer had it."

John nodded, "Right. I remember thinking at the time that after the streets had been swept clear of broken glass, after the last op-ed piece had been written and the numerous explanations had been offered, what we were left with was a graphic example of why we've been given the Tenth Word, and the consequences of ignoring it."

Sam said, "Absolutely. They were just a bunch of thugs. Hooligans—isn't that what they call them over there? Opportunists. No respect for other people's property."

"I must confess that I had similar thoughts as I scrambled the eggs for breakfast that morning," offered John. "I opened up some distance between myself and the mob, and was enjoying a sense of moral superiority. 'How can people do such things?'

"But when that thought about the Tenth Word popped into my head, all my moral indignation went out the window." John leaned forward. "You see, while I may not have been in the mob stealing and looting, nor, tragically, taking someone's life, I think such behavior does have its roots in the Tenth Word—'You shall not covet.' And coveting is something I'm well acquainted with. I imagine that the young woman interviewed on the radio didn't wake up one day and just decide, *I think I'll destroy some property today. I think I'll steal some stuff tonight.* Nor did someone wake up and say, *When I hit the streets tonight, I think I'll kill anyone who gets in my way.* The behavior of the mob, which we condemn, began with a desire. A desire I'm all too familiar with.

"I've had my old Harley out there," pointing his thumb toward the parking lot, "for twenty years."

Will interjected, "And it looks like it."

"I know it does," John shot back. "When I wheeled it out of the garage this morning, it was its usual temperamental self and took a while to get started. But as I rode over here I wasn't thinking about how beat up it looks. Or how I sometimes have to bump start it on cold mornings. I was just enjoying the beautiful morning and the brisk air on my face. And later on I'll feel those same things as I ride out into the country and maybe get my knee down around a few bends."

He paused. "But then I'll stop at my favorite little diner for lunch, and I'll pull up next to the cook's custom Night Train."

Jenny and Sam looked confused. Will said, "That's his dream bike."

"Right, sorry," said John. "Anyway, I'll get off my bike, and chances are I'll look at his ride and then down at mine, and some of the shine will get taken off the day. On my best days I'll just feel a twinge of jealousy. On my worst . . ."

Steve spoke up, "You're not the only one, preacher. I feel that way about my neighbor's car. It's all I can do to keep mine on the road. He seems to switch his out every other month." He looked around the group. "What about you all? What do you covet?"

"For me," said Rick, "it's my buddy's golf swing. I know it sounds stupid, but as much as I love the guy, when we play golf, more often than not I'm hoping he has a bad game rather than that I'll have a good one."

"My best friend's family." The attention turned to Jenny. "I love and hate being over there for dinner—it reminds me of everything I don't have in my own."

"Clothes," said Sarah. "Specifically, my sister's wardrobe. And, if I'm honest, the body it's displayed on."

"The way my family idolizes my brother." Carlos looked down. "I guess he'll always be the good son, and I'll always be the screwup."

There was an awkward silence, which Will broke. "It wouldn't surprise me to discover that your brother is envious of you." Carlos looked at him questioningly. "Being the 'good son' can be a heavy burden to bear," observed Will. The look on Carlos's face suggested he wasn't convinced.

Will turned to the wider group. "There's so much to envy, isn't there? Houses. Careers. Marriages. Children. Education. Beauty. Athletic ability. Physique. Skin. Hair. Talent. Good fortune."

"Mabel Lewis's Sunday school attendance record." Everyone looked at Sam. He shrugged. "Hey, nobody's perfect." They all laughed.

"OK," said John. "Back to the London riots. My guess is, Sam, that many of the people who hit the streets during those nights envied what other people had, which they saw was beyond their own reach. And so when the opportunity came to obtain the object of their desire, they reached out and took it—literally. And the frustration they felt was poured out in destruction of property."

"But . . ." began Sam.

John interrupted, "I'm not trying to justify their behavior. But that behavior began with the same feelings you and I have just admitted to. We may not be as different from the mob as we like to think we are."

He turned to the whole group. "Can I bounce some of the stuff off you I've been thinking about the Tenth Word?"

"That's why we're here, right?" said Steve.

"OK. It seems to me that covetousness—or envy—is a good place to start thinking about the Ten Words. Coveting opens the door to so much of what the other nine Words prohibit. Envying our neighbor's stuff can lead to stealing it—if not from our neighbor, from somewhere else. It can even lead to murder. Obtaining credit to purchase what we covet may involve deception."

"Yes, mister loan officer," said Steve. "Those numbers are solid."

Jenny added, "And it's not just from our side. 'Low APR'? Sure, till you miss a payment. 'Only 10 Easy Payments'? I've never made an easy payment in my life!"

John nodded. "Coveting our neighbor's spouse may lead to adultery. The Tenth Word opens up the world of all our disordered desires and all their repercussions. Here's the key, I think. The problem is not with desire itself. It's with the *object* of our desire: that which belongs to our neighbor. As the Book says, God may have made us a little lower than the angels, but our concern seems to be to climb a little higher than the Joneses. We become envious. My friend Matt defines envy with this equation." John stood and wrote on the chalkboard.

Envy = Desire + Resentment

Sarah laughed. "I'm going to have to remember that!"

Carlos elbowed Rick. "And remember, resentment is the number one offender, 'Tiger.'"[2]

Sam said, "So what you're saying is that it's not wrong that we want something. It's that we want it because our *neighbor* has it, and we resent them for having it."

"Exactly," said John. "We're jealous. We wonder, *How come they get to have that and I don't?* Something that is quite ordinary, say, a lawnmower, suddenly becomes extraordinary if our neighbor purchases a new one—especially if it's a ride-on. The problem is not primarily that I see him riding his mower and it makes me jealous: the problem is that I see him as my competitor and not my neighbor."[3]

"So," said Steve, "instead of being pleased for him, I resent him. Either because he has one and I don't, or because now that means I have to buy one."

Jenny spoke up, "That shouldn't surprise us though, right? Our entire economy relies on this dynamic. From the moment we're born, our desires are being shaped and molded by the world around us. And the world around us encourages us to covet—to want what other people have that we don't. We read magazines full of beautiful, shiny people who drive beautiful, shiny cars and have beautiful, shiny things, and we want what they have. We may love to sing 'America the Beautiful,' but we struggle to catch a glimpse of it between the billboards that litter the landscape. Advertising is a major national industry."

Will chimed in, "You could almost argue that it's a religion, in that it deals with questions of meaning and identity. Its high priests live on Madison Avenue, and we flock to the temple to worship the gods they bring to us—and get mad when we have to park in the furthest corner of the parking lot of the mall before completing our pilgrimage. Americans live with more abundance than at any time in history, and yet we're increasingly dissatisfied with what we have."

"And," added John, "that abundance actually fuels our dissatisfaction. The more things we have to compare with our neighbor, the more opportunities we have to come up short. Even if we get to the point where we have all that we could possibly want, the omnipresent advertising industry is there to fuel our seemingly insatiable desires."

Steve said, "My favorite news magazine has a section called 'And for those who have everything . . .' which features some absolutely ludicrous products. Which suggests to me that none of us will ever think we have 'everything.'"

John said, "Our economy is driven by covetousness. If we're not working more hours, we won't be able to buy more stuff, and if we're not buying more stuff, then the economy is going to lag. It's practically our patriotic duty to shop—on credit if necessary. And, until the recent global recession, it has always felt necessary. We are a nation of consumers."

Sam piped up, "Ain't that the truth. The days are long gone when we walked into the general store with our list of what we actually needed, gave it to the employee who walked into the back and came back with those items in a sack for us to buy. Some bright spark at Woolworth's came up with the idea of putting the merchandise out front where we could see it, touch it, smell it—desire it. And the rest, as they say, is history."

"And old history at that," said John. "Coveting what belongs to our neighbor is as old as humanity itself. God created the first humans and a world where all of life could flourish. God gave them every kind of fruit and vegetable to enjoy, except for that of just one tree. The man and the woman walked with God in the cool of the evening, and life was good. At least it was until Mad–hisssss–on Avenue showed up."

Steve groaned.

"And introduced envy into Eden. 'Look at what God has,' said the serpent. 'All that knowledge of good and evil. And he's keeping it all for himself. But if you eat this fruit you'll be just like him!'"

John picked up his Bible.

When the woman saw that the tree was good for food, and that it was a delight to the eyes, and that the tree was desirable to make one wise, she took from its fruit and ate; and she gave also to her husband with her, and he ate.[4]

Sam scratched his head. "Huh. I guess I never noticed that before. It almost sounds as if she hadn't really paid much attention to the fruit of the tree until the serpent pointed to it. As if she had no real desire to eat it until the serpent invited her to take her eyes off the abundance of the garden and look at the one tree she couldn't eat from."

Jenny chimed in, "It's like the serpent put up billboards to obscure all the other trees and then shone a spotlight on that one tree before saying, 'You deserve this. You need this. You have a right to this. You'll be just like God.'"

"That's a great visual, Jenny." John scribbled a note. "Life couldn't have been any better for them, but as envy reared its ugly head for the first time, they began to tell themselves the lie that eating the fruit would make their life better, and they let themselves believe the lie until they acted on it." He shook his head. "How many times have you and I done just that?"

"And so desire was let loose until it was consummated," John noted, "and as the juice dribbled down their chins an emptiness and fear was born in them. An emptiness and fear that I'm all too familiar with. What happened to them is what happens to us when we believe the lie: our world begins to crumble around us.

"And so it began. Coveting what belongs to our neighbor. In the garden it led to reaching for what wasn't theirs. Outside the garden, it led to murder." John turned the page. "The children of the first humans—Cain, the farmer, Abel the shepherd—bring an offering to God. It does not appear that God asked for an offering—apparently they just choose to make one."

Cain brought an offering to the LORD of the fruit of the ground. Abel, on his part also brought of the firstlings of his flock and of their fat portions. And the LORD had regard for Abel and for his offering; but for Cain and for his offering He had no regard. So Cain became very angry and his countenance fell.[5]

John commented, "It's not clear why God preferred Abel's offering over his brother's. But clearly Cain coveted the approval his brother received. God confronts Cain's anger and articulates the choice that lay before him. 'If you do well, will not your countenance be lifted up? And if you do not do well, sin is crouching at the door; and its desire is for you, but you must master it.'"[6]

"Again," John observed, "it's not clear what it would mean for Cain to 'do well,' but it appears that God is offering Cain the chance to gain the approval he covets, while acknowledging that Cain may well make a different choice."

Will shook his head sadly. "And tragically, Cain makes that choice, and his envy of his brother leads to murder. 'If I can't have God's approval, then neither can he.'"

John continued, "God comes to Cain and asks him where his brother is. And Cain's response gets to the heart of why I think we so desperately need the Tenth Word. 'I do not know. Am I my brother's keeper?'[7] When I read that this week, I found myself wanting God to respond like this: 'Yes! Of course you are your brother's keeper! Which means you should know where he is. That's what it means to be brothers!' And what it means to be neighbors. But Cain apparently saw Abel as his competitor for God's approval, not his brother, and so he killed him."

Reaching into his backpack, John pulled out another book and turned to the page he had bookmarked. "As David Hazony points out, the word play in Hebrew reveals the deeper truth behind Cain's response to God's invitation to come clean:

> The word 'keeper' (shomer) has already appeared once in Genesis in verb form, where Adam is put into the garden 'to work it and to keep it' (ul'shomro). Cain tilled the land like his father, working it to produce his own food, but he has failed . . . to be a keeper, a caretaker of humanity, [which is] to expand beyond our own selves and see to the flourishing of our world, beginning with our brothers.[8]

"Instead of keeping his brother, Cain has killed his brother. Because he coveted what his brother—his neighbor—had."

Carlos spoke up, "That's terrible. But a bit extreme, right? I mean, I would never kill someone to get what I wanted."

"I wonder," said Jenny, "if our coveting does sometimes lead to death and destruction, but we just don't connect the dots. Maybe this Word isn't only about my literal neighbor."

Blank looks greeted Jenny's comment.

Jenny leaned forward. "You said we're a nation of consumers. We want bigger houses, bigger cars, bigger everything. All that requires more and more energy. We have 6 percent of the world's population, but we consume 25 percent of the world's oil. We're addicted to cheap energy to keep our consumer lifestyle going. We'll go to war to keep it flowing, and tens of thousands of our global neighbors die. We'll blast the tops off mountains here to get the coal out cheaply, or frack natural gas out of the ground and pollute ground water sources for generations to come. And all this to power an economy that consumes more and more crap that comes in all kinds of packaging that we'll dump in the ground or ship to poor neighborhoods where we'll burn it and make people breathe all kinds of toxins."

Steve jumped in. "Don't forget bigger churches." He looked at John. "When the weather permits, I sit outside here on Sunday mornings and watch all those people drive out of the neighborhood to go to one of those megachurches. They drive by other churches to get there and then sit in their massive air-conditioned or heated auditoriums. No doubt they're singing about loving God and loving their neighbors, all the time burning up all that oil to sit in comfort for an hour or so. All while we've got people right here in this neighborhood who can't afford to turn their heat up—or even *on*—when it's freezing cold outside. Maybe you could preach on *that* this Sunday."

Jenny jumped in again. "Steve, I'm not just pointing my finger at other people. I'm pointing it right back at myself." She held up her cell phone. "I love my phone and all I can do with it. And I *know* the conditions the people who assemble it work in. I also know the toll in human life that mining the minerals for my phone takes and the impact it has on the environment. If geography no longer determines who my neighbor is, then my envy of friends' technology, my desire to have the latest version of that phone, my need to keep my home at a comfortable temperature—all those things contribute to the misery of my neighbors around the world. *And* right here in America. In some cases, it leads to their death."

Will spoke, "And what happens when our global neighbors get envious of *us*? Is there anyone here who thinks for a moment that this old planet can sustain that kind of consumption? I think Jenny's thoughts should give pause to any of us who are tempted to say, 'Well, a little envy never hurt anybody.'"

Sam turned to John. "Well, there's plenty to think about for your sermon. Got a Bible story picked out?"

"Unfortunately I'm rather spoiled for choice. The Bible is littered with stories about coveting what our neighbor has. Joseph's brothers covet the affection of his father, and plan to kill him because of it. King David covets his neighbor's wife Bathsheba, leading to coerced sex, adultery, deception and murder. King Ahab covets his neighbor's vineyard, leading to murder and theft. These are stories about people who have *everything* and yet are dissatisfied because they don't have what belongs to their neighbor. And you don't have to be the king of Israel to be caught up in that kind of dissatisfaction."

Steve said, "Here's a statistic you may find interesting: 90 percent of people who win the jackpot in lotteries—becoming millionaires in the process—*still play the lottery*. Despite having more money than just about everybody else in the world, these winners still want more."

"How much money is enough?" asked Sarah.

"Just a little bit more, according to John D. Rockefeller," Will replied. "Especially when it's just a little bit more than what my neighbor has."

John said, "C. S. Lewis wrote, 'Pride gets no pleasure out of having something, only out of having more of it than the next man. We say that people are proud of being rich, or clever, or good looking, but they're not. They're proud of being rich-er, or clever-er, or better looking than others.'[9] And we play the game along with them, envying those who have more and who *are* more than us. So no matter how much we have, it's never enough."

John turned toward Jenny. "You're absolutely right, Jenny. There's always the next generation of smart phone we need to upgrade to, usually after our neighbor has shown us theirs. I read an op-ed piece Zygmunt Bauman wrote following the London riots."

John pulled out the clipping and read, "It is the level of our shopping activity and the ease with which we dispose of one object of consumption in order to replace it with a 'new and improved' one which serves us as the prime measure of our social standing and our score in the life-success competition."[10]

Sarah spoke up, "But here's the question: once we obtain the object of our desire are we happy? Content, finally? No! And why not? Because we continue to compare ourselves to our neighbors, whether on our street, on our Facebook newsfeed or on the pages of our favorite magazines. Or, in my case, to my sister and her closet full of shoes. My friend Suzanne often says, 'Comparison is the thief of joy.' Yet knowing that and acting on it are worlds apart."

Will said, "This is the bitter irony of covetousness: it makes us blind to our own wealth, prevents us enjoying the beauty that is already ours."[11]

John responded, "And if covetousness prevents us from enjoying what we have, the resentment it breeds tells me that my neighbor shouldn't be able to enjoy what *she* has. I'm thinking of doing this pop quiz in the sermon—what do you think?" He stood up and started writing on the chalkboard. "When you see a friend's update in your Facebook newsfeed that consists of a photo and description of their new car, motorcycle, boat, boy- or girlfriend or whatever, or their latest vacation, or a meal at that restaurant you've been dying to try, or their child's latest achievement, which of these is your reaction?" He sat down, and they looked at the board.

A. That's fantastic. I'm so thrilled for them!
B. Must be nice to be them.
C. How many more times are they going to post on this?
D. Why can't I have that?
E. Unfriend.

Steve said, "I'll tell you something. If anyone answers 'A,' then that will just confirm my views about the depth of hypocrisy among church folk!"

John finished off his coffee. "Envy also has a darker side that often goes unnoticed. Because envy is not just about gratifying our desire to obtain what our neighbor has. It's also about diminishing our neighbor. This dark side manifests itself when we gossip about our neighbor. 'Did you see his new car? A Jaguar! Well, you know what they say about men and sports cars. Compensation for . . .' And we snicker and mock him, while simultaneously wishing we had that car sitting in our driveway."

"Or," Steve interjected, "we stop by to 'admire' his new car and casually mention that we're surprised he went with the Jag when *Car & Owner* gave it a less-than-stellar review. Not that I would ever do anything like that, you understand."

"This dark side manifests itself," John continued, "every time we delight in the downfall of someone we envy and find people to share our delight with. Even pastors aren't above this. I've attended many conferences over the years, and I think I'd be hard-pressed to think of one where someone didn't ask me this question: 'So, how many are you running in worship?' And before I realized I didn't have to play that game, I would say what our attendance was, and then one of two things would happen. If the other person told me they had less in attendance, then I would feel a little smug inside and spout some platitude about numbers not being important. Or if they had more in attendance, I would feel a little less than and spout some defensive cliché about focusing more on discipleship than getting people through the doors. And I would walk away and despise myself for even thinking and saying those things. Such is the insidious nature of envy.

"So, in the land of the free with a free-market economy and freedom to buy whatever we can afford (or qualify to borrow for), I wonder if the Tenth Word reveals that we are, in fact, slaves."

Carlos snorted. "I'm serious," John said. "We're slaves to our disordered desires that are nurtured and magnified every time we open a magazine or turn on the TV, and every time we drive down the highway or log on to the Internet. This overwhelming, continuous assault on our senses that tells us that we don't have enough and that we *are* not enough, takes healthy desire and transforms it into envy. The resentment it breeds drives a wedge between us and our neighbor. We're free to choose, and all too often what we choose is to be discontent with what we have *and* with who we are."

"That's what *I* do to myself anyway," said Sarah. "When I'm at a party, I immediately begin to compare myself with others. I check how my clothes measure up. My looks. And yes, my weight. And my enjoyment of the evening is affected by how I think I measure up.'"

Rick looked thoughtful. "I wonder if coveting turns us inward. It magnifies our self-centeredness and selfishness, which, as those of us wrestling with the bondage of addiction know all too well, 'is the root of our troubles.'"[12]

"I think you're right," said Will. "Coveting appears to be *outwardly* oriented—envy of what our neighbor has—but I wonder if it's really *inwardly* oriented, focusing on what we do *not* have. Isn't it really saying, 'I don't have what I need, and it's not fair.' It's not fair that I don't have it, and it's certainly not fair that my neighbor does. That kind of resentment put us in prison, and then gives the key to someone else. It's 'like drinking poison and waiting for the other person to die.'"[13]

John nodded. "That's how coveting affects us as individuals. But coveting also affects us as a society. When we see each other as competitors for limited goods rather than as neighbors living with enough, our sense of the common good is strained, if not destroyed. We've been raised on the American Dream, where with the right combination of hard work and luck—emphasis on hard work—we'll acquire a beautiful home and all the toys we could want, and become one of the legions of self-made millionaires. So it's no surprise that many of us are dissatisfied with the life we actually have. We watch the videos of the lottery winners with their oversized checks that are going to change their lives forever. Or we read about the starting salary of our favorite NBA or NFL player. Or we read a book or watch a video from the self-help section and discover the key to fulfilling our financial dreams, and we get a little starry-eyed. And we take one more step away from accepting our ordinariness."

"And," said Jenny, "we deny the fact that all of us sitting at this table are ridiculously wealthy compared to the majority of our global neighbors. We are the 1 percent. And we're miserable. That's the net gain of all our progress—more time to think about what we lack, and more money to try to fill that hole with stuff we buy. You can chart it from the 1950s—GDP has gone steadily up, and our happiness has gone steadily down."[14]

No one spoke for a while. Then Steve asked the question that was on everybody's mind. "Seeing that we've all pretty much admitted we covet our neighbor's ass, or in my case, his Jaguar, what can we do to change? What are you going to tell your people to do?"

John shook his head. "That's it, isn't it? It's always easier for me to diagnose the problem. It's another thing entirely to find the solution. This world, which I believe God created, is a desirable place, and that is both our glory and our damnation. We were made to desire, which is where we find our joy. But it's the excesses of our disordered desires that can lead us to live dissatisfied lives—to mistreat and oppress our neighbors and to lose all sight of the common good."[15] He turned to Steve. "Even us preachers."

John picked up his Bible again. "This guy James wrote a letter to people wrestling with these kinds of questions. At one point he writes this:

> *Those conflicts and disputes among you, where do they come from? Do they not come from your cravings that are at war within you? You want something and do not have it; so you commit murder. And you covet something and cannot obtain it; so you engage in disputes and conflicts.*[16]

"That's the human condition," John continued. "These deep-seated disordered desires that make us continually discontent with our lot in life. Which cause us to continually compare ourselves to others and come up short. Which make us resent our neighbor. And worse."

Steve said, "Well thanks for getting our week off to such a great start. And I thought *I* was the miserable one." The group laughed. Steve's face turned serious. "It's all very well to say, 'Thou shall not covet,' but how in the world do you actually do that? I mean, really. How?"

"Well," said John, "it's pretty obvious that coveting what our neighbor has is harmful in so many ways, but we just keep on doing it anyway. How can we do what those four words say when we're constantly bombarded with the exhortation to do the exact opposite?" John paused. "That's not a rhetorical question! If these Ten Words were given to that bunch of slaves to transform them into a people who sought the common good, how did they do that? How do *we* learn to embody this Word? Let me put it this way. When I get off my bike at the diner today, what can I do to keep from looking at that beautiful Night Train and then speaking gruffly to its owner when I place my order?"

Will responded, "G. K. Chesterton said, 'There are two ways to get enough, or to be content with what we have. One is to continue to accumulate more and more. The other is to desire less.' Clearly the challenge is learning to desire less."

Rick spoke up, "Well if we're talking about resentment, here's what I've learned in Alcoholics Anonymous. Make a gratitude list. And not just a 'first five things that come to mind that I'm thankful for' kind of list. A 'sit down and write out everything that I have to be grateful for' kind of list. I've also learned to name my resentments and think about what I have to be grateful for around them."

Steve stroked his chin. "Let me see if I understand what you're saying, Rick. So the next time I'm lusting over my neighbor's Jag, I maybe think about the guy waiting at the bus stop at the end of my street in the rain who would probably *love* to have my old car, and that would help me be thankful, instead of resentful?"

"Yeah. Something along those lines," Rick agreed. "Maybe you can try doing that this week and let us know how that goes."

"I don't know if a week is going to be enough time! I've been lusting after that car for quite a while," Steve observed.

Carlos spoke up, "Do the next right thing. And don't be invested in the outcome." He looked at Rick.

"That's right, Carlos. Maybe you have been paying attention to us old-timers." Rick looked around the group. "My sponsor used to ask me this question all the time. 'What if, when you woke up tomorrow, you only had those things you had remembered to be grateful for today?'"

Sam observed, "My house would be pretty empty, I guess. I don't recall ever making anything like a gratitude list. But I've got all the time in the world to make one today."

Sarah said, "I'm sure I have plenty enough shoes I can be thankful for when I lust after my sister's latest purchases. An 'experiment in contentment' would probably be good for me."

John looked at his watch. "Thanks for the suggestion, Rick. I'm hoping to find some tangible ways to begin to embody these Words—some practices, if you like. That's a great one to get us started. And thanks everybody for coming. I really am going to enjoy meeting with you on Mondays. And I'm sure my community will benefit greatly from what's going to come out of our time together."

Sam looked thoughtful. "You know when Jesus says, 'The meek shall inherit the earth'? I've always wondered what that meant. But after listening this morning and doing some thinking, I wonder if he's talking about people who don't have to own something to enjoy it."

Jenny's eyes lit up. "That sounds like one of my kids. He always wants to meet me at the arboretum because he says he loves being around all those beautiful trees and flowers. He never says, 'I wish

I had some of these in my yard.' He just seems content to be there. I've never thought about that before."

"Well, as you know," said Steve, "I like to have the last word, so here's another idea. I think I'm going to cancel my car magazine subscriptions. As much as I like reading them, they seem to fuel my dissatisfaction with my own car. And I'm sure they nurture my resentment of my neighbor's."

"I'm writing that one down, Steve—thanks." John stood up. "Well, I know most of you have to get to work, so let's wrap things up for this week. And the open road beckons me." He paused. "But please don't covet my day off." A chorus of groans greeted these words. "Next week we're going to be talking about the Ninth Word, which is about telling lies about or to our neighbors. Let's give some thought to where we see that in our lives and in our culture. See you then."

As John was zipping up his leather jacket, Will walked over and said, "You know, there's another practice you're already engaged in that can help with dissatisfaction."

"What's that?"

"The Eucharist. Communion. Or the Family Meal, as your community calls it. Our culture tells us to grab for what we covet, to seize it, to clutch at it. But every time we come to the Table, we're invited to come with open and empty hands to receive what will truly satisfy our hunger. And the amazing thing is that we call that small piece of bread and that sip of wine or grape juice a feast. Perhaps the Family Meal can change your normal experience of the meal you'll have at the diner today. After all, if you loved your neighbor as you love yourself, you might find joy and fulfillment in him having a Night Train." Will grinned broadly. "Or you could just huddle over your burger and fries and be miserable as usual."

John punched him on the shoulder. "I'll let you know which way it goes when I see you next Monday." He swung the backpack over his shoulders and put his helmet on, hoping his bike would start the first time.

2

From Deception to Truth Telling

The Ninth Word

> *People say believe half of what you see,*
> *son, and none of what you hear.*
>
> MARVIN GAYE,
> "I HEARD IT THROUGH
> THE GRAPEVINE"

> *You shall not bear false witness*
> *against your neighbor.*
>
> EXODUS 20:16

The espresso machines were gurgling merrily when Steve arrived at the coffee shop. He looked for the group and saw that everyone else had already arrived. Sarah caught his eye, and he waved to her and mimed drinking a cup of coffee to let her know he'd be over after ordering. Students from the private high school across the street were at the table next to them—unusual at this time of the morning. Steve got his cup of coffee and walked across to the students.

"What are you all up to?" he asked.

"Studying for a big test later this morning," a young man replied.

Steve looked down at the table. "Where are your books?"

"Busted!" laughed one of the young women. "It's more like a quiz, but we told our parents it was a big test so they would let us come here to 'study.' We really just wanted to hang out and grab a latte before school."

John pulled a chair out and with a grin called, "Come on, Steve— you're late."

The young woman said, "What are you doing?"

"We're having a little discussion group."

"Oh yeah? About what?"

Steve hesitated and then said, "Why don't you swing your chair around and find out?" He paused. "Unless you need to get back to your 'studying.'"

She laughed, then elbowed the girl sitting next to her. "You want to do a discussion group with me?" Her friend looked confused. "Sure you do," and she spun her chair around to join the group. She looked at Steve. "OK. What are we discussing?"

"First things first, young lady," said Sarah. "Introductions. I'm Sarah."

They went around the table giving their names before arriving back at the two new additions.

"I'm Ellie, and this is Yasmina. Now, what are we talking about?"

Steve said, "John, why don't you tell Ellie what we're doing?"

After John explained, Ellie said, "Huh. What commandment are you talking about today?"

Steve grinned. "Oh, I think you may find today's commandment interesting." She raised an eyebrow. Steve turned to John. "Why don't you show Ellie the commandment for today: maybe she can read it aloud for us." John passed her his Bible and pointed to the Ninth Word. Ellie read,

"No lies about your neighbor."[1]

Her forehead wrinkled. She looked up at Steve. "So we're talking about lying?"

"Well, this is awkward," said Yasmina.

Ellie's cheeks colored.

"Not exactly lying, Ellie. But, yes, we are going to be talking about deception. Are you still up for the discussion?" asked Steve.

She looked around the table and met the puzzled looks of the rest of the group. "I guess it probably wouldn't hurt, huh?" She offered Steve a wry smile, who smiled back.

"Probably not." He turned to John. "So what do you got for us today, preacher?"

John, still looking mildly confused, kicked off the discussion. "Well, the Ninth Word: 'You shall not bear false witness against your neighbor.' Out of interest, how many of you have ever been called as a witness in a trial?" No one responded. "Right. Most of us will never find ourselves in that situation. But I imagine that if we happen to, we believe we'd speak the truth. After all, we like to think of ourselves as being basically truthful people. Of course, we may tell a little white lie every now and then, but no harm, no foul, right?"

Ellie shifted in her seat.

"And yet," he continued, "even though we may think of *ourselves* as being truthful, what about others? Do we always expect people to tell us the truth?" This comment garnered some blank stares. "OK, let me try to illustrate what I mean. When you hear these words, how do you react?" He paused. "'This won't hurt a bit.'" A peal of laughter rang out from the group. "See? Any other examples you can think of?"

Steve jumped up and grabbed a piece of chalk. As he wrote on the board, he said, "A salesman told me this last week: 'Even *I* can't get this car for the price I'm offering you.'"

Sarah snorted, "Here's a good one. 'One size fits all.'"

The group fired off other suggestions, which Steve added to the list.

I'm here to help you.

Yes, I have done all my homework.

No, officer, I have not been drinking this evening.

I have no idea how that got in there.

The check's in the mail.

There was a brief pause before Ellie said, "Of course I love you," with just a trace of bitterness in her voice.

John continued, "When someone begins a statement with 'Trust me,' how likely are we to want to do that? There's a reason this joke keeps doing the rounds: 'How can you tell when a politician is lying? His lips are moving.'" More laughter. "Right. We laugh on cue, because we don't trust our elected officials to speak the truth. Nor many other people. Even though we tend to think of ourselves as truthful, by and large we don't expect the truth from others. With good reason, apparently. I read an excerpt from a survey conducted by the Josephson Institute of Ethics earlier this year which affirmed such mistrust." He looked down at his notes. "It states that 59 percent of American high school students say they cheated on a test during the past year. Twenty-one percent say they stole from a parent or other relative, and 80 percent say they lied about 'something significant' to a parent. However, 92 percent say they're satisfied with their own personal ethics and character."[2] He looked at the two students.

"Sounds about right," Yasmina shrugged.

"However," said John, "it's not just adolescents who are capable of that degree of self-deception. What kinds of situations might provoke a less-than-truthful response from adults?"

"'Enhancing' your résumé a little," said Steve. "So you stand out in a competitive job market. Or being 'creative' in explaining the gap in your employment record."

"How about padding the expense account a little with meals that weren't business related?" asked Rick. "Or adding a little extra when filling out insurance claims."

John nodded. "Clearly what we're doing is deceptive, but we often excuse it. After all, 'everybody does it,' right? 'It's no big deal.' 'People expect it.'"

"Certainly the major food companies believe we expect it." The attention shifted to Jenny. She leaned forward. "As more and more people are choosing organic food—what our grandparents just called 'food'—major agribusiness companies are jumping on the bandwagon. Are they doing that by removing or reducing chemicals from their products? Or changing other industrial farming practices? No, they're doing it by repackaging the same product and labeling it with the word *natural*." She looked around the group. "Now, *organic* and *natural* may sound similar, but in the world of FDA regulation they are worlds apart. However, the companies are banking on the fact that most of us don't know that. Or perhaps that we don't want to know that."

Steve spoke up, "I think I'm going to need an example before I buy that. No pun intended."

Jenny nodded. "OK. The clearest example is chicken. What used to be packaged as simply 'Chicken' is now 'All-Natural Chicken. No Steroids or Antibiotics Added!'—with a little asterisk after the words. Look for the information about that asterisk on the packaging, and this is what you'll find in tiny print. 'The FDA does not permit the addition of steroids or antibiotics to poultry.' The new packaging suggests that they chose not to do something other companies do, whereas in fact they're not permitted to add them by law."

Yasmina picked up Jenny's theme. "Sounds like my mom. When she checks out her options in the egg section at the grocery store, she gets all excited if they have 'cage free' eggs. I know she buys them with images in her mind of happy chickens roaming in and out of warm barns. But the reality is, the vast majority of those chickens never see the light of day. They live with about the same amount of space to move as caged hens do, breathing noxious fumes from their own waste and eating through mutilated beaks."

Sarah chipped in, "Or how about those enormous bags of chips that are emblazoned with the words 'Zero Trans-Fat!' or 'Cholesterol Free!' Suddenly it almost sounds as if those fat-laden food items are now healthy! And I confess I'm willingly deceived."

John jumped back in. "So, are the people in the marketing divisions of these major agribusiness companies just more cynical, devious, dishonest or even more cruel than the rest of us? I imagine that there must be at least one person in the marketing offices of those major poultry companies who keeps backyard chickens for fresh eggs for his own family. And I would bet the farm," eliciting a loud groan from Steve, "that those chickens are not kept in the same conditions as the millions of chickens that his company sells. He knows what the life of a genuinely 'all-natural chicken' can be."

Will chimed in, "Doesn't that reveal the incredible ability we have as human beings to distance ourselves from the truth of what we do? Our capacity for self-deception is quite remarkable. I don't imagine that this hypothetical marketing guy visits one of the plants his companies owns and then goes back to his office to figure out how to spin the deplorable conditions into something that sounds more wholesome for marketing purposes. I doubt if he has ever set foot on a corporate farm. His job is to present his company's product in the best possible light to maximize sales and shareholder return. He pays attention to cultural trends and notes the increasing market share of organic poultry producers. And instead of fundamentally questioning the way his company raises chickens—which is not his job—he comes up with a new idea for packaging that rides the wave of 'natural food' without actually changing anything about the chicken other than the labeling."

"And so," said Jenny, "he bears false witness against his neighbor—he deceives us." She chewed a fingernail for a moment. "But I suppose he can do that because he never thinks of us as his neighbors. I guess to him we are first and foremost consumers. Even if he does experience a brief twinge of conscience, maybe he convinces himself that what he's doing is no big deal. After all, most people *are* going to buy the cheapest chicken they can find, and at least with the new packaging they can feel a little bit better about their choice. Perhaps he's even able to convince himself he's doing us a favor. Maybe he is. We *are* consumers after all—and consumers with a tendency to allow ourselves to be deceived in such ways. Because we really don't want to pay the price of a chicken that has been raised the same way our imaginary marketer raises his own chickens."[3]

"That kind of deception isn't limited to agribusiness," Sam said. "I reckon there are plenty of companies or corporations 'bearing false witness' against us."

Yasmina leaned forward. "Isn't that what all the Occupy Wall Street groups were about? They were protesting the major banks, many of whom reaped vast fortunes from selling bad mortgages, repackaging the debt inside complex derivatives and selling them as reasonable investments, all the while betting against them." Ellie looked at her friend with her mouth agape. Yasmina responded, "What? My dad *is* a banker after all. We got the lecture."

"More than once, by the sound of it," Steve noted.

Yasmina blushed. "Yeah. Anyway, when this house of cards collapsed, causing a global recession, the banks were bailed out by their tax-paying neighbors—many of whom lost their homes because of the bank's deceptive business practices." She turned to John and said with some heat, "So it's not just adolescents who are capable of self-deception. Many of the bankers responsible still insist that what they did was standard business practice. Or, in other words, they are satisfied with their professional ethics. And, I might add, they continue to be handsomely rewarded for it."

John nodded. "You're right, Yasmina. OK, let's switch gears a bit. It's pretty easy for those of us who consider ourselves to be part of the 99 percent to disparage the 1 percent who have engaged in the kind of deception that has affected the common good in such devastating ways. But let's bring the Ninth Word a little closer to home. Let's talk about the specific kind of deception that I think lies at the heart of the Ninth Word, the primary way I think we bear false witness against our neighbor." He looked around the circle. "Gossip."

Sarah wagged her finger. "Mmm, mmm. You were just talking before—now you're meddling!" A peal of laughter rang across the coffee shop.

John continued, "This is my favorite definition of gossip: 'When you hear something you like about someone you don't.'[4] And then pass it on to someone else. Without necessarily checking its veracity or its context or the source of the information. No, we just send a text, usually beginning 'OMG! Did you hear . . .' Or we forward the email. Or link to the blog post. Or, most prolifically, we share it on our Facebook wall, and add to the litany of gossip that comprises so much of what passes for a 'newsfeed.'"[5] He picked up a book. "Ellsworth Kalas says, 'It may well be that no sin is so universally popular as the sin of false witness, the sin of slander, the defaming of other persons. This is partly because all of us have the weapon, and because the weapon is so immediately available.'"[6]

"Or," said Sarah, "as Alice Roosevelt Longworth articulated so eloquently: 'If you haven't got anything nice to say about anybody, come sit next to me.'"

More laughter.

John nodded. "Don't we tend to believe that this kind of behavior is not that big a deal? Especially when we're talking about a public figure. And we *love* to talk about public figures. Or, better yet, listen to cable news channel and talk radio hosts talk about public figures. Selectively editing speeches and video clips, we portray those we disagree with in the worst possible light. We impugn their motives, stereotype, lampoon and use derogatory language about them, all in the name of 'objective' journalism."

Will leaned forward. "Appear on MSNBC to explain why you understand the frustration of the Tea Party movement and you're a 'right wing nutbar.' Appear on Fox News to explain why you can understand the frustration of the Occupy Wall Street protestors and you're a 'left wing nutbar.' We might look on in disgust or delight, *but we're looking on.* The news media companies have our attention, and therefore they have an audience that can draw the advertising revenue that such companies need to exist. I think our appetite for gossip—as John defined it for us—fuels the ever-increasing polarization of political discourse in the U.S., and divides us as a people. 'But it's not that big a deal,' we say." Will leaned back. "I think we're selling ourselves way short on that one."

John took another book out of his bag. "David Hazony would agree with your sentiment.

> *Gossip is called* lashon hara, *'the evil tongue,' and the rabbis believed it to be one of the worst crimes against society. According to the Talmud, 'Anyone who speaks the evil tongue, God says of him: He and I cannot live in the same world.'*[7]

John looked around the table. "What do you think? Is Hazony overstating the case? Is gossip *really* one of the worst crimes against society? Is name-calling *really* that harmful?"

Sam spoke up, "How many of you can remember coming home from elementary school in tears because other kids had called you names?" A few nods in response. "And what nugget of wisdom did we hear, passed down from generation to generation?"

Sarah said in a sing-song voice, "Sticks and stones may break my bones, but words will never harm me."

"And did that make it all better for us? Did that help us the next time they called us those hurtful, lying and demeaning names?"

"No," said Yasmina. "I kept on internalizing those names, wishing the few friends I had would stick up for me. But they didn't." She looked down. "No, here's what I know from bitter experience: Sticks and stones may break your bones, but words will tear your heart out."

Ellie leaned across and threw her arms around Yasmina, who sat stiffly, continuing to look down at her hands folded in her lap.

After a few moments of silence, John picked up the Hazony book and read,

> *It's amazing how little heed we pay to so many centuries of Christian and Jewish teaching about the evils of derogating others. While we have fairly well committed ourselves to the value of life and the respect for property, the inclination to demean runs wild. Why?*
>
> *The most obvious reason is that whereas in crimes like murder and theft the harm is self-evident and well-defined, with negative speech it is easy to convince ourselves that there are no bad results, especially when the words are spoken in private.*
>
> *"The gossiper," the rabbis taught, "talks in Rome and kills in Syria."[8]*

"And," interjected Sam, "it's not just people we *don't* like that we do this to. We also gossip about people we *do* like. In my church we call that 'sharing concerns so others can pray for them.'" He shook his head. "Somehow I don't see Jesus pulling John aside and saying, 'In confidence, and strictly for prayer, but did you hear about Peter?'"

Rick said, "I tend to think of gossip as repeating private information to someone who is neither part of the problem nor part of the solution."[9]

Will asked, "How many of us have heard something about a friend or neighbor that surprised, shocked or even scandalized us, and then found that upon hearing the news our first impulse was to want to tell someone else?" A few heads nodded. "How many of us have acted on that impulse and even as we were repeating the information, ignored the nagging voice in the back of our head that was saying, 'You really should not be doing this'?" He paused. "And then wondered if people talked about us in the same way behind our back?"

He continued, "I wonder if social media has fundamentally changed the way we see each other. You don't have to be famous to be a public figure. We're all public figures on Facebook and Twitter. Which has created some distance between us and even our closest friends. So when their foibles and failures get posted on Facebook for all the world to see, instead of seeing these as burdens for us to bear out of friendship, they become things to comment on—or, heaven forbid, even 'like.'"

Ellie responded, "Yeah, I can't imagine what it was like when you could only be cruel in the *playground* at recess."

"I suppose," observed Steve, "that's also true for a bunch of the jokes we tell. Jokes that rely on stereotyping whole groups of people. There's a guy who comes in to my office once a month to clean the windows—his name's José. Nice guy, doesn't say much. When he's gone, one of my employees will tell some joke about Mexicans—nothing too offensive. I like to think it's just a bit of harmless fun, right? A bit of a laugh at the end of the week. I've even repeated one or two of them." He turned his coffee mug in his hands. "I wonder what those jokes reveal about me." He took a drink and looked off into the distance. Everyone else studiously avoided looking at Carlos.

"You're not the only one who does that, Steve." The group now turned toward Carlos. "I can't tell you how many times I've spent the night in jail and laughed at jokes about the guys in the next cell—because they tend to keep us segregated, y'know? And we use those jokes to put them down, to make us feel better about ourselves. All while I'm sitting in a jail cell because I was stupid enough to do drugs and get caught driving under the influence. Or worse. Who's the joke really on?"

Jenny said, "It's hearing your dad tell his poker buddies for the hundredth time, 'I believe a man's place is in the kitchen. Making sure the woman does the work right.' And them laughing as if he's said something funny. And me knowing what my dad was capable of doing if he thought she *wasn't* doing it right." She twisted her napkin in her hands. Sarah gently laid her hand over Jenny's.

John sighed. "So maybe the Ninth Word still has something to say to us. Because all these ways of bearing false witness against each other, whether through advertising or gossip or telling racist jokes, lead to one thing: the erosion of trust. And without trust, how is it possible to have any kind of genuine communication? How is it possible to have any kind of meaningful relationships with others?" He reached for another book. "Truth telling is thus not a general virtue so much as it is a necessity for maintaining harmonious relationships. It is one of the clearest manifestations of love of God and love of neighbor."[10]

He put the book down. "Is there any doubt that there is a crisis of trust in our culture? A crisis that leads to all kinds of divisions in every sphere of our shared lives? We make much of the fact that we live in a democratic society, and yet in a study I read just last week, 89 percent of those polled said they distrust government to do the right thing.[11] An astonishing nine out of ten Americans do not trust the government that 'we the people' elected to act in our best interests. As we enter each electoral cycle, we watch candidates from the same party sling mud at each other until the last one is left standing, and then we watch while the losers line up behind the winner to throw mud at the incumbent. Am I overstating the case? You've all seen the column in the local paper called 'Watchdog,' which investigates local political TV ads, statements made in debates, et cetera, and then reports on the truth of the claims made. How often does the sidebar read 'True'?"

Steve snorted. "Hardly ever. It most often reads 'partially true' or 'mostly false.'"

"Right. But it's not just our political institutions that suffer from a lack of truth telling and therefore trust. It's also true of our marriages, our friendships, our workplaces and our churches. It's not that we necessarily tell out-and-out lies to each other. It's just that we so often color the truth to best suit our purposes. We may try to convince ourselves that we're doing so in the other person's best interests, but if we have the capacity to be honest with ourselves, we recognize that we do so for our own sake. Whether that's to hide behavior we're not proud of, to hide our motivations, to divest the guilt we're feeling onto the other person or any of a myriad other reasons, we simply don't tell the truth to each other so much of the time."

Sam handed his mug to a barista for a refill, as John continued.

"Some of us have learned to avoid telling the truth because we've paid the price for doing so. And so we've created this culture of mistrust that erodes our relationships under the weight of all the forms taken by our deception, our lies, our gossip and slander. And as our mistrust increases, so does our fear of the other. Instead of seeing each other as neighbors, as diverse people sharing life and having a sense of the common good, we learn to fear each other. With a glance we determine that someone looks suspicious, threatening. Or we quickly apply labels to them such as 'stranger,' 'illegal,' 'terrorist' or, in the church's case, 'heretic,' because of the ways we talk about 'people like them.' There's no question that bearing false witness against our neighbor has profoundly affected us."

John threw his arms wide and laughed. "But, again, this shouldn't surprise us. Bearing false witness against a neighbor is as old as our story. The very first conversation found in Scripture begins with the serpent doing exactly that: 'Indeed, has God said, "You shall not eat from any tree of the garden"?'"[12]

He looked around the table. "If I can take us back to the same scene as last week, the serpent misquotes God and in doing so casts God in a much less generous light than God's actual prohibition merited, which was to forbid them from eating the fruit of just one tree, 'the tree of the knowledge of good and evil.'"

Sam interjected, "The serpent bears false witness. That's why he's called the 'deceiver of the whole world' in Revelation."[13]

"Indeed!" John continued. "Now, to this point the man and the woman had lived in this beautiful relationship with God and with each other, literally naked and unashamed. Absolutely vulnerable and absolutely OK with that. But now the serpent introduces doubt. 'Can you really trust God? How do you know God has your best interests at heart? God's holding this back from you.' So they go back to the tree. 'Hey, it does look pretty good, it's good eating, and if it's going to make us wise, well maybe we should have a little bite.' And the serpent's half-truth bears bitter fruit. No, they don't die immediately. But the second they take a bite of that fruit, something *inside* them dies. And when they realize what they've done, they try to cover their rears—literally—with fig leaves. When God shows up for their daily chat, they hide. God calls out, 'Where are you?'"

"Like God didn't know!" said Ellie.

John smiled. "How many of us hear those words spoken with an angry tone?" A few nods. "Maybe we hear the voice of our parents remembered from childhood. But I wonder if God speaks gently, invitationally. Giving them a chance to come clean. Perhaps God's words are an invitation to be found. But instead of telling the whole truth, the man says, 'I was afraid because I was naked; so I hid myself.'[14] God replies, 'Who told you that you were naked? Have you eaten from the tree of which I commanded you not to eat?'[15] And what does the man say from the bushes? 'That woman you gave me—she made me do it.'"

"Imagine that," Sarah intoned. "He blames his wife."

"Yeah," said Sam, "but she turns around and blames the snake."

"And," John continued, "with those words, the first human community is divided. That beautiful, vulnerable, shameless relationship gets torn apart. Technically, they *are* telling the truth. But in refusing to take responsibility for his own actions, the man bears false witness against his wife—his neighbor—by blaming her for the choice he made."

Yasmina asked, "So what would have happened if they had come out of the bushes and just said something like, 'We were hiding because we were afraid and ashamed because we did what you told us not to do'?"

John responded, "Maybe our story would have turned out very different. But they didn't. Instead they chose to remain hiding in the bushes and blame each other for what they themselves had done, and it all goes wrong from there. It all began with words."

Will interjected, "And it continues with words. A little half-truth here. A little deception there. A little doubt sown here. A little gossip there. A little rationalization, and slowly the trust necessary for relationships unravels. Everything comes undone. Every word of deception carries a price tag. Every lie. Every half-truth. Every untruth."

He leaned forward. "And here's the irony of our situation. When we bear false witness against our neighbor, we think our neighbor is the one who is going to pay the price. That's why we do it. We want to avoid the consequences we see we'd bear if we tell the truth, so we tell a lie, and we believe the other person pays the price for it. But the reality is, *we* bear the cost."

John looked down at his coffee mug for a moment, then said in a quieter voice. "That's something I know all too well. Early on in my life I developed this incredible capacity for deception. It began with lying in order to get out of trouble—blaming my brother for something I had done. Then I began to lie in order to get what I wanted, especially with girlfriends." He turned sad eyes toward Ellie, who held his gaze for a moment before looking away. "I learned to paint myself in a much better light than I merited—I hurt people with my actions, then convinced them that it was really their fault. I bore false witness to my neighbor over and over again. And it was exhausting.

"I also discovered that I no longer trusted anybody. Because I lied so frequently, I unconsciously began to assume that people did the same. Why would they be different from me? As I lied, I began to lose touch with what was really true. What actually happened. What was actually said. What I really thought. What I really felt." He looked around the table.

"Who I really was.

"I tried to convince myself that it really wasn't that big a deal. But lying is a bit like disabling the warning lights on your car: it gives the illusion that everything is OK and running smoothly until it all comes to a grinding halt." He looked down, and the group sat in silence for a while, unsure what to say. John looked up, offered them a rueful smile and then reached for another book.

"Just how many more books have you got in there?" asked Sarah. Her comment acted as a relief valve, and the group broke into laughter.

"Oh, one or two," said John. "Joan Chittister puts it like this, 'I simply no longer know myself; whether what I say is what actually happened, or what I wanted to have happened, or what I'm afraid happened or what I want other people to believe happened.'"[16]

Sarah said, "That sounds all too familiar. Wasn't it Abraham Lincoln that said, 'No one has a good enough memory to be a successful liar'?"[17]

"Right. We start telling stories and then we can't remember what version of the story we told to whom. How do we keep it all straight? No one has a good enough memory to do that, but you know what? We keep on trying. The words we use are so important because words are powerful. Words are sacred. God *spoke* the universe into existence."

Sam observed, "Just like John wrote: 'In the beginning was the Word, and the Word was with God, and the Word was God.' And 'the Word became flesh and blood, and moved into the neighborhood.'"[18]

"Yes, speech is sacred because it is godlike. With words we create our world. With words we give life or take it. And, sadly, all too often we take life." John shook his head.

"False speech destroys," he continued. "False speech undermines trust. It erodes the community, and it steals our credibility. You get caught in a lie once, who's going to believe you again? But truth and truth telling does the opposite. It *creates* trust between people. It builds up the community as we begin to trust each other, because what we say is what we mean and what we do. And consistently telling the truth begins to give us back our credibility in the eyes of those around us.

"Joan Chittister says this, 'Truth is its own reward. It requires no memory. No elaborate explanations. No conspiring confederates. And no fear of exposure.'[19] Telling the truth is liberating.

"How many of us want to live in that kind of freedom? Where we don't have to keep track of the conversations we've had and what we said to whom? Where we don't question what others say to us, because we trust them? Where we learn to speak the truth about others by refusing to pass on gossip about them. Not just sometimes but *all* the time. How would that change us? What would truth telling do for our families, our marriages, our friendships, our politics? What would it mean to begin to tackle the crisis of trust we experience by telling the truth, one conversation, one political ad, one chicken package at a time?"

Sam said, "Sounds like a plan to me."

"More than a plan," added Rick. "It's a way of life." He looked at John. "Or a practice, as you might say." He grabbed his Big Book and gave it to Carlos. "Find page 58 for me." He turned to the group. "You'll hear these words at the beginning of every AA meeting. This is how it works." He turned to Carlos. "Read the first paragraph for us."

Rarely have we seen a person fail who has thoroughly followed our path. Those who do not recover are people who cannot or will not completely give themselves to this simple program, usually

men and women who are constitutionally incapable of being
honest with themselves. They are not at fault; they seem to have
been born that way. They are naturally incapable of grasping and
developing a manner of living which demands rigorous honesty.
Their chances are less than average. There are those, too, who
suffer from grave emotional and mental disorders, but many of
them do recover if they have the capacity to be honest.[20]

"That's it, right there. A life of rigorous honesty. Because that's
what kills us—self-deception. It's not just about bearing false
witness against our neighbor; it's also about lying to ourselves."

"Exactly! That's great." said John, writing a note in his book.
"Now, we may like the idea of truth telling as an abstract concept.
We can see why it would be so beneficial for society if we all did
that. But as I've been thinking about this Word, there's still one area
where so many of us don't want to be told the truth. And that's the
truth of who we are."

"You're about to meddle again, aren't you?" said Sarah.

"Probably! How many of us are like those first two humans,
hiding in the bushes, trying in vain to cover ourselves up so that
others won't really see the truth about us? Or the truth of who we
think we are." John looked at Yasmina. "Or the truth we have come
to believe because of what other people have told us. Remember:
words are powerful, and they have the power to either give life to
someone or take it away. Perhaps the most powerful way this
happens concerns our identity—who we are. The beginning of the
Story tells us that we are created in God's image, yet so many of us
walk around with an image that is far from divine. Why is that?"

Jenny answered, "Because people have spoken words into our
life. People we love. People we trust. Our parents, our friends, our
relatives, our schoolteachers. And I daresay our preachers. And
these are the words that the kids I work with have heard: 'Hopeless.
Useless. Fat. Thin. Never going to amount to anything. Least likely

to succeed. Bottom of the class. Worthless.' If you hear those words long enough, you're going to internalize them. And they will become your truth."

John nodded sadly. "Don't we long to hear that we are beautiful? That we have worth, that we are good at something, that we are loved? For those of us who grew up in church, we want to believe that we are a child of God, created in God's image with everything that God has at our disposal. But instead, the message we often get is, 'No, you're this person. You're that person.' We take in the identity that other people forge for us with words. Not the truth, the deepest truth of who we really are, but what other people say we are. We take it in and it misshapes us, until, as you say, Jenny, it becomes our truth. That is, tragically, one of the most prevalent ways we bear false witness against our neighbor."

Several of the group were looking down into their coffee cups. Sarah spoke quietly, "And then we live out of that false identity. And we begin to try to cover up the pain we feel with all the crazy stuff we do. And we start making up our own stories about ourselves and about others, until we no longer have a clue who we really are."

Carlos turned to look at Rick. "Until someone tells us. Which in my case was when a roomful of family and friends took turns telling me all that my drinking had done to them."

Wide-eyed, Ellie said, "Wow. How was that?"

Carlos shook his head. "Well, I didn't thank them for it! At least, not then. They spoke the truth that I refused to see. But in that moment I didn't want their message. If I'm honest, I wanted to kill the messenger."

"Here's the rub," said John. "We can all agree that telling the truth is important, that doing so is essential for us to regain the trust necessary for healthy relationships and a healthy society. But, to quote a Roman governor who lived two thousand years ago, 'What is truth?'" Turning to Carlos, he asked, "If these Ten Words are given so that we might be free, what is the truth that is setting you free?"

Without hesitation, Carlos replied, "That I was alcoholic and could not manage my own life. That no human power could have relieved my alcoholism. And that God could and would if he were sought."[21]

John turned back to the group. "I wonder if there are two kinds of truth. There's the truth that *describes* reality, and then there's the truth that *transforms* reality." He glanced down at his watch. "We need to wrap things up, so let me run a last thought by you. I've been reading this book by Peter Rollins called *How (Not) to Speak of God*.[22] In it he talks about the classic ethical conundrum about bearing false witness: hiding Jews during the Second World War."

Jenny chimed in, "I remember that from intro to philosophy in college. When German soldiers knock on your door and ask you if you're hiding Jews, do you say no, which would be a lie but would save their lives? Or do you tell the truth and say yes, knowing that they would be taken and killed? We argued for two class periods about that."

"Right. But here's what Rollins says. To say that there are only two options is wrong. To say that your options are limited to either telling the truth, whereby the Nazis drag off the Jews to die, or lying to save their lives is to misunderstand the commandment—and the truth. Because there is a third way and it is this. When they ask if you are hiding Jews in your house, you say no, *and you're telling the truth*. Because the truth does not *describe* reality, the truth *transforms* reality. Because you know that if you allow the soldiers to take the people you are hiding away, not only will they die, but in doing so you will also allow the soldiers to do something that will deeply violate their own humanity. The truth, the truth that transforms reality, is to say no, and know that in doing so you are actually keeping the commandment."

Ellie, clearly confused, looked at Sarah, who smiled and shrugged as John continued.

"Some of the community leaders tried to put Jesus in a similar ethical conundrum. He had gone to the synagogue to worship on the sabbath day, and there was a person there who had been disabled from birth.[23] The leaders were looking at Jesus, wondering, *Are you going to heal him on the sabbath? Because that would be breaking the law, and then we've got you.* But Jesus spoke the truth; not the truth that describes reality but that transforms reality. He said, and this is my paraphrase, 'You tell me what's keeping the law; to let this man continue to suffer because it's the sabbath day or to heal him because I can and because God wants him to be whole?' The leaders respond by saying nothing, because at that moment they saw the truth about themselves."

John leaned forward. "Jesus sees the hardness of their hearts and is mad. He's mad because they are more committed to the letter of the law and miss the entire intent of the law, which is to set us free from all that keeps us in bondage. Free from all that makes us less than the humans we were created to be. How could they tell Jesus he couldn't heal this man when he had the power to do it, just because it's a certain day of the week? And so Jesus healed him. And do you know what the leaders did? They walked outside and said, 'Let's kill the messenger.'" He leaned back again.

"They can't celebrate what's happening in front of them, someone whose life is transformed, because they are not committed to the truth that transforms. So, like many of us, when people have spoken the truth we don't want to hear, we want to kill the messenger. And that's exactly what they ended up doing to Jesus. The one who said, 'I am the truth.' They said, 'Let's kill the truth.' And so, when we're faced with a situation where we have to bear witness to or about our neighbor, we are to speak the truth. That's the practice of the Ninth Word. Not the truth that merely *describes* reality but that *transforms* reality. Which means sometimes saying something we don't want to, and other times not saying something we *do* want to, because we know that to do so would harm the other. Even if what we said was 'the truth.'"

Steve said, "Sounds like you've got that sermon just about wrapped up already."

Everyone laughed, none louder than John.

"Not yet, Steve, not yet. But it certainly is helpful to talk it over with you all."

Ellie grabbed Yasmina's arm. "We've got to go." Then she turned to Steve. "Can we come back next week?"

Steve looked at John with a smile and answered, "I hope you will—but only if you'll tell your parents you're coming to meet us."

Ellie beamed. "Of course! Then I won't have to lie to get my latte." She laughed out loud. "What are we talking about next week?"

Steve turned to John, who said, "Theft."

3

From Theft to Generosity

The Eighth Word

> *If we look at mankind in all*
> *its conditions, it is nothing but a vast,*
> *wide stable full of great thieves.*
>
> Martin Luther,
> The Large Catechism

> *You shall not steal.*
>
> Exodus 20:15

The group assembled as John looked over some notes. Ellie easily won the prize for "Most Chipper." When everyone was seated, greeted and in the initial stages of caffeination, John leaned back in his chair. "Well, how did practicing rigorous honesty work out for us last week?"

Ellie led off, "When my mom picked me up from school that afternoon I told her that I'd lied to her about the test. She was so surprised by my confession that I guess she forgot to be mad at me."

As the ensuing laughter faded, she said, "But you know what? Having told the truth once, I caught myself about to lie or to spin the truth way more often than I would have thought. It's almost second nature to me—but I've never thought of myself as being a liar." Her voice took a serious tone. "Which has made me wonder what other ways I'm deceiving myself. And I guess I never paid much attention to just how mean my friends can be to each other, myself included. It's almost like a game—who can we get the rumor mill going on today?" She caught Yasmina's eye. "To be honest, I almost didn't come back this week. After all, ignorance is bliss." Then she laughed, picking up her cup. "But I've got my latte, so maybe it'll be worth it."

A couple of others disclosed their own experiments with truth telling before Steve said, "How about you, preacher? How did the sermon go Sunday? Did you have them wailing at the altar, crying out for God to forgive their lying ways?"

John laughed. "Not quite, Steve. But I did have some interesting conversations with people on their way out. This series is obviously striking a nerve with folks."

"I should hope so," said Sarah. "It's certainly doing that for me."

"Well, this week we're talking about the Eighth Word. I'd like to recite the pertinent verse from memory." He paused.

"No stealing."[1]

He stood to take a bow. "I've been working on that all week."

Steve groaned.

"So, if you've had any time to think about theft this week, what's come up for you?"

Sam spoke up first. "Well, I suppose most of us don't like to think of ourselves as being a thief, but I bet we all do it in some way or other. We don't call it theft, of course. We have different names for it. When I was a kid it was 'finders keepers, losers weepers' or 'borrowing without permission.'"

Steve leaped up and grabbed the chalk. "All right, how else do we avoid calling it stealing?"

> The five finger discount.
> Surplus to requirements.
> I meant to pay them back.
> They'll never miss it.
> Eminent domain, if you're the government.
> Creative accounting with offshore accounts.

"Right," said John. "We can rattle off a list quickly. Because we've all done it. Perhaps still do it. But like Sam said, we probably don't think of ourselves as thieves. Why is that? I've got a theory—and one that applies to more than just this Word."

He looked at them intently. "Rodent hairs."

This revelation was greeted with blank looks.

"Did you know that the FDA will only order apple butter to be pulled off the shelf if it has four or more rodent hairs per 100 grams? Or five or more whole insects, not counting mites or aphids? Only three rodent hairs or four bugs and you're spreading it right on your bagel this morning. That coffee you're drinking? If 10 percent of the beans were insect infested or had mold, you wouldn't be holding it.[2] But only 9 percent?" Ellie looked down at her latte and made a face. "And hotdogs. Don't get me started on hotdogs. If we took all the nasty stuff out there'd hardly be anything left!"

"Just out of curiosity, what's the connection between mold on coffee beans and being a thief?" asked Steve.

"I'm glad you asked. The reality is, when it comes to food standards, the FDA does not require absolute purity from bugs, mold or other contaminants. Some bureaucrat decided that there's an acceptable level of impurity we can live with." He leaned forward. "I wonder if we don't think along similar lines ourselves. So, for instance, rather than maintaining the absolute standard suggested by the Eighth Word—no stealing—we have decided what constitutes acceptable levels of theft that still enable us to not think of ourselves as actually being thieves. And we do the same thing in most areas of our lives, right?"

"Most of us know when we're doing it, because our conscience tells us. But then we rationalize our behavior: 'It's not really stealing. They'll never miss it.'" He gestured at the chalkboard. "Or pick any other justification from that list. And eventually our conscience stops being pricked when we bring home a box of pens from the office 'so we can work at home.' We'll tell ourselves that it's just one of the unspoken perks of the job—and not really stealing."

John leaned back again. "I did a little research, and recent studies indicate that four out of five people think it's all right to steal from their employers. One in three people have stolen something from a store. We defraud the IRS out of an estimated $30 *billion* a year. All while telling ourselves we're not *really* stealing."

"That puts me in mind of a story I heard once," said Sam. "Seems like someone sent an anonymous note to the IRS, along with a $100 bill, that read, 'I have trouble sleeping because of my conscience. Please find enclosed $100. If this doesn't cure my insomnia, I'll send you the rest.'" Everyone laughed.

"But," said John, "what price do we pay when we continually downgrade our conscience? How many rodent hairs are we willing to live with?"

Will spoke up, "And what do we get when you add your rodent hairs to mine? And everyone else's? In this coffee shop? In this city? In this state? In this country?"

Steve picked up his paper, then dropped it back on the table. "I guess we get some of the headlines in here."

Sarah piped up, "What about being a victim of theft? Has anyone here been stolen from?"

Yasmina responded, "When I was in fifth grade, Sally Jones stole my lunch money every day."

"One time I was living in a halfway house," Carlos said, "and someone kept stealing my smokes at night. Never could figure out who it was. But it made me so mad—we were supposed to be helping each other out, not stealing from each other."

"I got scammed out of a considerable amount of money recently," said John.

Heads swung in his direction.

"When I was in seminary, I became friends with a pastor from Nigeria. I hadn't heard from him in quite some time, then out of the blue he friended me on Facebook. He had a couple of photos posted and some information about the seminary where he was teaching. Nothing out of the ordinary. Then a few weeks back I got an email from him saying his wife was very sick and needed treatment immediately. They had been able to raise some money but still needed a couple of thousand dollars to pay for hospitalization. She was on expensive drugs to prevent any further deterioration, and so the sooner they could get the balance, the better."

"Tell me you didn't send the money," said Steve.

John smiled sheepishly. "Not immediately. Of course, I had my doubts, but it clearly seemed to be him. I admit, I wondered for a moment when he asked that I wire the money to him personally after I offered to wire it directly to the hospital, but I've never been to Africa and just assumed that was the easiest way for him to make sure he got the money." He shook his head. "The guy who did the wire transfer even asked me if I really knew the person I was sending the money to. Anyway, when I got a message through Facebook the next day asking for more money as the cost had gone up, I got that sick feeling in my stomach and pretty soon realized I'd been had. I was so mad! Not just because this guy had stolen from me but he obviously knew my friend—enough at least to set up a false Facebook account for him. I posted a warning on the wall, and sent a message to all the mutual friends I had on his account, but whoever it was deleted the post and unfriended me straightaway."

"How do you feel about it now?" asked Steve.

"Stupid, more than anything. I really thought it was my friend. But I confess it's given me pause when people show up at the church building asking for help with rent or utility bills. I guess I'm a lot more suspicious now." Heads nodded in understanding.

"My house was burglarized once." Everyone turned toward Sam.

"It happened ten years or so ago. I got home late one night and the house was dark, which was odd because I always leave a couple of lights on. At first I thought the power was out, but everyone else's lights were working. Anyway, I unlocked the door, and when I flipped the light switch nothing happened. I walked through my dark house to the back, and then heard and felt glass crunching underfoot." Sam sighed. "They'd broken a back window to get in. My breaker panel is on the outside of the house, and they'd thrown them all. I guess that was to cut power to any alarms or motion detectors I might have had. Which I didn't. Never thought they were necessary."

"Did they take much?" asked Sarah.

"Not really. It looks like something spooked them. Every drawer in the house was pulled out and my stuff tossed—even the bed mattresses were flipped. But they wound up only taking some computer equipment and some loose cash lying around. The police thought they might have been looking for drugs or guns."

Ellie leaned across and touched Sam's forearm. "How did you feel?"

He patted her hand. "Pretty violated, to be honest. After that, whenever I pulled up in the drive, I wondered if they had come back. It took a while for me not to feel a little scared when I first got home.

And mad that someone had been in my home uninvited, y'know? Strangers pawing at my stuff. Making a big mess. I got off lighter than most, I know. They didn't take anything I couldn't replace.

"But I started paying a lot more attention to people in the neighborhood after that. If I didn't recognize them and thought they looked a bit shifty, I'd sometimes follow them in my car. Making sure they weren't up to anything bad." He shook his head sadly. "But I eventually stopped that. That's no way to live—full of fear and distrust."

"That could have been me," said Carlos. "I've sat in enough meetings to know that if I kept down the path my addiction takes me I could have ended up breaking and entering to get money. Or worse. Hell, I already *was* stealing. Taking people's pain pills from their medicine cabinets when I was using the restroom. Lifting bottles of liquor from their wet bars. You don't realize just how much you've done until you do a fourth step and write it all out. And then when I did my fifth step and read it to Rick, I learned all the other ways I'd stolen as well."

"What do you mean?" asked Ellie.

"After I'd gone down my list, which I thought was pretty thorough, Rick said, 'Well, that's the *stuff* you've stolen. What *else* have you stolen?' I didn't understand what he was asking. Then he said, 'I want you to think about how much time you've given to your addiction. How much time have you spent drunk or high? How much time have you spent hung-over and barely functioning? How much time have you spent thinking about partying? Or planning your next bender? Or sitting in jail? Because that's time you stole from your family. Time you stole from your friends. Time you stole from your employers. Time you stole from your community, by failing to participate.'

"He told me to make another list, and write all that down. I went back to the halfway house and sat down for hours and made that list. And when I realized how much time I'd stolen from others, that was what broke me. It was much worse than the dollar amount of the stuff I'd stolen. That's something I can do something about. I'm making amends where I can—paying people back. But I can never give that time back to my family. Or my friends. Or to God, who has given me so much—and which I totally wasted."

An awkward silence fell on the group as Carlos looked into the bottom of his empty coffee cup. The silence was broken by Steve, who spoke up in a gruff voice. "Well, Carlos, hearing you talk makes me wonder if I'm not much different from you." Carlos looked up at him. "Oh, I don't mean that I've stolen bourbon from friends. Or that I'm an addict. But I've stolen a whole ton of time from my family." He paused, as if deciding whether or not to elaborate on his statement. He saw the hopeful expression on Carlos's face, and then continued.

"Most of you know me. Or at least you know my company. Well, it's no secret that I'm proud of what I've built up here. Started from scratch thirty years ago. I employ a bunch of people, and I have a great staff. I believe in our products. My family has never wanted for anything, my kids all graduated from great schools, and all but one work in the family business.

"But truth be told, I sometimes wonder if I really know my kids. When they were young, I was already heading to the office when they woke up, and only made it home for dinner with them once or twice a week. Sure, their dad took them to their ballgames on the weekend, but I was barely present, thinking about new product lines or wrestling with logistical problems." He shook his head. "I told myself I was doing it all for them. And maybe I was." He looked at Carlos.

"But I bet you if I made a list like yours and added up all the hours I was at work before and after everyone else was in the office, and the hours I was thinking about the business while I was at home, and the nights I was entertaining clients—all time I stole from my family—I'd be shocked." His shoulders slumped. "Or maybe not. I guess I've always known in the back of my mind the truth of what I was doing." He looked up to see Yasmina's compassionate expression, and straightened his shoulders. "Oh, my kids turned out all right. They have us over for dinner pretty regularly, so I guess they're not too resentful!" He laughed briefly before looking down. "But even though I've given them all I could, what have I stolen from them in order to do so?"

"Thanks, man," said Carlos. "I appreciate your honesty." The group nodded their agreement. "It's hard enough to admit the truth to yourself, let alone anyone else. So, thanks." He held up his cup. "I need a refill. Can I get anyone anything?"

Steve added, "And I need a smoke."

"OK," said John. "Why don't we take a quick break and then pick things up again in five minutes."

When the group settled down again, John asked, "So, why do we steal stuff? We've talked about the euphemisms we give for stealing so we can deceive ourselves into thinking we're not really stealing. But even when it's obvious that we are, in fact, stealing, clearly lots of us do it anyway. Why?"

Ellie got the ball rolling. "Because we want something and can't afford to buy it?"

"OK," said John. "But why not wait till we can afford it and *then* buy it? Or, if we'll never be able to afford it, just give up the idea of having it? Why do we *steal* it?"

"Because sometimes you've just *got* to have the latest Ugg boots," Ellie stated. "And if your parents won't spring for them . . ."

"Conspicuous consumption," said Jenny. "After all, the one who dies with the most toys wins. Or so they say."

Will observed, "Rudyard Kipling said this to the graduating class of a prestigious medical school: 'You will go out of here, and very likely you'll make a lot of money. One day you'll meet someone for whom that means very little. Then you will know how poor you are.'"[3]

John jumped in. "That gets to the heart of this, I think. We're going to talk about the Second Word—idolatry—a few weeks from now, but I think it's directly linked to this Word. Now, talking about idols might conjure up images of wooden figures carved by primitive peoples representing a god of some kind, but I think the idols we have are quite different. An idol is something, often good in itself, which we worship instead of God. There's no question that one of the biggest idols in our culture is money or wealth. We worship it in the sense that we make it the biggest priority in our life and give it ultimate value: something we are willing to sacrifice for. The drive to possess more begins with what we already have and can be all-consuming."

Sam said, "It's no wonder that Jesus said, 'You cannot serve God and wealth.'"[4]

"Right," noted John. "You cannot serve both God and property. Which may well be the basic claim underlying the prohibition against stealing. I wonder if theft can also involve deception, because we don't understand whose stuff it is ultimately. The psalmist says, 'The earth is the LORD's, and all it contains.'[5]

"Even for those of us who do believe in the Creator, we still seem to think that what we possess is our stuff. My personal property, for me to dispose of as I want. And if I'm really spiritual, then I tip, I mean, tithe, 10 percent to God. After taxes, of course."

Sam leaned forward. "I heard a great sermon about that a long time ago. This guy was talking about the tithe and then pulled out his Bible and read some passage about how the people of Israel were supposed to give God 10 percent of everything—produce, livestock, even wine. But as he kept reading, turns out what they were supposed to do with all that food and booze was throw a big party in Jerusalem!"[6]

Steve snorted, "I bet you didn't hear that sermon in *your* church!"

"Actually, I did. Our preacher invited him to come speak. He was pretty famous, I think. But that ended up being the first *and* last time he was invited." He laughed. "Anyway, this guy went on to say that we have it backwards. We give 10 percent to God and think the remaining 90 percent belongs to us. But he was saying that it *all* belongs to God, and that Israel got to party with the 10 percent to celebrate God's provision for all their needs. Because God had given them enough to live on as a people, and everyone would have enough as long as they took care of each other. They were supposed to make sure the poor were fed, immigrants weren't exploited and the priests got their share. So no matter how successful each individual family or town was, they understood that God had entrusted them with the land to provide for everyone. And if someone's crop failed, then their neighbors fed them."

Rick spoke up, "That's why I love the Lord's Prayer. Because Jesus told us to pray like this: 'Give *us* this day *our* daily bread.' Now I know most people probably pray that personally, asking God to take care of *my* needs or my family's needs, but what if God literally meant 'Give *us*—*all* of us'? And what if God has indeed given us— the whole earth—all that we need to live? Then that means if people are hungry while my pantry is full, then I have to ask myself, *Whose bread do I have?*"

"And," said Sarah, "whose shoes do I have in my closet?"

Will leaned forward. "I believe it was Saint Basil who said, 'When someone steals a man's clothes, we call him a thief; shouldn't we give the same name to one who could clothe the naked and does not? The bread in your cupboard belongs to the hungry man; the coat hanging unused in your closet belongs to the man who needs it.'"[7]

"Are you looking all this up on your iPhone under the table, or are you really just a walking book of quotations?" asked Ellie. The group broke into laughter, and Will held up his empty hands with a smile.

John said, "I spoke on this theme one Sunday at church a couple of years ago, and the following week, a young woman came up to me after the service and said that was the first time she had ever been to church. I asked her what led to her coming that morning, and she told me her story.

"She had recently finished a lengthy stint in federal prison, and had been released to a three-month program at a facility that brings a van to our Sunday service. She arrived at the halfway house with literally nothing except the clothes on her back. Apparently her roommate at the program had come on the van the previous week, listened to the sermon and when she got back she went to her closet and divided the few clothes she had into two piles and gave this young woman half of them. When she asked her why she did that, her roommate said something like, 'That's just how we roll at my church.' That was enough for her to come check us out."[8]

"Wow," said Yasmina. "That's amazing."

"I know. And very humbling. I went home that afternoon and walked into my closet, and saw for the first time just how much money I spend on things I really don't need. And how little I give to others who don't have access to the kind of resources I have."

Will leaned forward. "As I've been thinking about the Eighth Word this week, I revisited something Paul wrote to the church in Ephesus. I think it nicely pulls together what we've been talking about." He turned to Ellie with a smile. "And as I don't have it memorized, would you mind reading it for us?" He handed her his Bible and pointed to the verse he was referring to. Ellie took it and read, "He who steals must steal no longer; but rather he must labor, performing with his own hands what is good, so that he will have something to share with one who has need."[9]

Will thanked Ellie. "Paul's call to the thieves in the community is really interesting. He doesn't say, 'Get a job so you can support yourself.' He says, 'Get a job so you can help support others.' Paul addresses the two kinds of theft we're talking about here, sins of both commission and omission. It's not enough to just not steal: we also have to not withhold what we have from those in need. Even if we stopped all the ways we take what isn't ours, most of us have a very long way to go when it comes to hoarding—stealing from those who need what we have."

"That sounds more like socialism than Christianity," said Steve.

Will laughed. "I know it does." Then his face turned serious. "Which is really sad. If those of us in the church were taking Jesus seriously, maybe people would say that it's socialism that looks like Christianity."

It was quiet for a moment, then Jenny spoke up. "What about all the ways we steal from people that aren't so obvious?"

"What do you mean?" asked Ellie.

Jenny turned to face her. "Have you ever been in a clothing store and looked at the price of something and thought, 'How can they sell it for that?' Because it's so cheap?"

"Sure. Especially during sales."

"Right. Have you ever tried to find out why they can sell clothes for so little?"

"No. I've never really thought about it, I guess."

"It's because those clothes are often made by children. Kids who work sixteen hours a day for peanuts. Or by workers in factories where they have no rights, who can lose what little pay they get for making mistakes, who get short—if any—breaks, and who rarely see the light of day, literally. Factories where the fire exits are often chained shut to prevent theft, so that when poor wiring or decrepit equipment starts a fire, hundreds of people die in agony.[10] All so you and I can find 'bargains' and fill our closets with clothes we don't need and will hardly ever wear. You don't have to shoplift in order to steal from others. Every time we buy that kind of clothing we're stealing people's dignity and their right to a fair wage. They're modern-day slaves."[11]

John interjected, "You may be interested to know that what you're talking about is probably closer to the meaning of 'don't steal' than shoplifting is. In the rabbinic tradition the Eighth Word is not about stealing stuff but rather about kidnapping.[12] It is about the theft of a person, as indicated in other parts of the Torah." John reached for his Bible. "For instance, in Deuteronomy 24:7, we read, 'If a man is caught kidnapping any of his countrymen of the sons of Israel, and he deals with him violently or sells him, then that thief shall die.'"[13]

He put down the Bible, and picked up another book. He found the place he wanted. "'Stealing a person's freedom is virtually always a matter of economics, the theft of a person for economic gain, turning the stolen object into a human machine of productivity.'"[14]

"The beginning of the story that leads to the Ten Words is the selling of Joseph into slavery by his brothers, one of whom asked, 'What profit is it for us to kill our brother and cover up his blood? Come and let us sell him.'[15] Joseph ended up a slave in Egypt, and four hundred years later his descendants—now freed slaves—receive this Word, which says, in effect, 'No more stealing people for economic gain.'"

"No more slavery," said Yasmina.

"Exactly. Although it took us several millennia to figure that one out."

Jenny added, "But don't forget: there are more slaves in the world today than at the height of slavery in America."

John shook his head sadly. "We're still dehumanizing people, turning them into something to own and exploit, like any other possession. We may think the meaning of 'No stealing' is obvious, but it began with slavery." He leaned forward. "What's interesting is that there is no object to the word *steal* in the commandment itself. The rabbis inferred the object—people—from other commandments in the books of the law, but the lack of an object in the Eighth Word opens up the trajectory of meaning to more than just the person being stolen. It also prohibits any act that would rob a person of their property or their life. Especially if that property is the means of their livelihood." John opened his Bible again.

"So, a couple of chapters later we read that it is forbidden to steal oxen or sheep, animals a person keeps for work or food. If the thief is caught, he or she has to make economic restitution.[16] Then there are all kinds of commandments about not stealing from your employees by not paying them fairly or by withholding their wages."[17]

Yasmina asked, "What does that look like today? How do we steal people's oxen? How do we steal from workers?"

Jenny spoke up again, "By demanding ever cheaper goods at the store, like I was saying. This country was founded by Puritans, right? We've all heard of the Protestant Work Ethic and the virtue of thrift. That's in our DNA. So we shop at those huge megastores that—because of their sheer size—can buy goods and services at the cheapest possible price. And they can sell them at that price because they find countries with the cheapest labor—whether it's exploiting kids or not. They buy goods that can be made so much more cheaply there than here because the countries where they're made don't have labor laws or the kinds of environmental protection laws that keep the costs much higher here. So those stores sell goods far cheaper than anyone else can, and we feel good because we're being frugal by shopping in those megastores. But the reason we're able to save money is because we're part of a system that is doing all the things you're telling us the Eighth Word says we should not." She paused for breath. "And I bet hardly anyone in your church ever thinks about *that*."

John nodded his head. "You may well be right, Jenny. But not after this Sunday's sermon!"

Sam, with a sparkle in his eye, said, "I've got a title for your sermon." "Oh yeah?"

Sam winked at Steve. "Jesus was a socialist."

John laughed. "Or, at least, 'Moses was a socialist.'"

He turned back to Jenny. "I want to pick up on what you were just saying. Because I do think it's important. When I get up to speak on 'Thou shall not steal,' most of my congregation are going to be thinking about theft of private property. But like you said, there's a much wider meaning for this Word. And the fact of the matter is, we are *all* implicated in a global economic system that is deeply unjust. And even if it *is* the best possible system—which I'm not convinced it is—the church at least ought to be offering an alternative. But, sadly, we're not."

He glanced down at his watch. "Wow—this morning has flown by. We need to wrap this up. Over the years I've learned that the most important question to wrestle with in a sermon is, 'So what?' Not necessarily to answer the question but to send people out asking it. So, in these last few minutes, let's talk about a couple of things. What are the consequences of *not* keeping the Eighth Word as we've been describing it? And what practices are we going to adopt to try to keep it? We've already talked about weakening our consciences by using euphemisms for stealing, but what other consequences are there?"

Sarah began, "Shoplifting and employee theft raises the price of things in stores."

Steve offered, "How about health care fraud? I've seen that estimated at $400 billion a year."[18]

Sam said, "Like I said, when my house was burglarized, I began to be suspicious of strangers in the neighborhood. I'm sure that's why people who can afford to, live in gated communities. Then the guards at the entrance keep the strangers out. But I don't want to live suspicious of others, afraid of being stolen from. It seems like what you're saying, John, is that we need to take responsibility for the well-being of our economically deprived neighbors, not wall ourselves off from them."

"Absolutely," Jenny said, "Theft weakens our social bonds, violating trust. When lobbyists spend millions to weaken regulatory agencies, reduce environmental protection and expand tax breaks for corporations and their other wealthy clients, the cost to society is a lack of trust in our democratic institutions, and other structures designed to hold community together. If we come to believe that honesty does not pay, then why not 'get yours'? How about those for some of the consequences of violating the Eighth Word?"

"Amen," said John. "One last thing before we get to the 'what can we do?' question. Nearly every commentary I read on the Eighth Word talked about the inequitable distribution of wealth that results from our failure to keep it. The ever-increasing gap between the wealthy and the poor, both in this country and around the globe, can arguably be directly traced to our refusal to practice the Eighth Word, for all the reasons we have been talking about.

"OK. Here's where the rubber hits the road. What are *we* going to do to keep the Eighth Word? What practices can we adopt?"

Rick leaned forward. "John, you talked about how being ripped off in that scam negatively affected the way you viewed the people who came to your church for financial help. I can't begin to tell you the number of times those I've sponsored in AA have stolen from me. It would have been easy for me to have become cynical, and stop taking risks on people who were early in recovery. But my sponsor told me that every time someone stole from me, I needed to find someone else to help out financially. Because what's worse than being stolen from is to let the thief steal your desire to be generous. To let the thief steal your desire to help your neighbor. To let the thief steal your ability to trust others and, I guess, to trust God."

"Wow," said Yasmina. "That's awesome. Do you actually do that?"

"Oh, you can be sure it sometimes takes me a while to get there, but I do eventually. Because I know that for me, if I stop trying to help others, then I'll just get back into being old selfish and self-centered Rick, and that way of living never worked too well for me."

Carlos spoke up, "Something that's helping me is making amends for what I've done. Making restitution to the people I've stolen from. Actually admitting what I've stolen and then planning how to pay it back. Which is really hard when you don't have much to begin with."

He turned to John. "And that story about the girl in the halfway house. Man, that's convicting. There's always someone who's got less than me. I'm always looking at the people who have a lot more than me and thinking I'm so poor. I guess I want to learn how to live like this," Carlos spread his fingers wide, "so I can not only receive from God, but can also let it flow through my hands to people who need it. I've spent too much of my life living like this," he clenched his hands into fists, "trying to hold on to what little I had." He looked at Sarah. "You're not the only one who needs to ask 'Whose shoes do I have?'"

Jenny said, "One of the most important things we can do is think about what we're buying. To ask, 'Why *is* this so cheap? Whose right to a living wage or healthy working conditions or basic human dignity am I stealing by buying this product?'" She held up her coffee cup. "It's choosing fair trade or direct trade coffee." She nodded at Steve. "It's choosing to buy local when you can, supporting businesses that employ your neighbors and hopefully who treat their employees well, like Steve here."

"Now you're going to make me blush, Jenny," said Steve. "But while I do appreciate your sentiment, I don't think it's always as simple as that. I agree—it's terrible that the cheaper goods most of us buy are made by children and adults who are exploited. But what's the alternative? If we stop buying from them, what happens to those kids and their families? There's a reason those factories don't seem to find it hard to maintain their workforce. For people living on a dollar a day, three dollars a day is a huge jump in income. Even if it's still unjust." Seeing Jenny about to jump in, he added, "I'm not defending it. I'm just saying that it's not always as cut-and-dried as we like to think."

John spoke, "Well, it's been another cracking conversation—thanks so much for being here and helping me think through these important questions." Turning to Jenny, he said, "If distance no longer determines who my neighbor is, then we *do* need to keep asking the questions you're asking. If the earth truly is the Lord's and God has given us enough for everyone to live a full life, then we *do* have to ask, 'Whose shoes do I have?' And then we need to ask the systems question, 'Why don't they have their own shoes?'"

He turned to Carlos. "And I love the image of coming to life with open hands. It's what I love about the Eucharist. We come to the Table holding out empty hands. Even those who may have much come as those who appear—and truly are—poor and in need of what only God can give. Part of which is to realize that we all eat from the one loaf that God gives, and that one loaf, when shared, is enough to feed us all."

He pushed his chair back and stood up. "OK. One last idea. What if, sometime this week, we were all to take a walk through our homes and pile up everything we could find that we had not acquired honestly? Office supplies we've brought home, 'because everyone does it.' Things we'd bought where we knew the price was too good to be true, but didn't ask questions."

"What if we actually did that?" said Ellie. "Seriously, what if we all went through our homes and identified what we'd stolen and brought it here next week?"

"What would we do with it?" said Steve.

"I could take it to Goodwill," said John.

Steve laughed, "I suspect the pile we could come up with together wouldn't fit on the back of your bike!"

"Probably not. But it's a thought, isn't it? This is one of the few Words where we can actually make restitution—make right what we've done. Either by returning what we've stolen to the owner or giving it away in service of those in need."

Sarah stood up. "I'm in. And how about we also look at the stuff in our houses that we *didn't* steal, and ask, 'Who does that really belong to?' And then maybe take the time to give it to someone who really does need it. To love our neighbor as ourselves, right, John?"

"Sounds good to me, Sarah."

Ellie asked, "Hey—what are we going to be talking about next week?"

"Sex."

As John saw Yasmina and Ellie's eyebrows raise almost simultaneously he attempted to backpedal. "Well, not sex in general. Specifically, adultery." Feeling the stares of everyone in the group, and with color rising in his cheeks, John looked at the two students. "I feel like I should ask you to bring a note from your parents." Which caused Ellie to almost spray John with the dregs of her latte as she burst out laughing.

"Oh, I think we'll be OK."

As the girls headed for the door, Sarah put her arm through John's. "What I wouldn't give to be a fly on the wall in *her* house at dinner tonight." John looked at her with a puzzled expression. Sarah grinned. "Can't you just hear it? 'So, how was the group this morning dear?' 'Great, Dad. I have to go through our house and find all the stuff we've stolen and take it with me next week, when we're going to be talking about sex with the pastor.'"

Everyone roared with laughter. Steve slapped John on the back. "Who knew that Mondays could be so much fun?"

4

From Betrayal to Fidelity

The Seventh Word

> *Twenty miles away she waits alone for me,*
> *but when I try to picture her,*
> *you're the one I see.*
> DEL AMITRI, "BE MY DOWNFALL"

> *You shall not commit adultery.*
> EXODUS 20:14

When John walked into the coffee shop, he was greeted by the sight of a small mountain of consumer goods piled up in a corner. Steve got up from his seat, beaming from ear to ear.

"What do you think, pastor? Bunch of guilty consciences out there, huh?"

John looked somewhat stunned. "This is all from our group?"

"No! I thought your idea was a good one, so I've been talking about it with some of the other regulars all week. I asked the owner if people could leave their stuff in the corner, and she was totally up for it. I guess once stuff started showing up, the word got around, and, well, as you can see I guess we *are* just a bunch of thieves after all!"

John surveyed the pile of office supplies, clothes, towels, pirated DVDs and the like, and then shook his head. Steve put his arm around a mannequin draped in a plush bathrobe. "This is my personal favorite."

"Wow. That is quite something."

"I've got a couple of my guys coming by later today to pick it all up and take it to the Rescue Mission's thrift store down the street. They should be able to do some good with all of this!" exclaimed Steve.

As John started to walk to where the rest of the group was seated, Steve put his arm out to block his way. "Aren't you forgetting something?" John looked at him blankly. "Well, where are your stolen goods? Or didn't you find any?"

"Oh, right. Actually, I've already taken mine to Goodwill. I realized I wouldn't be able to get everything here on the bike this morning."

"I'd like to have seen your pile!"

"Oh, it was mostly clothes. The result of me standing in my closet and asking 'Whose shirt do I have?' But I assure you, there were a few items in the boxes whose provenance was questionable."

Steve slapped him on the back. "Glad to hear it, preacher. Now let's go talk about sex."

As John sat down, Ellie said, "Can you believe how much stuff is out there? I told my friends at school all about it too. I think most of the DVDs and stuff came from them. And those really cute skirts. It's totally cool!"

Sarah said, "Needless to say, you can put me down for most of the shoes." She looked at Rick. "I had to do a little grief work before I could bring them here. And pray the Serenity Prayer a few times while I piled up the shoeboxes. It was a lot harder than I thought it would be." She laughed. "I guess I need to do some Tenth Step work."

John took his first sip of coffee. "Well, let's just jump right in, shall we? Question: if we took a quick poll of the folk in here and asked them to name one of the Ten Commandments, which one do you think we'd be most likely to hear?"

Sam responded first. "Thou shalt not commit murder."

John nodded. "Any others?"

"Thou shalt not commit adultery," said Jenny.

"Sure. Why do you think those two would be the first to come to mind? Rather than say, for instance, 'Thou shalt not steal' or 'Thou shalt not bear false witness'?"

Yasmina, twisting her hair with one hand, said, "Well, stealing and lying are nowhere near as bad as taking someone's life, so I think people would tend to think of murder first. And adultery . . . well it might be because we're all so obsessed with sex. Or maybe because of how devastating that kind of betrayal must be."

"Maybe it's because it seems so commonplace these days," said Sarah. She turned to John. "If half of all marriages in the U.S. end in divorce, how often is adultery part of the picture?"

John leafed through his notes. "Depends on which studies you read. It seems that one in five Americans, and two in five people around the world, have extramarital affairs. But this is all based on self-reporting, so I think it's safe to say that the actual numbers are even higher."[1]

Ellie chimed in. "Well, if what our friends tell us goes on in their families is anything to go by, I bet you're right. I don't think it's that big a deal anymore."

"But it *is* a big deal," said Jenny. "At least in America. Just ask any politician caught with his pants down. That's what will make the news—way before the media reports on any legislation he may be involved in."

Sam piped up, "But those facts are important. They speak to character, and that is essential in elected office."

"I think people in America might agree with you," responded Jenny. "But not in some other countries. I remember reading a former French president's memoirs, in which he detailed all kinds of sexual encounters he had while in office—his literal office—and the French public kind of went 'Ho hum.' The last Italian prime minister's sexual antics are almost cartoonish, but it wasn't that behavior that lost him the election."

"And this is all nothing new." Everyone turned toward Sam. He shrugged. "It's not like the people in the Bible were much better. When I wasn't cleaning out my closet this week, I was thinking about the Seventh Word. And the trouble I see with it is that hardly anyone in the Bible seems to have actually kept it. Let's start with King Solomon. Seven hundred wives. And a few hundred concubines."[2]

Ellie almost sprayed her latte over Carlos. "What! How does that work?" She paused. "Actually, I don't want to know how that works. Eww!"

"His old man, King David, took the wife of one of his generals and then had him killed to try to cover it up.[3] Abraham gave his wife, Sarah, to the king of Egypt, pretending she was his sister. Sarah later gave her servant, Hagar, to Abraham as a concubine. Jacob married two sisters. The twelve tribes took the wives of the men they killed in battle when they entered the Promised Land. So, we've got old Moses coming down the mountain with this Word, 'Do not commit adultery,' which then just seems to have been roundly ignored by most of the major characters in the story."

"You're absolutely right, Sam," said John. "Although, as a side note, I find the list you just gave us one of the most compelling reasons for me to take the Bible seriously. We hear these people's stories—warts and all. Most of them have clay feet. Hardly the kind of spiritual giants you might expect to find in a holy book. You'd think God would have cleaned their stories up a bit! But that's a conversation for another day."

He turned to Jenny. "And you're absolutely right as well, Jenny. Outside of conservative America, adultery seems to just be part of life. Although not every country is like France. A few are on the complete opposite end of the pole. Let's not forget that people are being stoned to death for adultery in some Middle Eastern countries. Actually, when I say 'people,' I mean 'women.' While we may wink at 'indiscretions' here, in other countries, men are murdering women who have been caught in the act of adultery."

"Which sounds like another story out of the Bible," said Sam.

"Yes," said John. "I can guess the one you're referring to, and I plan on coming back to that later. But I want to focus on the original meaning of the Seventh Word first. Because it appears to be somewhat different from the ways we think about adultery today."

Jenny piped up, "Absolutely." Everyone turned toward her. "So I did some research this week. I Googled 'adultery laws in the Bible' and started to read some of the other passages. What I read was really troubling."

"I'm intrigued," said Steve.

"OK," she continued. "So we tend to think of adultery as having to do primarily with sex, with violating a monogamous relationship, right? But the people who received the Ten Words knew little of monogamy—men had lots of wives. The way I read it, marriage in the ancient Near East seems to have been primarily an economic affair, not an emotional affair. Wives were a man's property. They bore his children, which preserved the bloodlines of inheritance and maintained a clan's hold on its property. Thus, for a man to have sex with another man's wife—with the possibility of her becoming pregnant with his child—threatened the integrity of the family line and potentially the wealth of the tribe."

Jenny turned to John. "So, is that right? Is adultery really about stealing another man's property, rather than someone cheating on their spouse?"

"That's a really good question, Jenny, and a fair one, given what the Torah—the first five books of the Bible—says about all this." He scratched his chin. "Now, here's the question I have in response to yours. If a woman was seen *only* as a man's property in biblical law, then presumably adultery could have been covered by the Eighth Word—the prohibition against theft. If that is the case, why is it necessary to spell it out in a separate Word? I did some research myself, and I found this helpful." He pulled out a book. "This commandment is an explicit claim that the sexual activity between a man and a woman who are married is central to the relationship and may not be disregarded."[4]

"That commentator's thought suggests to me that this is *not* just about taking another man's property. I do think the married couple's sexual relationship is very much in view here. It seems to me that the aim of the Seventh Word is to protect the marriage of one's neighbor. It affirms the sacred character of marriage and the centrality of sex to the relationship. While those listening to these words may have thought first of their own marriages, I wonder if the exhortation is actually to take responsibility for the well-being of your neighbor, which would go along with the words we've talked about so far—'Don't envy your neighbor,' 'Don't lie about or to your neighbor,' 'Don't steal from your neighbor.' And now, 'Don't have sex with your neighbor's spouse.'"

"It's important to remember the big picture for these Ten

Words: the formation of a people from a bunch of former slaves. The formation of a people who will work together for the common good, not just their own self-centered needs. Those of us who are married may hear this Word and think it's about the protection of *my* marriage, about my need not to stray and destroy *my* marriage. But what will ultimately protect my marriage is my *neighbor* keeping this commandment by refusing to commit adultery with my spouse, and by me doing the same. By the creation of a society—a community—where people protect their neighbors. Not least by refusing to have sex with their neighbor's spouse."

"But what if the spouse doesn't care?" asked Ellie. "Or if they're both doing it? You know, open marriages. If both the husband and the wife are doing it, then no one's getting betrayed, right? And if no one's getting hurt, then is it really wrong?"

Sam grunted.

"I'm just saying," retorted Ellie.

Will spoke up, "We say that so often, don't we. 'As long as no one's getting hurt, it's OK.' It seems to me we may not know that someone's getting hurt right at that moment. In my experience we don't realize just how much damage we can do to each other—and ourselves—until much later."

Sarah chimed in, "And the ripples of the affair spread out far beyond the spouses. If the affair rocks the husband or wife's world, then those same waves can hit their kids just as hard. Then they spread out to two families, to friends, to neighbors. When it happens in an office or a church, it can draw lines where none existed before as people side with one or the other of the spouses."

"So why do we do it?" asked Sam. "Not just today, but back in the Bible? Why do people commit adultery?"

John said, "Here's one answer to that question that I heard last week." He looked around the group. "I dropped into the Rescue Mission for lunch last Thursday. I sat down at a table and got drawn into a conversation with three folk who live in the same apartment complex down the street."

"One of them was talking about his neighbor who had to leave town for a few days. He was saying that he has noticed that his neighbor's wife has had a couple of male visitors 'that I don't think are friends with her husband, if you know what I mean,' and how he thinks that's just not right. To which his friend responded, 'Well, you know what the Bible says about women like her. She tempts weak men by saying,

I have perfumed my bed
with myrrh, aloes and cinnamon.
Come, let's drink deeply of love till morning;
let's enjoy ourselves with love!
My husband is not at home;
he has gone on a long journey.'"[5]

"You're making that up!" said Sarah.

"No," said John. "I must say I was impressed that he had that particular text memorized! And I couldn't help but wonder why. But he wasn't done yet. 'This is the way of an adulteress,' he quoted from memory:

She eats and wipes her mouth
and says, 'I've done nothing wrong.'"[6]

"So, once again, it's the woman who's to blame, huh?" said Yasmina. "Like those poor, weak-willed men just couldn't resist her 'spices.' *That's* why men commit adultery?"

"Well, at least according to my dining companion."

"Who *was* quoting the Bible, though, right?"

"Yes. Although it was a pretty select choice of all that the Bible has to say on the subject." John turned to the group. "But what do *we* think? What's behind adultery—why *do* we do it?"

For once, there was prolonged silence in response to a question, until Carlos said, "Umm, because people aren't getting it at home?"

Sarah reached across the table and swatted him upside the head. Carlos blurted out, "What? What did I say?"

Sarah smoothed out her dress as she resumed her seat. "Young man, there are ladies present." Sam laughed out loud, which he promptly tried to cover with a fit of coughing.

Rick said, "I do believe you're blushing, Carlos."

Carlos, looking quite uncomfortable, said, somewhat defensively, "Well, *isn't* that why people cheat on each other?"

"I don't think Sarah was questioning the reason you gave, more the way you worded it."

"Oh." He turned to Sarah. "Sorry."

"On behalf of the ladies present, I accept your apology." Before he looked away, Sarah winked at him. He smiled sheepishly in return.

Sarah then turned to the group. "While I may not appreciate the way Carlos phrased his answer, I think many men justify their behavior in that way. I remember reading *People* magazine when I was getting my hair done a while back, indulging in a little celebrity gossip." She turned to John. "That was obviously long before our conversation on the Ninth Word."

"Obviously," said John.

"The actor in question, who was in divorce proceedings, admitted to, and I quote, 'adultery by diminished responsibility.' Apparently his sex drive was just 'too high' for one woman."

"And," said Yasmina, "apparently his self-restraint was 'too low.'"

Sarah nodded. "That same thought did cross my mind."

John said, "OK, so one reason people commit adultery is because of a lack of sex in their marriage. What else?"

"Boredom," said Rick. The group's attention shifted to him. "After a while—maybe years—I guess the excitement and newness and exploration wears off and sex becomes routine. Even something you do because you know you ought to, not because you necessarily want to. All that passion and fire seems to fizzle out. Especially after you have kids! Sure, in the moment it can still feel good—even wonderful. But those moments can all too easily become further and further apart, until you realize you haven't made love for months.

"That's why I'm not convinced adultery is always about lust. I think it can often be more about *longing*. A longing for the excitement, the passion, the fire of the early days of dating. The excitement of getting to know someone new, learning about them, wooing them. Intrigue. The stuff that gets evoked when you catch the eye of a beautiful stranger in the street who gives you a smile and suddenly this flood of longing overwhelms you, almost out of nowhere. A longing that makes you want to turn and catch up to the person and, I don't know, get a cup of coffee and hear their life story." He looked around the table. "Adultery isn't always about sex. Or, at least it doesn't always start there."

Steve spoke into the awkward silence that followed Rick's words. "You know, this hasn't always been my locale." The table's attention shifted to him. "I used to get my early morning caffeine fix at another coffee shop in town. Obviously I wasn't the only regular. Among the others was a young woman, who, like me, came in to read the paper and have a cup of coffee before work." He took a moment to look each person in the eye.

"You know me, I love to talk about the headlines. I discovered this young woman did too. We started talking. Laughing about the foibles of our fellow humans. Getting angry about the things our fellow humans do to each other. I found myself looking forward to seeing her, to getting her opinion on things." He paused. "Then I found myself just looking forward to seeing her, period. Then I was thinking about her during the day. Sometimes she was the last thing I thought about before going to sleep."

With a catch in his voice, Rick said, "What happened?"

Steve lifted his eyes to Rick's face. "I told my wife."

"What!" Ellie blurted out. "Whatever did she say?"

Steve turned to Ellie. "She suggested I find another coffee shop."

"Wow," said Yasmina.

"Yeah, wow," said Steve, quietly. Then he lifted his coffee cup and said with his more customary bluster, "And, I must say, the coffee is much better here."

There was another moment of quiet before Ellie said, "This is really heavy."

"But really good," said Yasmina. "Thanks, Steve."

He shrugged.

"You know," said Rick, quietly, "I think the Ninth Word is part of all this too. Adultery involves a lot of deception. Not just all the lies about where you've been and who you were with. It's also about self-deception. The things we tell ourselves to rationalize, to justify our behavior, to quiet our conscience. It's not just a 'fling.' Or a bit of a romp. Or a harmless bit of fun. It's not true that it doesn't mean anything. Nor that this is 'true love.' We try to tell ourselves that it's beautiful and not sordid. But it's none of those things. It's betrayal and hurt and loss of integrity."

More silence.

"I wonder if adultery doesn't always have to involve another person," said Yasmina.

"Huh?" said Carlos.

She turned toward him. "Don't you think that a job or a promotion, a hobby or a sport, or an obsession of some kind can be 'the other person'? I think a husband or wife can be pouring all their emotion and energy into something other than their spouse, practically ignoring them, and those things can be much harder to deal with than sex, because there's nothing wrong with them—at least on the surface."

"That's really insightful, Yasmina," said Sarah, raising an eyebrow. Yasmina held her gaze for a moment, then looked away.

Sarah turned to Jenny. "You're looking thoughtful, Jenny. What's on your mind?"

"Honestly?"

"Of course."

"I was thinking a couple of things. One, I'm pretty amazed at how willing you all are to share such personal, and, I imagine, painful stories about yourselves. And how grateful I'm becoming for this group." She tilted her head back and blinked her eyes rapidly. "The other thing I'm wondering is what part our culture plays in adultery."

She leaned forward. "The issue with adultery is fidelity, right? We break the vows we made to the other, the 'forsaking all others' promise, the 'till death us do part' promise, the 'I'm staying with you come what may' promise. Those promises are a commitment, a covenant, right? And therein lies the problem—because our culture, I think, is increasingly commitment-phobic."

"Go on," said Sarah.

"Just look at my friends. They never commit to anything. I can organize a Facebook event for a project in the neighborhood, and a bunch of them will click on 'Maybe' rather than 'Going'—just in case something better turns up. They like to keep their options open—just in case. I've got a friend who's been with this great guy for five years, and he keeps asking her to marry him, and she keeps saying no. I think she's mad, but when I asked her why she won't commit, she said, 'What if I say yes and then meet someone who's even more amazing?'"

"Isn't that why people sign them prenuptial agreements?" asked Sam. "Till death us do part. But just in case . . ."

Steve interjected, "Lawyers. Putting the money into matri-money since the nineties."

Jenny groaned, eliciting a grin from Steve. Then she turned to Sam. "You're retired, aren't you, Sam?"

"Yup."

"How long had you been at the company you retired from?"

"Let me see now. I guess it was right at forty years."

"And how many jobs did you have before that one?"

"Maybe a couple, right out of high school."

"Right. Some of my friends seem to change jobs more often than I change underwear." She looked at Sarah. "No offense, Sarah."

"None taken. Although I hope that's an exaggeration! And by the way, I have friends who change churches about as often, because, and I quote, 'my needs weren't being met there anymore.'"

"Really? Huh. Anyway, we'll move to new cities and states over and over again for employment. Just about the time we're making real friends we'll up and move for a job that we believe, or at least hope, is better than the one we're currently in. Or that will pay more. Or is more secure. Or will look good on the résumé."[7]

As Steve began to interrupt, Jenny waved her hands. "I know, I know. Some people have no choice. I get that. But many do have the choice to stay, but they choose to move on. So," looking around the group, "why should it be any different in marriage? I think we live in an adulterous age. If we think the grass is greener on the other side of the fence, then let's just hop right on over. And don't even get me started on politics."

Steve said, "Oh, I'll go there with you, Jenny!"

She smiled. "OK. Twist my arm. How many politicians make all these promises about what they'll do when they get elected, and then once we jump in bed with them, they hop out the other side and break all the promises they made?"

"All right," said John. "Let me see if I can summarize what I'm hearing. You're saying we either commit adultery because we're in a sexless marriage or we're not satisfied with marital sex or because we have a longing for the intensity of the early stages of a relationship, and because we're affected by a commitment-averse culture. Is that a fair summary?"

"Sounds good to me," said Sam. He looked at John. "And I bet over the years you've heard plenty of stories when you're counseling members of your congregation whose marriages are on the rocks 'cause one of them's been unfaithful. I know you can't talk about it, but if I was a gambling man, I'd bet that you've heard all kinds of attempts to justify the cheating. How many of them have said something about having sexual needs that aren't being met at home? Or that the other person really listened to them—unlike their spouse—which is what they were really looking for, but somehow ended up in bed. Or some such excuse."

Will leaned toward Sam. "And the saddest part of all that is that they're *right*. Some of us *do* live in sexless marriages where our sexual needs go unmet. Some of us *do* live with a spouse who will not communicate with us, and we desperately need an understanding and listening ear. Some of us *do* need a lot of physical affection, and our spouse doesn't provide it. Those are legitimate needs. Yours and my generation may not have the same divorce rate as the younger ones, but I'll tell you this: a lot of people our age had—or still have—utterly miserable marriages because *we* had those same needs and just buried them. Sure, we may have celebrated our golden anniversary, but there wasn't much of a marriage to celebrate beyond sheer longevity."

Ellie spoke up, "So, what are you saying? If I get married one day and whatever needs I may have aren't being met, my options are to gut it out and be miserable or cheat on my husband and get divorced? Why would anyone ever get married?"

"A lot of people are choosing *not* to get married for that very reason, Ellie," said Will. "However, I'm not sure it's an either-or situation. At least, I hope it's not. I think one of the great challenges of marriage is what to do when legitimate needs aren't being met— especially given that the person not meeting those needs usually promised 'to love and to cherish' us when we got married. So we have a right to ask them to meet the needs they can. Or work on learning how to if they can't. But there's the rub. Because *we* made that same promise to *them*—that we would love and cherish them. Regardless of whether they keep their promise to us.

"So when we're faced with our legitimate but unmet needs and decide to look elsewhere to get them met, we're breaking covenant with our spouse—and ourselves. We may feel 'alive' or 'free' or 'fulfilled' in this adulterous affair, but the truth is, all too often what we discover later on is that our freedom is really slavery. Slavery to our needs, to our passions, to deception and everything else that comes with an illicit affair. And here's the irony: we're not only cheating our spouse; we're cheating ourselves. We're not only cheating our spouse out of the fidelity we promised; we're cheating ourselves out of our own integrity. We're not only breaking faith with him or her: we're breaking faith with ourselves."

John spoke up, "One thing I've learned from all the marriage counseling I've done over the years is this: adultery is rarely what destroys a marriage. It's usually a sign that the marriage was *already* struggling, if not dying. And, likewise, stopping an adulterous affair does not *save* a marriage, unless the couple takes it as a warning to see what's really wrong in the marriage."

He turned to Will. "I think the reasons you gave for adultery are very plausible. And can be equally as true for the church as for the wider culture. Yet I confess there's part of me that, frankly, expects 'the faithful' to be just that: faithful. And clearly many of us are not. So I've been wondering this week why that is."

"And?" Sarah queried.

"I wonder if it's because the way the church tends to think about sex and marriage is a bit messed up."

Steve interrupted, "This just in: local pastor admits the church is screwed up about sex. We'll have more on this breaking news story at ten."

John smiled wryly. "Yes, I realize that may not be a shocking confession to most of you around the table. What I'm trying to say is that I think the church's understanding of sex and marriage has been increasingly shaped by the culture and less so by the Bible."

Jenny said with a grin, "So, you're ready to find a couple of extra wives then, John?"

John laughed. "You guys—cut me some slack, would you! Here,

let me read you what Elaine Storkey has to say on the subject." He picked up a book, and flipped to the page he wanted.

> *It would not be an exaggeration to suggest that in spite of even the most lavish and detailed wedding preparations, every marriage in Britain and America today gets off to a bad start. That is because the very meaning of what those two people are doing is fundamentally out of step with the ethos of contemporary society.*[8]

"So," said Jenny, "I'm not the only one who thinks that way then."

"No. Although it's too easy to blame the collapse of marriage solely on our sex-obsessed, commitment-averse culture. I think the blame can also be laid squarely at the foot of the church for failing to help people have a clear idea of what marriage is about, *including* our own members. Three-quarters of couples get married in a church, but I wonder if even those couples who do some kind of premarital counseling have any idea of what marriage really is about."

"OK," said Ellie. "So what is marriage about?"

"Obviously that depends on who you ask. Or what books you read. My guess is you could walk into the bookstore down the road and find a whole shelf full of books on marriage—what it is, how to improve yours, etcetera. I'm sure we could take a quick poll in here and get as many answers as there are people. Some might say it's the answer to loneliness. Others, that it binds two people in love together. Or that it offers financial and legal benefits for couples. Or that it creates a stable basis for having kids. Not all of those were the case when the Seventh Word was being written, as Jenny pointed out. The question is, what does the Seventh Word have to say to us about marriage today when we no longer marry for the sake of inheritance or family perpetuity?"

John continued, "From my understanding of Scripture, marriage is about more than just the couple's emotional or financial or children's well-being. Those are all important, for sure. But clearly just the *fact* of being married does not automatically lead to those things. I wonder if marriage creates the framework in which those things are possible. That it's only within the security of mutual lifelong commitment that our marriages—and our children—have a chance to flourish.

"I also think that the Seventh Word tells us that in marriage men and women have the opportunity to mirror in our lives and relationships some of the fidelity God has shown to us. Certainly the Bible is full of the imagery of marriage as a picture of God's covenant love for God's people. Time and time again God's people broke covenant with God, running after other gods for their security, committing adultery. Yet God kept wooing God's people, trying to win their love and affection, rather than filing for divorce, if you like."[9]

"I don't get what you're saying," said Ellie.

"What I'm trying to say, Ellie, is that all the things we're looking for in marriage only come when we are faithful to the covenant we make when we get married. Not just in terms of sexual fidelity but all the things involved in out promise to love and cherish each other. To want them to be happy, not just for my needs to be met. Here," picking up another book, "let me read you what Joan Chittister says: '"You shall not commit adultery" is the word that calls us to truly care about the people we say we love. Not to use them. Not to exploit them. Not to ignore them. Not to patronize them. Not to manipulate them for the sake of our own satisfaction.'"[10]

"To love your neighbor—your spouse—as yourself," said Sam.

"Exactly," replied John. "Especially when it comes to sex. There's no question we live in a sex-saturated culture, but I don't think the problem is that we think about sex too *much*. Rather it's that we think about it so *poorly*. If sex is all about personal satisfaction and fulfillment rather than a vulnerable self-giving to one another, then why wouldn't someone go elsewhere if they aren't happy about their marital sex life?"

He turned to Carlos. "If sex is about '*getting* some' rather than *giving* some, then why not look elsewhere? How many movies or novels or country songs, for that matter, portray adultery as normal—if not downright unavoidable? How many portray sex as something that happens when two complete strangers who have just met fall into bed and, with no fumbling or awkwardness or pain or mess, experience ecstasy before falling asleep with smiles on their faces? Sex is so one-dimensional in the movies. It's almost a caricature of sex as the vast majority of us experience it. I can't tell you the number of times either my wife or I have said, 'Well—they never show *that* in the movies.'"

"TMI!" yelled Ellie, putting her hands over her ears, much to the amusement of the rest of the group.

"Sorry, Ellie. What I'm trying to get at is this. I'm convinced that sex belongs in marriage, not because I'm a prude or 'unliberated' or *old*, but because of the safety that a loving and permanent covenant provides. The safety that makes possible the kind of vulnerability that we long for—to be 'naked and unashamed' with another person, just as the first couple were described. It enables us to come together and feel secure enough to be utterly vulnerable and give ourselves to another, even as they give themselves to us. My wife and I stopped talking about 'making love,' which sounded like we were about to construct something, and started talking about 'growing love'—nurturing our love, tending to each other, not thinking of sex as an end in itself but as part of the fabric of our relationship."

"That all sounds beautiful and right," said Jenny. "But it just doesn't ring true for me. You've told us that members of your church still cheat on their spouses, so obviously even if they agree with you about what marriage is, that wasn't enough for them."

"You're right, Jenny. And that's why I said that I think even church members' understanding of sex and marriage has been shaped more by our culture than by Scripture. And the simple fact that all too often we fail to acknowledge that marriage is hard work. Because it's about self-giving, self-denial, selflessness—the exact opposite of the majority of the cultural messages we're exposed to every day." He reached for yet another book. "I really like how Ellsworth Kalas writes about that:

> *In most cases we mistake the wrapping for the gift. It's the wrapping, after all, which is given all the play in our popular culture—the seductive body, the insistent persuasion, the intrigue of the forbidden. Perhaps we shouldn't be surprised that these are the elements that our culture emphasizes, because it is so much easier to show a well-turned thigh or a rippling pectoral than a lifelong loyalty. It's very hard for a camera to say, 'For better, for worse, for richer, for poorer, in sickness and in health,' because such words have to be lived out over months and years."*[11]

Steve gestured at the pile of books in front of John. "Speaking of gifts and wrapping, I think we should all chip in and get John a Kindle for his birthday so he can give his back a break." John looked at the growing pile of books in front of him and shrugged.

"OK," said Jenny, "so what about married couples where one person's needs for sex or affection or communication aren't being met? What is that person supposed to do? Just be faithful—and miserable—like Will said?"

"That's a great question," observed John. "And one that countless books have tried to answer. I think a couple simply acknowledging that reality is a huge first step toward changing things. Counseling can help. Taking small steps toward meeting the other's needs can get us moving in the right direction. Being patient and kind, and trying to understand why our spouse is hesitant or unable to meet our legitimate needs—all those things are the hard work of marriage."

"Well, John," said Sam, "looks like you've got all kinds of stuff you could talk about on Sunday. I'm not sure I'd know how to turn all this into a thirty-minute sermon!"

"Me neither, Sam. Although as I've thought about it this week, I'm leaning toward one of two directions."

"Which are?" said Sarah.

"Well, I thought about beginning with Jesus' words on the Seventh Word from the Sermon on the Mount: 'You have heard that it is said, "You shall not commit adultery." But I tell you that anyone who looks at a woman lustfully has already committed adultery with her in his heart.'[12] And then talk about the seriousness of breaking covenant, the importance and challenge of fidelity that we've discussed today."

"Or . . . ?" asked Sarah.

"Or I was thinking of telling the story of the woman caught in adultery from John's Gospel."

"I don't think I know that story," said Jenny.

Yasmina added, "And I don't think I'm going to like it, by the sounds of it."

John looked at his watch. "Wow. We're past the hour already. You got a few more minutes?"

"Absolutely," said Sarah. The rest of the group nodded their agreement.

"OK. So, Jesus is teaching in the temple. The Bible scholars and Pharisees drag in a woman, stripped to the waist, and stand her before Jesus. Then they say, 'Teacher, this woman was caught in the very act of adultery. In the Law Moses commanded us to stone such a woman.' They turn to the crowd and say, 'What do you say?'"[13]

"Excuse me, but where the hell is the man?" asked Jenny. "I'm assuming if she was caught in the act, there *was* a man present?"

"I know. This is wrong on *so* many levels. It wouldn't surprise me if the reason the guy isn't there is because the Pharisees set the whole thing up just to trap Jesus in public, and the woman is just a convenient victim. Because Jesus is in a pretty tight spot here, everyone in the crowd is waiting to hear how he'll answer the Pharisees."

"So," said Yasmina, "what did he say?"

"Nothing."

"Nothing!" said Jenny.

"Nothing. Because Jesus knew that this wasn't about adultery. It wasn't even about this woman. It was about *him*. He knows if he says, 'Don't stone her. How can you even think of doing that?' then they'll say, 'Well, then how can you call yourself a teacher of the law, because Moses clearly says that's what we should do?' And if he says, 'Go ahead and stone her.' then the crowds are going to say, 'We thought you were different than all of them, but maybe you're just the same.' Whatever he says, it's a lose/lose situation for Jesus."

He turned to Jenny. "So he just ignored them. He knelt down and started writing in the dust at his feet. The only time in all of the Gospels that Jesus writes something, he doesn't write it on papyrus, he writes it in the dust, for the wind to blow away his words. Obviously the Pharisees weren't satisfied with this response. They demanded an answer. So Jesus straightened up and said, 'I'll tell you what. If you have never sinned, then go ahead, pick up a stone and throw it at this woman.'"

"Wow," exclaimed Ellie. "Then what happened?"

"One by one, beginning with the oldest ones there, everyone walked away. Everyone. Not just the woman's accusers. Everyone. Why do you think that is?" He looked around the table. "When Jesus said, 'If you're without sin, throw the first stone,' I think everybody had a moment of clarity. I think they all realized, *I'm as messed up as this woman. I have given myself to things that have taken away my integrity, whatever they are. I have given myself to things that promised freedom and only brought me bondage. I have been selfish, self-centered, self-absorbed.* And suddenly everyone is stripped as naked as that woman is. They're all adulterers."

John leaned forward. "Where does adultery begin? Does it begin with our genitals? Or does it begin here," he thumped his chest, "with our heart? The heart that God wants to capture with God's love; because if God can capture our heart, then nothing else can get a hold of it. The deepest truth of ourselves, as human beings, is that we were created to love and be loved by God, and that we want to be captured by God's love.

"Underneath all the crazy stuff that we do to try to meet this desire to be loved, to feel connected to something, to feel affirmed and accepted just the way we are; all those things that lead some of us to commit adultery, underneath all that is this hunger to be loved that God has put inside each one of us. And the trouble is, we feel this desire, this God-given desire, and we look for it to be met, in the words of the country song, 'in all the wrong places.'"

Will spoke quietly, "Every man who knocks on the door of a brothel is looking for God."[14]

"Right, Will. When we knock on those doors, we're looking for God. The trouble is, if we walk *through* those doors, most of us find hell. We become slaves. The freedom that I was supposed to find with this new person, the freedom that I was supposed to experience with this great sex, ultimately cannot deliver what it promises. All too often I'm still left with those same needs, only now I'm facing the loss of my integrity. Realizing that I've gone back to slavery, and not freedom."

No one spoke for a while. Then Yasmina asked, "Is that the end of the story?"

"No," said John, leaning back again. "Jesus said to the woman, 'Where are your accusers? Is no one left to condemn you?'" He paused. "I've often wondered if she had her face buried in her hands, afraid to look, but when she lifted it up to steal a look, she realized that everybody had gone. Then she said, 'There's no one. There's no one, Lord.' 'Then neither do I condemn you,' said Jesus.

"And then he says this: 'Go. Sin no more.' And this is what I hear in those words: 'Don't give your heart away, don't get captured by what promises so much but can deliver so little. Let your heart be embraced by God's love, and embrace the freedom that God wants you to live in. Don't become a slave again.'" John folded his hands on the table. "Or something like that."

"For what it's worth," Rick offered, "I hope that's the story you tell on Sunday."

"I'm with Rick," Yasmina seconded.

"Me too," Ellie chimed in.

Will spoke up, "Can I offer a thought before we go our separate ways? If these Ten Words are practices we are to adopt so that we seek the common good together, loving God and loving neighbor, what could we do to keep this Word?" He reached across and picked up one of John's books. "If I remember rightly . . ." he thumbed through the pages, "yes, here it is. 'Chains do not hold a marriage together,' Simone Signoret wrote. 'It is threads, hundreds of tiny threads, which sew people together through the years.' It's weaving those threads that counts."[15]

"That's beautiful," said Sarah.

"And a good word to end our time together," John added. "Thanks so much everybody. This has been really wonderful."

"Well," said Ellie, "I think I just about survived the sex talk. What's up next?"

John smiled. "Oh it'll be another light subject. Next week we'll be talking about the Sixth Word, 'Do not kill.'"

As the group began to push back from the table, Steve grabbed Rick's elbow. "Got time for another cup of coffee?"

Rick held his gaze for a moment. "Sure. I'd like that. I'd like that a lot."

5

From Violence to Peace

The Sixth Word

I wear the black in mourning
for the lives that could have been.

JOHNNY CASH,
"THE MAN IN BLACK"

Thou shalt not kill.

EXODUS 20:13 KJV

As a curl of blue smoke drifted skyward from the tip of his cigarette, Steve heard his name called and looked up from his paper. He saw Rick crossing the parking lot toward him. "Morning, Rick. How's things?"

"Better than I deserve, no doubt." Rick sat down at the picnic table across from Steve. "Thanks for getting here a little early so I can check in. And thanks again for asking to hear my story last week. It was good to speak some of that stuff out loud again."

"No worries. Well, no point beating around the bush. How have things been at home this week?"

"OK. I spent a bunch of time thinking about the fact that I'm still married, which is pretty much a miracle. I mean, after all that my wife put up with during my drinking, for me to have an affair in sobriety . . . Well, I thought that would be the final nail in our marriage's coffin. But certainly things have never been the same since. I know I've got a long way to go to regain her trust.

"But knowing that and accepting that? Well, that's my work to do. And, man, I tell you, it's hard work some days. If I'm honest, I just want her to get over it. Forgive and forget and all that. Which I know is utterly unfair and is all about my selfishness. And I've got enough years in the program to know that if I dwell on that too long, then I'll end up in trouble."

Steve raised a questioning eyebrow.

"Oh, I don't think I'll drink over it. At least it won't start with that. But sitting in there last week," gesturing with his head toward the coffee shop, "talking about all that, I had this moment of clarity when I realized I am fully capable of deceiving myself into justifying another affair. And if I were to do that . . . well, I remember the look on my wife's face when I told her the first time, the pain of betrayal I saw in her eyes. And the pain I felt because of my complete loss of integrity. I don't think I'd survive that again."

"So, what are you doing about that?"

"Talking to my sponsor, that's for sure. And I've been thinking about that quote Will read last week. About the threads that hold a marriage together. Our marriage almost came unraveled because of my affair. I need to start reweaving some of those threads—and drop any expectations I have that my wife should do the same. And I realize that it *is* the little things that are going to make or break our marriage. So I've been thinking about what I can do to show her that I do love her, that I know her 'love language'—those things that make her feel loved. And try to do them.

"I've also been thinking about the things I do to self-sabotage that. Things like driving home from work and wondering if I'll get a hug when I walk in, needing that physical, tangible affirmation and evidence that she still loves me. Then getting myself all worked up about it to the point where I decide that she's not going to hug me, so I'll walk through the door and blow right past her rather than risk feeling rejected. I know, I know, crazy. But there you have it."

"So, what did you do differently this week?"

"When I caught myself thinking that way, I called myself on it and stopped that stinkin' thinkin' right there. Then when I got home and greeted my wife, I just asked her if I could have a hug."

"And?"

"The first couple of nights it was kind of awkward. Like we had forgotten how to do it if it's not spontaneous." He gave a wry smile. "But on Friday when I walked into the kitchen, she looked at me, and before I could say anything, she just held her arms open and stepped toward me. That felt huge."

"I bet it did."

"Yeah."

They sat in silence for a while and watched as the other members of the group began to arrive. As they stood to go in, Steve placed both hands on Rick's shoulders and looked him in the eye. "Whenever you need a hug, don't hesitate to ask." Rick held his gaze for a moment before pulling him into a bear hug. Then they walked inside.

When everyone was seated, Steve said, "Well, preacher, how'd it go yesterday?"

"Pretty well, I think. I did some thinking and praying after we met last week, and decided to go with the group consensus. So I told the story about the woman they dragged before Jesus. As I looked around the congregation while I was speaking, a few people didn't meet my eye. A few did, some through tears. And I bet when I check my messages tomorrow, I'll be making a few appointments for marriage counseling. At least I hope I will."

John sighed heavily. "But obviously the movie-theater shooting overshadowed everything else.[1] We had a time of silence to pray for the families of the victims of that senseless killing. And for the family of the young man responsible for their deaths—I can't begin to imagine what they're all going through."

Yasmina said, "It's been all over my Facebook newsfeed. People have some pretty strong opinions about what happened *and* what should happen now. And they're not expressing them in very nice ways. I almost shut it down yesterday."

"I'd say it's almost ironic, given the Word we're talking about this morning. But if it is ironic, it's also tragic. A tragedy that gets played out every day. So, let's get to the Sixth Word, shall we?" John picked up his Bible and found the text.

"Thou shalt not kill."

Will raised an eyebrow. "That doesn't sound like the version you normally read."

"That's because it isn't." He held up the Bible. "This is the good old King James Version."

"I think that's the one I have," said Jenny, "because that sounds like what I read. Is there a difference between the versions?"

"There is. I normally read the New American Standard Bible. It translates the Sixth Word like this: 'You shall not murder.' So do two other popular versions, the New International Version and *The Message*."

"But don't they mean the same thing?" asked Sam.

"It kind of sounds like they do. But I'm beginning to think that 'Do not kill' is quite different from saying 'Do not murder.' But before I say more about that," turning to Yasmina, "how about you tell us what your friends are saying on Facebook."

"Well, at first it was pictures of candles and stuff, people saying, 'Pray for the victims,' you know, that kind of thing." She chewed a fingernail for a moment. "But then someone shared a photo from a gun rights group that said something like 'One person with a concealed handgun could have stopped this.' Then it was my gun-control friends' turn, and they started posting stuff about banning assault weapons—or all weapons. That's when the comments started getting nasty—two groups of people with *very* different views arguing back and forth and calling each other names. Honestly, I thought it was pretty tasteless, given what had happened. I mean, a bunch of people are dead, for goodness' sake."

John nodded. "I know. I admit I have strong feelings about all this and what we could do as a society to address the questions it raises. I posted my thoughts on my Facebook wall yesterday, knowing that I have good friends on both sides of this particular fence. The discussion was heated, although civil, for the most part."

He looked around the table. "Over the last few weeks, we've talked about the fact that people can come up with all kinds of reasons to ignore or dismiss the Words we've discussed so far. But my guess is most people would say 'Do not kill' is so basic to human society that there's not much to talk about. If we're going to live together, then it starts by not killing each other. It's a no-brainer, right?

"But then we start reading our Facebook walls, and suddenly it's not quite so simple. Even among my own congregation it's not a simple matter. There are some members who will strenuously invoke this commandment against abortion but not think about capital punishment—and vice versa. I read this yesterday, and I wanted to read it to you." He picked up a book.

> *Of all the commandments, "Do not kill" is the one we keep least carefully, most cavalierly. We make up reasons all the time to kill: we kill to preserve the state; we kill to protect the self; we kill to punish wrongdoers . . . we kill to enforce authority. We kill for political reasons. And, finally, we kill whole segments of society— strip their lands, rape their forests, soil their air—to satisfy whole other segments of society. "You shall not kill"? Hardly.[2]*

He looked at the faces gathered around the table. "So, is Joan Chittister right? Although we might think 'Don't kill people' is a no-brainer, do we really come up with exceptions so easily?"

Yasmina waded in. "Well, that was the topic of conversation on my wall. Everyone agrees that what that guy did was evil, but when it comes to *stopping* people like him, well, clearly there's a whole slew of my friends who think killing someone to stop them killing someone else is just fine, even a person's civic duty, should they happen to be carrying a weapon."

"I don't know what I think about having everybody carrying guns," said Sam. "I reckon if there'd been a few concealed weapons holders in that movie theater and they'd pulled their guns when that guy opened fire, they would have just added to the chaos. I mean, who's the bad guy you're supposed to shoot? Which muzzle flash do you aim at through the smoke? And anyway—he had all that body armor on, like he was expecting someone to shoot back. I think there'd be a lot more people dead if that had happened."

He leaned forward. "But surely that's why we have capital punishment, isn't it? To stop someone from killing again. And to send the message that killing is not acceptable. That's what's probably going to happen to this guy, after all."

"Not any time soon, though," said Jenny, "given the state of our criminal justice system. Which means you can forget the whole deterrent argument—it's not exactly 'swift and certain punishment,' is it? And anyway, don't you think that's kind of wrong-headed? 'Do not kill.' Unless, of course, it's to send the message that killing is wrong." She pushed back from the table. "It's a bit like spanking your kids to teach them that hitting people is wrong."

"Well, that worked for me," said Sam, gruffly.

Jenny laughed and leaned across to pat him on the arm. "I bet it did, Sam." More soberly, she said, "But capital punishment is obviously not working as a deterrent. Which is why more and more countries are abolishing the death penalty. The U.S. keeps some pretty unpleasant company when it comes to capital punishment. Only China, Iran, Iraq and Saudi Arabia kill more of their own citizens than we do, with Yemen and North Korea close behind. So we're right up there with the 'Axis of Evil' when it comes to the death penalty."

"And don't forget that justice is certainly not blind when it comes to race," added Sarah. "You're much more likely to be sitting on death row if you're black or if you killed a white person."

"And you're *not* likely to be sitting on death row if you're wealthy," said Jenny. She turned to John. "I'm all for taking the Sixth Word and applying it to capital punishment."

Ellie spoke up, "And don't forget about all those people who were proven innocent later. Some spend decades on death row before being set free."

Yasmina turned to John. "Well, I think Joan what's-her-name is right. 'Do not kill' is yet another commandment we choose to ignore or justify breaking on a pretty regular basis. Just look at today's paper. What's the news, Steve?"

"Let's see. Front page is obviously about the shooting in Colorado. Inside, let's see . . ." He began to flick through the pages. "20-year Sentence in Group-Home Beating Death. More Fighting in Syria. Attacks Across Iraq Kill 30. Ceremonies Across Norway Remember 77 Massacre Victims. President Apologizes for France's Role with Nazis."[3]

Sarah shook her head. "And every day it's the same. There's so much killing, so much death. Last year there were something like 35,000 deaths by firearms in this country. If the numbers are the same for the first half of this year, that's more Americans shot dead—the majority by their own hand, mind you—in the past eighteen months than were killed in the whole of the Vietnam War."

Jenny observed, "We have this whole cult of violence thing going on. The blockbuster movies portray it for our 'entertainment.' We'll weep over movies like *Saving Private Ryan*, put yellow ribbons on our cars with 'support our troops' on them, then pass the homeless veteran struggling with PTSD, drug addiction or whatever without even seeing him. We have this . . . this . . . this myth that war is noble, that soldiers are warriors, able to be shot at and shoot back for a year, then come back home to their family twenty-four hours later and be just fine."

Yasmina leaned forward. "What a bunch of crap. Do you know that more active-duty American troops have committed suicide this year than have been killed in battle?[4] 'Support our troops'? Who's actually doing that, huh?"

Crossing her arms, she sat back in her chair. Jenny put her arm around Yasmina's shoulders and pulled her in for a side hug. Yasmina offered her a weak smile before looking around the table. "I'm sorry."

"Girl, you ain't got nothing to be sorry for," said Sarah. "I like to see young women get riled up about something worthwhile."

"So what does 'Do not kill' mean for soldiers?" asked Rick. "Or for war as a whole? I mean, that's kind of the point of war isn't it—killing the enemy? Does this mean we should have just let Europe burn during the Second World War? That we should have left Saddam Hussein in power?"

Seeing Jenny about to respond, John jumped in quickly. "I think that raises a whole bunch of other questions that might be important but might also take us down a rabbit hole that runs very deep." He turned to Jenny. "Can we agree that *why* we choose to go to war with certain countries is a very different question than *whether* the Sixth Word prohibits going to war?"

"I'm not sure it is," said Jenny. "I think the first question is absolutely relevant to our conversation. Isn't that what 'just war theory' is all about? The question of when the use of lethal violence is permitted in order to save life?" She sighed. "But I think you're right in that most of the wars we've engaged in over recent history have been political, and then we've just tried to claim the moral high ground for them after we've already made the decision to go to war."

Will spoke up, "I read the memoirs of a Roman Catholic chaplain who served during the Vietnam War. Obviously, he was well-versed in just war theory, and I imagine he could have questioned whether the Vietnam War fit the criteria." He reached for a book.

"Don't tell me you haven't memorized this quote?" asked Ellie with a grin.

Will laughed. "No, not this time, Ellie. I'll just have to read it. 'The point is that war as a human enterprise is a matter of sin. It is a form of hatred for one's fellow human beings. It produces alienation from others and nihilism, and it ultimately represents a turning away from God.'[5]

"So for at least one theologian, war is clearly a violation of the Sixth Word." Turning to Yasmina, Will said, "He had something else to say that I think you'll appreciate. He noted that when soldiers came out of the jungle, they'd often visit the local brothels. His fellow chaplains despaired of this behavior and lectured the soldiers about it at Mass. This troubled our chaplain, who reflected on that fact in this way: 'How is it that a Christian can, with a clear conscience, spend a year in a war zone killing people and yet place his soul in jeopardy by spending a few minutes with a prostitute?'"[6]

"Exactly," said Yasmina. "Are all these homeless vets messed up because they paid for sex a couple of times or because of what they did and saw in battle?"

Sam piped up, "If that was the case, why weren't a bunch of GIs living on the streets after World War Two? Is it a generational thing? Or a drugs thing?"

"Which came first—the drugs or the warfare?" asked Jenny. "Maybe the drugs were how they coped with what they saw and did in Vietnam. Or from going house to house in Afghanistan today. Which seems to be a very different experience from being in France in the Second World War." She sighed heavily. "But then again, I've never been in any of those places. What do I really know?"

Yasmina turned to John. "So all those books you're reading," pointing to the small pile on the table in front of him, "What do they have to say about war?"

"Quite a bit, actually." He picked up the largest book. "I'm loving this particular commentary. It's really thorough and very thought-provoking. Let's see now . . ." He flicked through the book. "Ah, here it is."

> *If many wonder whether the sixth commandment has anything to say about war, that is a very natural question. By definition, such killing is planned, intentional, [has] an aspect of enmity, and involves all sorts of devices to plot and plan the death of an enemy. One may not easily rule the killing of war as outside the prohibition against killing in the commandments.*[7]

He picked up another, slimmer volume. "Now these two guys note that by telling God's people not to kill, the Sixth Word is going to put them at odds with every government on earth! However, they're not big fans of discussions about just war theory or whether war is ever an option. Here's what they say: 'Our time might be better spent wondering how we might change the church to be the sort of place that produces and supports non-violent people.'"[8]

"I like these guys already," said Jenny.

"OK," said John. "Let's see where we are in our discussion. So far we've talked about or mentioned murder, carrying guns to prevent murder—or gun control to do the same—capital punishment, abortion and war. Are we missing anything?"

"What a depressing list," said Carlos. "I hope we *haven't* missed anything."

No one added anything else, and so John continued, "I wanted to come back to the difference between 'Do not kill' and 'Do not murder.'"

Sam leaned forward. "Using *murder* makes sense to me. All the commandments we've been talking about are about how we treat our neighbor. I don't *accidentally* commit adultery with my neighbor's wife. I don't *accidentally* steal from or lie about my neighbor. And I don't *accidentally* kill my neighbor." He paused. "Well, I guess I could. But then, how could God command, 'Do not *accidentally* kill your neighbor'?"

"That's kind of what I've always thought too," said John. "But it's been interesting doing some reading about this Word. Apparently the Hebrew verb is quite rare—the majority of times it shows up elsewhere are in just one chapter, Numbers 35." He looked around the group. "Without trying to turn this into a seminary class, basically that verb is used in several ways in that chapter. It's used to describe someone intentionally killing another person—or at least someone striking another person with a hand-tool knowing it could result in his or her death; it's used for someone who accidentally kills another person and also with reference to the act of execution. In other words," picking up the large commentary, he read, 'Both *accidental* and *legal* forms of killing can be and are described by *the same verb* the Decalogue uses to prohibit killing another person.'"[9]

He put the book down. "Which makes me wonder if we really can translate that verb in the Sixth Word as 'murder.' It seems all kinds of killing might be in view."

"But that doesn't make sense," said Sam. "Why would God say 'Do not kill' if the word can mean 'Do not execute'? Because God then goes on to give commandments to execute people who kill someone!"

"Yeah," said Carlos. "How does that fit in with what Jenny and Ellie said about the death penalty?"

"*And*," continued Sam, "what about all the times when God tells the Israelites to kill people? Is that giving them a free pass to break the commandment? Is killing OK if it's divinely sanctioned?"

"That's the terrorists' justification," said Carlos.

"And the crusaders, right?" added Jenny. "Not to mention the churches that allow people to carry concealed weapons into worship services. Or that ask God to bless us in the wars we're fighting. Seems like 'Do not kill' doesn't apply then, huh?"

John leaned forward. "I've got a shelf of books on those kinds of questions back home. And here's what I'm convinced of. Anyone attempting to use these kinds of texts to justify any kind of violence or warfare today is ignoring the vast majority of the Bible. *Nowhere* in the New Testament do you find Christians killing people. All the killing is done *to* them—sometimes sanctioned by the legal authorities—and it's never seen as a positive thing." He sat back. "After all, Jesus himself suffered capital punishment."

Jenny paused. "OK. Change of pace. Here's what I've been thinking about this week." She looked around the table. "I know we're looking at these commandments in reverse order, but as I was reading the Ten Commandments in my Gideon Bible, I was struck by something. It seems like keeping the Words we've already discussed begins with this Word, right? I mean, 'Don't kill your neighbor' is pretty much saying 'value and protect human life.' And then we move out from there to specific ways to do just that—don't steal from them, don't sleep with their spouse, don't lie about them. But if we don't value our neighbor, if we don't think we should protect them, then what motivation is there to do those things?"

"That's great," said John. "And it ties in well to the story I'm thinking of preaching from this Sunday." He took a swig of coffee. "So, there's this king of Israel, Ahab. And he's married to this woman, Jezebel."

"Mm, mm," said Sarah. "She is a piece of work."

"She certainly is," John acknowledged. "So, King Ahab has his eye on a neighbor's vineyard. He thinks it'll make a nice spot for some raised beds for his veggies. So he asks his neighbor, Naboth, to sell it to him. Or exchange it for one of the king's own vineyards. But Naboth turns the king down, because it's his family's land, his inheritance, and it's not for sale.[10]

"Well, King Ahab doesn't take that too well. He goes home and basically throws himself a little pity party. Jezebel walks in and asks him what's wrong, and he tells her. She says, 'Are you the king or not?' And before he can answer, she says, 'Don't worry—I'll get that vineyard for you.'

"So, the story begins with Ahab coveting his neighbor's vineyard. As the story unfolds we're going to move through the rest of the Words we've been looking at. Jezebel gathers the important people of the city along with Naboth. Then two men she has paid off confront Naboth, and accuse him of cursing God and the king."

"Bearing false witness," said Sam.

"Exactly. The people then drag Naboth out of the city and stone him to death. And Jezebel gives the vineyard to her delighted husband."

"So they stole his land, and had him killed," said Carlos. "I guess if she'd slept with him first, we'd have covered all the bases."

"Quite," said John.

"Did they get away with it?" asked Ellie.

"Well, the prophet Elijah confronts Ahab in his newly stolen vineyard. He tells him that because of what he has done, he and Jezebel will lose their own lives. Now, clearly there's an element of power involved in this story. But it begins with Jezebel's assumption that Naboth's life neither has value nor is to be protected. And it was murder by capital punishment—something numerous regimes around the world today inflict on their people."

"Well, this is all very interesting," said Ellie, "but it feels a bit, like, removed from where I live, you know? These are all 'issues.' What does 'Do not kill' mean in my day-to-day life?"

"Great question, Ellie," said John. "And one that's always at the forefront of my mind when I'm preparing to preach. The 'so what?' question, right? I wonder if we could pose that question to Jesus. What does he have to say on the subject?" He picked up his Bible and opened to a bookmarked spot.

> *You have heard that the ancients were told, "You shall not kill" and "Whoever commits murder shall be liable to the court." But I say to you that everyone who is angry with his brother shall be guilty before the court; and whoever shall say to his brother, "Raca," shall be guilty before the supreme court; and whoever shall say, "You fool," shall be guilty enough to go into the fiery hell.[11]*

"Whoa," said Yasmina. "Jesus just turned the heat up on this commandment! 'You shall not kill' becomes 'you shall not be angry with someone'? How does that work? I mean, who doesn't get angry every now and again?"

"Really?" said Ellie. "Jesus said being angry with someone is the same as killing them? That's crazy talk!"

"Well, Ellie, you're not the first person to make that observation," said John. "Jesus does kind of raise the bar on this one, huh?"

"Raise it? You'd have to be in zero gravity or something to get over that bar!" responded Ellie.

"So what do you think of Jesus' take on 'Do not kill'?"

"Other than the fact that it's utterly ridiculous?"

"Sure. Other than that."

"Well, like, I suppose a lot of murders are committed by angry people. Maybe that's why he said it? Kind of like, stopping it before it goes too far maybe? I don't know."

"Sounds good to me," said Sam. "I guess I've been so angry with people that I've wished them dead. Not that I'd ever take matters into my own hands, I hasten to add."

Will leaned forward. "Karl Barth might have something to say to you about that." He opened his notebook.

In most of us the murderer is suppressed and chained, possibly by the command of God, or possibly by no more than circumstances, convention, or the fear of punishment. Yet he is very much alive in his cage and ready to leap out at any time.[12]

Will looked up from the notebook. "How many times have we heard, 'I didn't mean to do it. I was just so angry'? Or 'I just got into this blind rage, and I couldn't help myself'? So, in our anger, sometimes we kill. In our hate of another, sometimes we kill. We might dismiss our own anger by saying, 'Well, I've never killed anyone,' but Jesus won't let us get away with that. Because, as always, ultimately it's not about what we do, it's about what's going on inside us. Moses revisits the Ten Words in Leviticus 19, and says this, 'You shall not hate your neighbor in your heart. . . . You shall not take vengeance, nor bear any grudge against your fellow Israelites, but you shall love your neighbor as yourself.'[13]

"Anger is a tricky thing. Of course, we all get angry, and many times rightfully so. Jesus himself got angry on occasion. But all too often our anger takes on a life of its own. I don't think that it's simple anger that Jesus is talking about. It's anger with an attitude, an orientation toward the other person that wishes them harm."

"I think I get what you're saying," said Yasmina. "Long before someone might try to hurt someone—even kill them—they got angry with them and did not find a way to deal with that anger, right?" She twirled her hair with her fingers for a moment. "It's like this guy at school. He did something a while back that really hurt a good friend of mine, and I was mad. I couldn't let it go. Still can't, I guess. Every time I see him, that anger comes back with a vengeance. Sometimes my fists clench without my realizing it. He's probably forgotten all about it, but I haven't." She looked around the table. "I don't think I'd ever hit him or anything, but, well . . ."

"Well," said Ellie, "if he never apologized or tried to make it right, you should be angry. At least, that's how I see it."

"But I don't like feeling the way I do when I see him. I'm not a violent person. At least, I like to think I'm not. I guess I just want him to hurt like he hurt my friend."

"An eye for an eye . . ." said Sam.

"Ah," said John. "I wondered if that would come up in this discussion. 'An eye for an eye, a life for a life.' The *lex talionis*."

"The what?" asked Ellie.

"It's a legal principle that states that the punishment should be identical to the offense. Hence, an eye for an eye, et cetera. It originates in the Torah, where it can be found in several passages. For some people it's the justification for capital punishment—a life for a life."

Sam added, "But it started earlier than Moses. It's right there in Genesis 9, in the covenant God made with Noah."

> *Whoever sheds man's blood,*
> *By man his blood shall be shed,*
> *For in the image of God*
> *He made man.*[14]

"A life for a life."

"It might be worth taking a look at the whole of that covenant," said Will. He looked around the table. "Most of us are probably at least somewhat familiar with the story of Noah's ark." Heads nod. "But do you know *why* God sent the flood, which wiped out everyone except for Noah's family?"

"Because the hearts of men were wicked," said Sam.

"Sure. But what explicit reason did God give Noah for the coming catastrophe?"

"Err . . . I guess I don't know."

"If I could . . ." said Will, gesturing at John's Bible. John passed it across the table. Will read, "Then God said to Noah, 'The end of all flesh has come before Me; for the earth is filled with violence because of them; and behold, I am about to destroy them with the earth.'[15] For the earth is filled with violence because of them."

Will laid the Bible down. "Beginning with Cain killing Abel—brother killing brother—humans have brought violence into God's world, destroying God's shalom, God's peace. I think it's *that* reality that lies at the heart of the Sixth Word—our tendency to respond with violence when provoked. So, after God carries out judgment on our violent selves, he makes a covenant with Noah."

He turned to Sam. "Part of that covenant is that in addition to plants and fruit, we are now given permission to eat animals. Instead of the harmony of the Garden, God says that now the animals will be afraid of us—and rightly so, given that we're about to start eating them. And so God introduced a concession to the story—the right to kill a living creature. However, God made it very clear that that right did *not* extend to killing another human being, by saying three times that if someone's lifeblood is spilled, God will require a reckoning. It is only then that we read the verse that you quoted.

"I think the point is not that God authorizes us to execute murderers, but to recognize that all life belongs to God and that murder is a violation of God's right, and the only way to respond to such a violation is for the life of the murderer to be taken. God sets up a legal mechanism for God's people to do just that in the law God gives to Moses." He looked around the table. "The tension lies in the fact that human legal processes are flawed, as Ellie pointed out earlier. And so in trying to affirm God's claim to human life by killing the murderer, we always run the risk of violating God's claim on the accused person's life by killing an innocent person.

"And Sam gave us the reason why life is so valuable that a person's life must be taken who themselves have taken another person's life: because human beings are made in the image of God. And that person is protected by the One whose image he or she bears."

Ellie said in an exasperated tone, "I'm totally confused. Are you saying that a life for a life is legit? Or not?"

Will laughed. "I'm sorry, Ellie. I don't always make sense to myself! What I'm trying to say is, rather than taking that verse to mean we can execute murderers, it reminds us of how far we are from the life God intended us to share together. A life of peaceful coexistence."

Sarah said wistfully, "And the lion shall lie down with the lamb."

"Hey, I've seen paintings of that," said Ellie. "Is that in the Bible too?"

Will said, "It comes from the prophet Isaiah's vision of what life was once like, and if you believe him, what life will be like again one day. 'And the lion will eat straw like the ox. . . . They will neither harm nor destroy on all my holy mountain.'"[16]

Carlos said, "What, we'll all be vegetarians?"

It was John's turn to laugh. "Would that be so terrible, Carlos? You know, the rabbis said that all those weird food laws in the Torah were meant to make Israel vegetarian."

"But what *do* we do with murderers then?" asked Sam.

Jenny weighed in. "How about life in prison? And I mean *life*. And anyway, aren't Christians supposed to be about redemption? Surely killing a person is saying nothing else can be done with him or her. Is that what you really believe?"

Steve weighed in, "A life sentence is certainly cheaper than putting someone on death row."

Rick rubbed his chin. "What if the story you told on Sunday is not just about adultery?"

"Go on," said John.

"Well, if I remember it right, Jesus said something like, 'Let the one without sin cast the first stone.' It seems like he's not questioning the law. He's not saying what she did wasn't wrong." He paused. "But he's making sure she doesn't die for what she did."

"And," said Yasmina, "I think he's telling all those people there that they have no business pointing their fingers at her, when they're no better themselves."

Sam said slowly, "Take the plank out of your own eye first."

Yasmina looked confused. "Something else Jesus said. Before you try to take the speck out of someone else's eye, check your own first."

John said, "Jesus said all kinds of things that seem appropriate to the discussion about capital punishment. 'Turn the other cheek.' 'Put away your swords.' And as he was being executed, he said, 'Father forgive them, they don't know what they're doing.'"

John glanced up at the clock, then turned toward Ellie. "I'm not sure we really addressed your question." She shrugged. "No, it's important. What *does* 'Do not kill' mean for us in our everyday lives?"

Sarah spoke up, "Well, the Words we've talked about so far are all about loving our neighbor, right? And if Jesus raised the bar on this one, as we said earlier, then *not* killing my neighbor is about as low as that bar can go. I don't get to take any credit for that." She paused, then said with a laugh, "Even if I've been sorely provoked a time or two! No, the way I see it, this is not about me *not killing* my neighbor. It's not even about doing all I can to not *harm* my neighbor. I wonder if this is really about me wanting *life* for my neighbor—the same kind of life I want for myself."

She leaned forward. "Maybe this commandment is telling us that failing to support the families and children of our society with health care, housing, food, education, day care and just wages—the things that constitute the essentials of the dignified human life—is at least as much a sin against life as war, abortion, euthanasia and all those other things we discussed will ever be."[17]

"Preach it, sister," said Jenny.

"Oh, I am, girl! I'm sick and tired of listening to members of my family go on about their being all 'pro-life'—by which they mean, anti-abortion—and how their church is for family values, and then they sit on their hands while the young girls in my neighborhood who don't know no different end up pregnant and get caught in the same cycle of poverty their momma did. And all the church will do is tell them not to have an abortion, and feel all righteous for 'saving a baby's life' when they do keep the child. But then do squat to help that child grow up with all that their own kids have. It's like my Al Anon sponsor always says, 'I don't get to claim a double for being born on second base.'"

Will spoke up, "Many of the Reformed catechisms form their questions about the Ten Commandments around what the commandment requires, and not just what it forbids. If I recall from my confirmation classes, the Heidelberg Catechism says,

> *Is it enough, then, if we do not kill our neighbor in any of these ways?*
>
> *No; for when God condemns envy, hatred and anger, God requires us to love our neighbor as ourselves, to show patience, peace, gentleness, mercy, and friendliness toward him, to prevent injury to him as much as we can, also to do good to our enemies.*"[18]

"Wow. Pretty impressive," responded Ellie.

Will shook his head. "Only if I do it, Ellie. Only if I do it."

Jenny spoke up, "Here's my answer to your question, Ellie. Tomatoes."

"Tomatoes?"

"Tomatoes. You know. Those shiny, uniformly red, plump, tasteless things at the grocery store you buy to put on your burgers in December."

"Oh, *tomatoes.*"

"Right. So, those likely came from Immokalee, Florida. They're picked by hand in thirty-two pound buckets by migrant farm workers, some who are literally slaves. They get paid fifty cents per bucket—the same rate as their grandparents made three decades ago. To make minimum wage they have to pick two and a half tons of tomatoes *every day.* You know what thirty-two pounds of tomatoes costs in December? About eighty bucks. How do we love those neighbors as ourselves? So they can live? So *they* can afford to buy those tomatoes if they want to?"[19]

Will picked up the Bible from the table. "There's part of a letter that one of Jesus' friends wrote that ties in what you're pointing out with what we've already discussed. Let's see . . ." Flicking through the pages, he found the place.

> *Everyone who hates his brother is a murderer; and you know that no murderer has eternal life abiding in him. We know love by this, that Jesus laid down His life for us; and we ought to lay down our lives for our brothers and sisters. But whoever has the world's goods, and beholds his brother in need and closes his heart against him, how does the love of God abide in him? Little children, let us not love with word or with tongue, but in deed and truth.*[20]

"So," John said, "if I can try to sum up. It seems the trajectory of the Sixth Word is more than simply not hurting others. It is about insisting on *life* for them—'to love our neighbor as ourselves.' And Jesus ramps that up even more by telling us that our neighbors include our *enemies*.[21]

"Yet, as is sadly all too evident, we're so full of fear and envy and violence that loving our neighbors is hard enough, let alone loving our enemies. In many ways we're no further along than that bunch of slaves hearing these Words for the first time. Perhaps that's why the Words are so blunt. 'Do not kill.' Not much nuance or qualification or equivocation for us to argue over there. Just, 'Do not kill.'"

He laughed. "Both Calvin and Luther said that God spoke to us like little kids. If we're going to keep this Word, then we're going to need patience and understanding, empathy, and courage—all virtues that take a long time to acquire. So for now God speaks to us like little kids, 'How about you don't kill each other for starters.'"

He turned to Yasmina. "So, your anger at this classmate. Clearly you don't want to feel that way, and yet it bubbles up from somewhere inside you, right?"

"Absolutely."

"My guess is that around this table you're not alone in that experience. And recent events show all too tragically that there are people who have those feelings, and it drives them to do terrible things."

He sighed. "But whenever I talk about loving our enemies and nonviolence, someone will say something like, 'So, if someone broke into your house and threatened your family, what would you do?' A question, to be honest, which has never really helped me as I wrestle with the implications of this Word. And which takes me back once again to the context of these Words."

"These Ten Words would shape the community of God's people. But the community would also be the rationale for these Words." Seeing a few blank looks, he leaned forward to explain further.

"Without a community trying to live out these Words *together*, they just sound idealistic or heroic, right? Something great, but which I can dismiss with all the exceptions we've listed. 'Do not kill . . . unless you're the victim of a home invasion.' You get what I'm saying. Yes, they're addressed to each individual standing there— and, I believe, to us today—but those individuals will eventually become a people who, as they keep these Words, among other things will learn to practice nonviolence, a people who will nurture patience, empathy, courage, contentment, generosity and all the other virtues necessary to fulfill *all* these Words.

"We can point our fingers at the 'monsters' who do things like we saw in Colorado last week. We can wring our hands over all the varied kinds of violence we do to each other. We can bemoan the fearful and violent nature of our society. But for me, I point a finger right back at myself and at the church. We are as much to blame for our violent culture as anyone else. For this reason: we have failed to be a community of nonviolence as the natural outcome of our worship of the Prince of Peace, who laid down his life for his enemies and suffered violence at their hands. Without responding in kind." John reached over and picked up the Bible. "If your enemy is hungry, feed him, and if he is thirsty, give him a drink; for in so doing you will heap burning coals on his head. Do not be overcome by evil, but overcome evil with good."[22]

He turned to Yasmina. "I'm not sure you can just stop feeling angry all by yourself. But what if you were part of a community that took this Word and all its implications seriously, and together we worked to find healthy ways to deal with our anger, the violence that lurks just below the surface in so many of us? Not to become a place with no conflict whatsoever. But a people who know how to confess our part in conflict when it arises, and who are swift to move toward reconciliation with the other. A people who confront wrongs and who seek forgiveness. A people who don't resort to violence to deal with conflict."

Yasmina smiled. "Are you inviting me to your church, pastor?"

John laughed. "You're always welcome, Yasmina. But I'm not sure my church is quite to that place yet." His face became serious. "But if there's any hope for us, it's the kind of people we must become."

Ellie said, "There's just so much hate. So much fear of people not like us, you know?"

"I do know. Even in the church, sadly. But I know this. The best protection against hatred is to cultivate affection for the people we live with. *Especially* those who are not like us."

"To love our neighbors as ourselves," said Jenny.

"To love our neighbors as ourselves."

Ellie grabbed Yasmina's arm and stood up. "Come on, we're going to be late." She turned to John. "What are we talking about next week?"

"The Fifth Word. Honor your father and your mother."

"I'm sure Yasmina's mom will drop us off early then," she said with a laugh and a wave as they walked out together.

As the rest of the group got to their feet, Jenny turned to Sarah. "I may just have to miss next week."

Sarah stopped still and looked Jenny in the eye. "I think it's time you told me your story." Jenny looked at her shoes for a moment, then lifted her eyes to Sarah's.

"Maybe it is."

6

From Obligation to Respect

The Fifth Word

And it's you when I look in the mirror,
and it's you when I don't pick up the phone.

U2, "SOMETIMES YOU CAN'T
MAKE IT ON YOUR OWN"

Honor your father and your mother,
that your days may be prolonged
in the land which the LORD
your God gives you.

EXODUS 20:12

Sarah eased out of her car seat as Jenny rode up and locked her bike to the rack. Sarah walked across to greet her. Jenny looked up and smiled.

"Surprised to see me?" asked Jenny.

"Not really. Although I admit I'm glad you decided not to miss this morning. I think it will be good for you—and hard, I'm sure. But I think you have a lot to offer the group about this particular Word." She looked into Jenny's eyes. "Thank you, again, for trusting me with your story." She held out her arms, and Jenny stepped into her embrace, leaning her head on Sarah's shoulder.

"I wish I didn't have so much to offer."

"I know, I know," said Sarah, gently stroking Jenny's hair. "But you're not alone any more—not like when you were a child. At least, you don't have to be."

Jenny pulled out of Sarah's arms, looked into her face and offered a tenuous smile. "I know. But it's hard. I've learned to be self-sufficient. And not to trust anyone. And to work hard for kids who don't have anyone to advocate for them." Her face hardened. "Like I didn't. If they gave me nothing else, my parents gave me that."

"No! You gave *yourself* that gift, Jenny. And it has served its purpose, getting you to this point. But there are so many other gifts waiting for you, gifts that only come as we learn to trust. As Bono sings, 'Sometimes you can't make it on your own.'"[1]

"You like U2?"

Sarah put her hands on her hips and wagged her head. "What? Too *old* for rock and roll? Not my *style*? Girl, it's all about the lyrics. And Bono? That man sings truth. Even when it's painful truth." Jenny blushed lightly. Sarah laughed. "Ah, don't worry. I'll get over your unintentional slam." She gestured across the parking lot as Ellie and Yasmina hopped out of an SUV and entered the coffee shop. "Looks like it's time to get started."

As they walked down the sidewalk, the SUV pulled up alongside them, and the driver leaned out of the window. "Excuse me. Are you Sarah?" Sarah looked at the woman. "Why yes, I am. At least, I'm *a* Sarah." The woman smiled and turned to Jenny. "And you must be Jenny." Jenny nodded. "Yasmina has told me all about your little group. I know she especially likes you two. She says you're really on her wavelength." She sighed. "I wish I were. Even just a little. Oh well—parents can never be right at this age, I guess." She noticed their expressions and laughed. "Oh, don't mind me. Just another chauffeur, chef, cleaning lady whining about their teenager." She pulled off, waving out the window. Sarah and Jenny looked at each other for a moment before bursting into laughter.

The group gathered around the table seemed a little subdued as the women took their seats. Jenny said, "What's up?"

Steve held up his newspaper and pointed to the headline. "Gunman Kills 6 at Sikh Temple."[2]

Jenny slumped into her chair. "Oh no. I hadn't heard."

"Someone else who must have missed 'Do not kill' in Humanity 101," said Steve.

"And someone else with easy access to an automatic weapon," said Yasmina. "I just don't get why we need those things."

John said, "How about we have a moment's silence for the victims and their families before we start this morning?"

"Sounds appropriate to me," said Sam.

The group sat quietly, each lost in their own thoughts, their moment of silence punctuated by the hiss of the espresso machine. After a minute or so, John said, "Well, it's kind of hard to change pace, I know, but let's take a look at the Fifth Word." He handed his Bible, flopped open to the text, to Rick. "Perhaps you'll do the honors this morning."

Rick found the commandment and read, "Honor your father and

your mother, that your days may be prolonged in the land which the LORD your God gives you."[3] He handed the Bible back to John.

"Thanks, Rick." John addressed the group, "So, what are your thoughts on this Word?"

Ellie jumped in straight away. "OK, I'll ask my usual question. What does it mean to 'honor' your mom and dad? Is that the same as saying, 'obey'? Like, no matter what they say? Because I don't know if I'm down with that."

"That *is* the first question, isn't it? What *does* it mean to honor our parents?"

"Well," said Sam, "I can tell you, that's exactly what I heard growing up in church. 'Children, obey your parents in the Lord, for this is right.'[4] I think the apostle Paul went on to quote the Fifth Word—probably to add some weight to his words. So yes, I guess I still hear 'obey' in my head when I hear 'honor your parents.'"

Sam scratched his head. "Still, it seems to me that's a good thing. What do we really know when we're little kids? We *need* to be told what to do—especially if we're doing something dangerous. I don't know about all these ideas about 'talking things through' with little kids. If they're doing something they shouldn't, I don't want to have a discussion about why they should stop. I just want them to stop when I tell them to!"

Ellie countered, "But I'm *not* a little kid. Although my parents treat me like one sometimes. And then it always boils down to 'Young lady, you will obey us on this.'"

"Well, it looks to me like they don't treat you *too* shabbily. Good school to go to, nice clothes, that latte you're drinking. And you've got good manners. Well, most of the time." Ellie laughed, despite herself. "Seems to me they're not doing too bad a job of raising you. Even if you think they're cramping your style from time to time, or whatever it is you call it these days."

"And they're pretty cool," said Yasmina.

"Well, *you* don't have to live with them."

"I know I don't. But I'm serious. I don't mean 'cool' like they're into your music or they let you get a tattoo."

"Exactly."

Yasmina laughed. "I mean 'cool' like they, you know, care about people. And not just their family and friends." She chewed a fingernail. "Remember last weekend when they took us to the movies?"

"Well, duh. It *was* last weekend."

"Well, instead of dropping us off outside the theater like they wanted, you *insisted* they park at the restaurant they were going to, and then we walked across the parking lot to the theater."

"Well? Getting dropped off outside makes me feel like I'm a little kid."

"Do you remember that guy walking up to your dad and asking for a dollar so he could get some food?"

"Vaguely."

Yasmina turned to the group. "Do you know what her dad said? 'How about you come in with us and we'll order you something to take out.'"

"He's always doing stuff like that. One time a guy actually sat down in the booth with us at McDonald's for a while. It was weird."

"Maybe. But I think it's cool. He doesn't treat people the way most of us do. He actually *sees* them, tries to help them. At least give them something to eat."

"Sounds like he's setting you a good example," said Sam.

Ellie shrugged. "I suppose."

"I should think it would be easy to honor a father like that," said Sam. Ellie did not respond. No one spoke for a few moments.

"So what about a father who molests his little girl?"

Jenny's words sucked the air right out of the room. As the members of the group either met her gaze or looked away, she wrung her hands before staring down at her coffee cup. Then, with a glance at Sarah, she continued.

"What about a father who rapes his little girl? How does that daughter honor her father? How does she honor the mother who allowed it to happen?" Sarah took Jenny's hand and squeezed it tightly as Jenny, tears rolling down her cheeks, met the gaze of those gathered around the table, landing finally on John's face, whose lower lip was quivering. "That's my question about this commandment."

As the group sat in silence, Jenny's face was not the only one wet with tears. The silence was broken by the sound of Sam's bar stool scraping slowly on the floor as he gingerly stepped down from his perch. He walked around the table to where Jenny was sitting and, his knees creaking, knelt down at her side. She turned to look at him, their faces just a few inches apart.

"I don't know how that daughter honors her father," he said, with a catch in his voice. "And I don't know that she should." A solitary tear traced the path of one of his face's many wrinkles. "And I think I want to give you a hug, but I don't know if that would be OK." Jenny held his gaze for a long moment, then threw herself into his arms with a loud sob. He held her stiffly for a few moments, then gently patted her back. "You dear girl. You dear, dear girl."

Ellie leaned across the table and laid a hand on Jenny's arm. "Have you tried counseling? Or therapy or something? That might help."

Sarah said gently, "She doesn't need you to fix her right now, Ellie." Color rose in Ellie's cheeks as she sat up and placed her hands back in her lap, looking down at the floor.

After a while, Jenny eased herself out of Sam's grip and wiped her face with the handkerchief Will held out for her. "Well, I'm all snot and tears now." She caught the eye of a person in line, who quickly looked away. She turned back to Sam. "Thank you. You're so kind."

"And stiff," he said gruffly as he pushed himself upright. She stood up with him, and turned to the group. "If you'll excuse me, I'll be back in a minute." She headed to the restroom, as Sam returned to his stool.

Steve, watching her walk away, said fiercely, "I tell you, men like that should be . . ."

"Strung up?" Sam finished for him.

"Yes. Or worse." Then his shoulders slumped forward. "But I guess we covered that last week." He looked at John. "This is not exactly what I signed up for, preacher."

John cast a look in the direction Jenny had gone, then turned back to Steve. "I imagine Jenny might say the same, Steve. And I can't tell you the number of times I've said those same words in my prayers."

He watched as Jenny got another cup of coffee before returning to the table. As she sat down he said, "You OK, Jenny? Is there anything else you want—or need—to say right now?"

"Oh, I think I'm done for right now." She looked around the group, offering each person a gentle smile. "So, how about we hear from someone else? Who else has a question?"

"Well, it's quite a change of pace," said Sarah.

Jenny said, "I'm ready for that."

"So, my question is about aging parents. How do you honor your parents when they can no longer safely drive? Or when you think they can't cope at home any more, but whenever you bring up the subject they get angry and cut the conversation off right there? I'm afraid my mom is going to hurt herself—or someone else—one of these days."

"Good question," said John. He surveyed the group. "Any more?"

Carlos said, "Well, it's nothing personal like Jenny or Sarah, but as I was reading the Word for this week, I was wondering what it means when it says that your days will be prolonged in the land. I didn't get that."

"Great," said John, "I guess this is the first time we've had a commandment which adds a promise for keeping it. Can I jump in with some thoughts here?" Nodding heads greeted his question.

"As always, I think it's helpful to remind ourselves of the context for these Ten Words. When God spoke these Words to that group of former slaves gathered there at Mount Sinai, it wasn't just instruction in personal piety but a way of life for a people. It was the way they were to structure their common life to ensure that everyone in the community flourished. It was the way that they would learn to love God and love their neighbors as themselves."

"The majority of people standing there were adults, and so even though we may hear this Word and picture young children doing what their parents tell them . . ." He looked at Ellie, who nodded, "the Word is primarily addressed to the adult children of older parents. Being a 'child' does not put you in an age category but a *relational* category. And 'loving our neighbor' naturally begins with those closest to us—our family—and moves out from there."

Will spoke up, "The visual image most of us have of the Ten Commandments is two stone tablets, because that's what Moses received from God on the mountain. Or perhaps what we've seen in courthouses, right, Steve?" Steve harrumphed.

"Now, the church has tended to divide those two tablets thematically: the first has to do with our obligations to God, the second with our obligations to our neighbor. The five Words we've talked about so far, along with this one, form the 'second tablet,' what it means to love our neighbor. They are all expressed negatively—'Don't envy, don't steal, don't lie, don't cheat, don't kill'—except for this one, which says 'Honor your parents.' This Word seems to me to be the 'bridge,' if you like, between the two tablets. Because in some ways our parents take the place of both neighbor and God, in that we live with them and they exercise authority over us when we're young."

"And when we're not so young as well," muttered Ellie.

Will gave her a sympathetic smile. "And so, in many ways, when we're little kids we learn both to love God and love neighbor in the home." He turned quickly to Jenny with a pained expression on his face. "At least, that's what's supposed to happen. But that obviously depends on the parents.

"The way I see this Word drawing together love of God and love of neighbor, especially the vulnerable neighbor, like aging parents, can be seen in one of the prophet Ezekiel's indictments of the rulers of Israel." He reached for John's Bible.

> *They have treated father and mother lightly within you. The alien they have oppressed in your midst; the fatherless and the widow they have wronged in you. You have despised My holy things and profaned My sabbaths.*[5]

"It seems that the bad treatment of parents led to the bad treatment of the weaker and more vulnerable members of the community. A lack of respect and care for aging parents, as well as for the Fourth Word—keeping sabbath—bodes ill for those at the bottom of society's ladder."

Sam spoke up, "Absolutely. I think that's what's wrong with society. Kids don't seem to learn to respect—to honor—their parents, so why would they show respect to anyone else? Whether that's teachers, police officers, employers or," turning to Yasmina, "street people for that matter."

"But what if our parents don't deserve our respect?" said Ellie.

Will replied, "I think that's why it's important for us to remember the story behind these commandments, as John keeps reminding us. The purpose of these Ten Words is for every member of the community to flourish. That will never happen if the way we treat each other is based on what we think the other person *deserves*. The flourishing of the community will be worked out as each of us are attentive to the good of the other *regardless* of whether we think they deserve it or not. In this case, our neighbor also happens to be our parent. And so we are to love them, not, perhaps, because they have some inherent right for us to treat them well simply because they are our parent. But because God has given us the responsibility to treat them well because they are our closest neighbor. Does that make sense?"

"I think so," said Ellie.

John jumped back in. "That also gets to Carlos's question. Because this is a commandment with a promise, as he pointed out. 'Do this,' says God, 'and your lives will be prolonged in the land which I am giving you.' Now, in the ancient Near East—and in much of the world today—economic security in old age was not about private pensions or Social Security, but about having lots of children who would care for you as you were no longer able to care for yourself. The well-being of aging parents was—is—dependent on their children caring for them. How would they enjoy longevity—both as individuals and as a people—in the Promised Land? By each successive generation living out this Word. So the son or daughter who honors their parents becomes the father or mother, who in turn is honored by their children."

Will added, "And note that the Word says 'Honor your father *and your mother*.' It's my understanding that all the other law codes we have from this era only talk about showing honor to your father—after all, they were all patriarchal societies, including Israel. But God requires them to show honor to their mothers as well."

"OK," said Ellie. "So back to my first question. What does 'Honor your parents' mean? Is it just caring for them when they're old? What else?"

John said, "Here's where it's helpful to look at the Hebrew word we translate as 'honor' and see what light it sheds on what this Word might mean. The Hebrew word is *kabbed*, which literally means, 'to make heavy.' So, the word seems to suggest that to honor one's parents is to treat them as persons of great weight, as people of high regard. Which seems to broaden rather than narrow the scope of what we are to do to keep this Word."

Ellie's forehead wrinkled. "I guess what I'm saying is that I wonder if the Word means that in *every* situation we treat our parents with great respect."

"OK," said Sarah. "So getting back to *my* situation. I think my mother is a danger to herself and other drivers every time she's behind the wheel of her car. And when I say behind, I mean she's looking *through* the wheel of her car. How do I show her great respect *and* still take the keys away?"

"Have you talked this over with her already?" asked Rick.

Sarah turned to face him. "Well, I don't think we've 'talked it over,' but I've told her several times that she needs to stop driving. And every time I do, she's told me I need to keep my nose out of her business."

"I wonder if treating her with respect is trying to see things from her point of view rather than from yours."

"What do you mean?" queried Sarah.

"Well, what are you asking her to give up?" responded Rick.

"The keys to her car!"

"That's all? I think you're asking her to give up *much* more than that. Namely, her independence. And not just in the sense of being able to get around on her own terms, in her own time. Giving up her keys would be the first of what will be many losses as she continues to age. How scary must that feel? If I were her, I think I'd want to hold on to those keys as long as possible. But I get that you are convinced it's not safe for her to drive anymore. So, I guess the question is, how do you show her great respect while trying to take those keys away?"

Sarah chewed a nail. "Well, I guess I usually bring it up if I've watched her pull up to my house in that big old car of hers and nearly clip my neighbor's car as she tries to parallel park. Or when I go with her to the store and it seems like I have to dig my fingernails out of the dashboard by the time we get there because we've had so many close calls." She paused. "Which was probably not the best time to have that conversation."

"*Probably?*"

"OK, *definitely* not the best time! I get what you're saying. Hmmm. I wonder if I should talk it over with my sister and then the two of us set a date to sit down with Momma and talk things over with her. Tell her that we know how hard it must be to think about giving up her car—and her independence. Show that we recognize what we're asking her to give up, rather than just telling her what to do."

"That sounds like treating your momma with respect," said Ellie. "Giving her honor."

Sarah nodded. "But I *am* getting those keys!" Rick looked at her. "OK. We'll see."

"Listening to you talk," said Yasmina, "makes me think of a story I read in literature class last semester." The group's attention shifted to her.

"It's one of the Brothers Grimm tales. Let's see if I can remember it." She twirled her hair with a finger for a few moments before beginning. "So, there's this couple with a little boy, maybe four or five years old, and the husband's father is getting old, so the elderly father moves in with them. Whenever they eat dinner at the table, the old man slops food off his plate, either onto the tablecloth or onto himself. This offends the wife, so she moves him onto a stool in the corner, where he eats out of an earthenware bowl."

"One evening, his hands trembling more than usual, he drops the bowl and it smashes on the floor, sending soup and broken pottery everywhere. The wife jumps up and yells, 'If you're going to eat like a pig, then we'll have to give you a trough.' So they made a little wooden trough, and he had to eat from it."

"One night after dinner they noticed their son playing very intently with his wooden blocks. When his father asked him what he was doing, he said, 'I'm making a trough to feed you and momma out of when I get big.'

"The wife and husband looked at each other for a long moment, then burst into tears. They went to the corner and gently led the old man back to the table, and from then on he ate with the family off a plate, and they never complained again about him spilling food or dribbling down his clothes."

"Whoa," said Ellie.

Sarah sniffed loudly. "I can tell that I might need to find that story and keep it somewhere close at hand."

Yasmina continued, "But it's not only about family, right? These Words were for a nation, a society, like John keeps saying. I know some people are quick to apply the Ten Commandments to what other people do in their bedrooms or at their doctor's offices, trying to pass laws to restrict both of those, right? But what about this one? What laws, or systems are in place to help—or hinder from—people keep *this* Word?"

"Have you got something in mind?" asked John.

"How many offices have onsite daycare for kids, or help offset the cost of daycare, so parents can hold down a good job? Well, what about people who are caring for elderly parents with, say, Alzheimer's? What about providing daycare for them, so they can work and still 'honor their mother and father'?"

"Great question," said John. "And a great idea."

Steve turned to John. "Can I push you a little on this one, preacher?"

"That depends on how big a push we're talking here, Steve!"

"Not too big, I think. You must have members of your congregation with elderly parents."

"Absolutely. And many of those elderly parents are members too."

"Right. So what do you tell those people to do when they come to your office because they've got this huge decision to make about whether to put their parents in a home or not? Or they need to but just don't have the finances to do so?" He paused. "Here's the push—it's the money question. Do you tell them to stop giving to the church so they can take care of their parents?"

"That's a good question, Steve. Honestly, in most cases where there's that kind of financial struggle, people stopped giving to the church long before they come to see me. At least giving to the church budget. As far as I'm concerned, taking care of their aging parents is absolutely still giving to God's work."

"I'm not sure some of those preachers on TV would agree with you on that. Seems like every time I'm flicking through the channels and find one, he's saying that people need to give God what they've got, even if they can't afford it, and then God will provide what they need—and more! And when they say 'give to God' they mean 'give to my ministry,' not to someone who may actually *need* the money."

"That's nothing new though, right, pastor?" said Sam.

John raised an eyebrow questioningly.

"Does the word *qorban* ring any bells?"

"Ah, right. Now I get you."

"Well, I don't," said Steve. "What's Sam talking about?"

"He's referring to a story about Jesus," said John. "Once again, Jesus had run afoul of the Pharisees and the scribes, the experts in the law, and they were accusing his disciples of not doing what they were teaching the people to do to keep the law.[6] Jesus calls them out on their hypocrisy, saying that all these 'laws' they've come up with for the people to keep were not always in line with the commandments. In fact, sometimes—like in the case of *qorban*—the scribes were twisting the law to their own advantage and missing the intent of the law. Creating loopholes if you like. Loopholes that give the impression of keeping the law, but really are not doing so.

"At the heart of the law, as we keep seeing, is God's desire for us to be set free from all those things that enslave us, that prevent us from flourishing as human beings living in community. The scribes and Pharisees added all these other layers of laws around God's law—ostensibly to help people to not break the law—but which in fact put people in even more bondage. At one point Jesus railed against these experts in the law saying, 'Woe to you! For you weigh people down with burdens hard to bear, while you yourselves won't lift a finger to help them.'[7]

"In this case it appears that the law experts had come up with a law taken from a concept called *qorban* or 'gift.' If someone declared something to be *qorban*, that meant it was devoted to God, and could not be used for its otherwise intended purpose. Apparently the scribes were encouraging people to do this. So, in the case Jesus describes, if a son declared the resources he had to care for his parents to be *qorban*, they could not ask for or expect any assistance from him."

He leaned forward. "But get this. The son did not actually have to *give* that money to God, either as a gift to the temple treasury or whatever. He just had to declare it *qorban*. But if he had a change of heart later and wanted to help his parents, the scribes would not allow him to. Their law 'trumped' the Fifth Word. So after calling them out, Jesus then basically said to the scribes, 'And you people do that a lot.'"

Will chimed in, "I wonder if that's why the Fifth Word isn't spelled out for us. Maybe God knew that if the law said, 'Here's how you're going to keep this Word,' we would start looking for loopholes or exceptions. Perhaps in being forced to ask, What does it mean to honor our parents? we're already cultivating the attitude we're going to need in order to keep the Fifth Word. At its most basic level, it means caring for aging parents, as Jesus indicates in this story."

John looked up from taking notes. "That's great, Will. All right, so that's *qorban*. What else comes to mind as we think about the Fifth Word?"

"Well," began Carlos. "Again, this isn't very serious, but I confess I get really annoyed with my parents around technology. They're hopeless! They have a great cable package, with TiVo and all that, but they have no clue how to use it. I'm always having to go over and show them what to do or help them find something they've recorded." He paused. "I guess I can be pretty short with them sometimes."

"Tell me about it," said Ellie. "I set my parents up with Skype so they can talk to my older sister, who moved out of state to go to college, but my mom still can't figure it out. Either the video or audio isn't working, or she hasn't plugged the camera in right and guess who has to come running to fix it for her?"

"Ah, the hardships of youth," said Sam. "What a burden we old folk are on you poor young'uns."

Ellie leaned forward, about to respond, but Sam's broad wink made it apparent he was just teasing her, and she settled back.

Will said, "You bring up something important for us to consider, though, Carlos. Our society is so technologically driven that yesterday's knowledge, the kind Sam and I might have, is often considered merely quaint if not obsolete. And all too often it appears in dismissing our knowledge, *we* get dismissed as well. A lifetime of discernment now considered useless. It started when we couldn't learn to program a VCR. Now Ellie here probably doesn't even know what a VCR is. I fear that ageism is on the rise even as some other 'isms' appear, thankfully, to be on the decline. And my concern is that ageism will mean the loss of decades of accumulated wisdom as we celebrate the now, the new, the 'hip.'"

"Haven't we always worshiped youth, though?" asked Sarah. "Don't you think at least some of this disdain for . . . the more mature members of society, shall we say, is about our fear of losing our own youth?"

Yasmina spoke up, "I think Sarah's right." She turned to Ellie. "Look at our classmates' moms. They're all wearing the same clothes we are, their hair is cut the same way. They even wear the same perfume."

"And," said Ellie, "how much money do you think they spend on anti-wrinkle cream, or anti-aging lotions? Or gym memberships so they can fit in *our* jeans? It's like they're afraid of looking their age."

"Perhaps they're afraid of losing their youth," said Sarah. "Or their vitality, their health. It's not like I can't relate to that."

"And it's not just your moms," said Rick. "It's all of us. We all seem so afraid of growing older. Of growing old." He slipped a thumb under his belt. "So when I have to use a different hole, it's not just a reminder that I'm eating too much. It's also another re-minder that my body just won't put up with the same kind of abuse it did when I was young. Which means I'm getting old." He grinned. "I mean, old-er."

"And few of us like being reminded of that fact," said John. "But what does this obsession with youth cost us? Not just as individuals but as a society? What kind of insecurity are people living with when finding a new wrinkle is a minor catastrophe? What does it say about the value we place on old age?"

Will leaned forward. "We so often talk about the importance of being 'productive members of society.' Now, while we may disagree on exactly what that means, that belief has profound ramifications for those people who feel that they are no longer productive. And if age is the reason for that, then there's no recourse for them to pursue. But what if wisdom is just as important as the ability to swing a heavy hammer? Or to design an app?" He looked around the table. "I wonder if the Fifth Word has wider implications than even the aging members of our society. What if it's a call to refuse to look down on or speak derogatively of *any* members of our com-munity who have lost much of their commercial worth? Especially those on whom our own life has depended?"

"How is all that insecurity working out for us?" asked John. "I mean, other than for the beauty and cosmetic surgery industries, of course? How can we learn to accept the aging process—which, after all, is inevitable? What would it be like to grow old and not feel insecure about that? To not believe that we'll be obsolete one day. That we'll have something to offer when we're drawing a pension. Or have to move back in with our kids. That we'll still be who we are, when we are, and have worth."

A heaviness seemed to hang over the table for a few moments before Ellie said, "OK, so before we have to go to school, I want to come back to obeying our parents."

"I'm glad to hear it," said Sam.

"You know what I mean. What am I supposed to do to honor them when all they're interested in is for me to obey them—especially when what they're asking is stupid?"

"While you're under their roof, I guess they have the right to tell you what to do," said Sam. "Even if it is 'stupid.'"

"Just because they have the right to doesn't make it right, though!"

Will stepped in. "Sam, what was that verse you quoted earlier?"

"Children, obey your parents in the Lord, for this is good."

"Right," said Will, picking John's Bible up from the table. "But Paul doesn't stop there, does he?" He found the passage Sam had quoted. "'Honor your father and mother (which is the first commandment with a promise), so that it may be well with you, and that you may live long on the earth.'" He paused, then read on, "Fathers, do not provoke your children to anger."[8]

Will placed the open Bible down on the table. "What do you think of that, Ellie?"

"Ha! Can you show me where that is, so I can read it to my mom and dad tonight?"

"I hope you'll read the whole of the passage and not just that last bit, though," interjected John. He turned to the group. "The passage Will read does get to what I think this Word, ultimately, is about. I think it's meant to create a reciprocal relationship. The parents' care for their children leads to the children's care for their parents, down through the generations. But obviously, it's very tempting for some parents to pull 'the God card' with this Word and say, 'Not only will you obey me because I'm your parent but because God says you have to.' Which reveals the somewhat ironic nature of the Fifth Word.

"In other places in the Torah this Word is expressed in negative forms." He pulled out some notes. "For instance, in Exodus 21 we read, 'Whoever strikes father or mother shall be put to death.' And 'Whoever curses father or mother shall be put to death.'[9] So here's the irony: this Word, which is supposed to *protect* people from abusive behavior, is the one Word most open to being used to *promote* abusive behavior." He sighed, and cast a quick glance at Jenny before saying, "It's hard enough for young children to say no to a parent. It's even harder when that parent uses God to enforce their will.

"But apparently parents were just as likely to do that in the first century as they are in the twenty-first. So in another letter Paul makes a pragmatic appeal to them: 'Fathers, do not exasperate your children, so that they will not lose heart.'"[10]

"What does that mean?" asked Ellie.

John answered, "I think it means something like, 'Parents, if you keep angering or frustrating or abusing your children, one day they will give up on honoring you. And then who will take care of you?'"

"Not me," said Jenny in a barely audible voice.

The group fell silent again.

She wiped the back of her hand across her eyes and said to herself, "OK, Jenny, you can do this." She reached for Sarah's hand before continuing. She looked at each person around the table.

"I left home as soon as I was able to. And I haven't spoken to either of my parents from that day to this. I have one brother—he's younger than me—who still lives in the same town as they do. We talk regularly, so I know how they're doing." She paused. "And they're not doing well. My dad has cancer, and it doesn't look too good for him."

"How does that make you feel, hearing that?" asked Ellie, hesitantly.

"Honestly? I don't know how I feel about it. I've tried not to think about or feel anything for that man for years now." She turned her coffee cup around in her hands for a moment. "No, I do know how I feel about it. My brother's my only family. As far as I'm concerned I don't have a father or a mother to honor."

Carlos said, "Can I say something, Jenny?" Jenny nodded. "This may sound kinda strange, but I wonder if you honored your father by leaving home." Jenny tilted her head, confusion and anger flashing across her face. "Let me explain," said Carlos. "Now, I'm sure you were just doing what you needed to do to survive, but it's also kinda like you were saying, 'I won't let you do that to me anymore. And I won't let you do harm to yourself by doing it.'" He paused. "I think you were protecting both yourself *and* your dad, whether you knew it or not."

Ellie asked, "Like what John said about the people hiding the Jews from the German soldiers?"

"Yeah, just like that."

Jenny wiped her eyes. "I can tell you I was not thinking at all about 'protecting' my dad from himself. My mom was the one who should have done that—she should have protected *me*—and she failed. So it's a nice idea, Carlos, but I don't think I can claim that I kept the Fifth Word in hindsight." She paused. "And even if I could, I'm not sure I want to."

"It's just a thought."

Sarah squeezed Jenny's hand until Jenny turned toward her. "Do you want to know what I think?"

Jenny offered her a weak smile. "I don't know. Do I?" She paused. "OK, what do you think?"

Sarah held Jenny's eyes with her own as she spoke. "You cannot undo what your father did to you. But what you can do, and what I believe you have done, is turn that abuse into compassion. Not only for yourself, so you can begin to heal, but for others as well, especially those who have suffered as you have.

"I wonder if your ability to be patient and understanding and, yes, loving with the kids you work with—kids many of us would probably write off with a look—is because you can empathize with them. Your pain enables you to not only feel their pain but also to want to protect them, nurture them—all the things you should have had, but never did."

"I know that's true," said Jenny. "As some of them come to trust me and open up—tell me about what goes on in their homes—man, I just want to wrap them up and take them home with me. Which

I can't do. But what I *can* do is try to get them out of the situation, and then do my best to make sure they don't get lost in the system. So yeah, I know the biggest part of why I do this is because I wish someone had done it for me."

"Here's what I would add to that," said Sarah. "I wonder if this life of compassion that you're leading, which has risen from the ashes of your suffering, is a way to honor your parents even as you rise above them. It is one way to honor the gift of life they gave you, without honoring what they did to you. And, I believe, it is part of your own healing process. Which I want to talk about with you later."

"I don't know about all that."

"I know you don't. At least, not yet." Sarah smiled and gave Jenny's hand another squeeze.

Sam coughed. He looked at Jenny. "I know these Words we've been talking about are all about loving our neighbors as ourselves, but I reckon what Sarah's talking about falls under the category of loving your enemies. And that ain't never easy."

"No, it ain't, Sam," said Jenny.

John leaned forward. "Jenny, thanks so much for making yourself so vulnerable with us. And if you ever want to talk . . ."

"Thanks, John," said Jenny, lifting up Sarah's hand, "but I think Sarah has me covered in the talking department for now."

"That's great. You're in very good hands."

"I know."

Looking at her watch, Yasmina said, "So what are you going to talk about on Sunday?"

"I don't know. I had thought about telling the story of Ruth and Naomi, simply because I think Ruth is the exemplar supreme of how to keep the Fifth Word. But so much stuff has come up in our discussion, I'm not so sure now."

"Isn't Ruth the one who said to her husband, 'Where you go, I will go'?" said Ellie. "'Your people will be my people. Your God will be my God.' Something like that?"

Yasmina said, "You never cease to amaze me, Ellie."

"Well, duh! It's only read at, like, every wedding I've ever been to."

"I try to steer couples away from that text," said John. "Because the story is actually about a daughter and her mother-in-law. And it's a really pivotal story in the whole narrative of the Bible. Because if Ruth had not gone with her mother-in-law back to the land of Israel and married Boaz, well, no King David. That's part of why I thought about speaking about her."

He continued, "But I also love Ruth's story because this Moabite woman, this 'outsider,' models to the 'insiders,' God's people Israel, what is expected of them."

"Like the good Samaritan story," said Sam.

"Exactly. So when we might be tempted to shrink the circle of protection that the Fifth Word creates to the nuclear family, Ruth takes us outside the biological family to care for her mother-in-law and, even outside her own people, a 'foreigner.'"

He looked at his notes. "But then, I've also been thinking about Jesus' apparent mixed signals about honoring parents, which I know people have questions about."

"What's that about?" asked Steve.

"Well, for starters, when Jesus called his disciples to follow him, some of them literally walked away from their fathers. James and John left their father standing there alone, holding his torn-up fishing nets and watching them walk away from the family business.[11]

"A little later on, Jesus is teaching the crowds when his mom and brothers come to get him. Just before that story, Mark tells us that they had already tried to force Jesus to come home because they were worried about him. Their exact words were, 'He has lost His senses.'[12] So, on this occasion, when someone tells Jesus that his family are outside to take him home, he says, "'Who are My mother and My brothers?" Looking at those who were sitting around Him, He said, "Behold, My mother and My brothers! For whoever does the will of God, he is My brother and sister and mother.'"[13]

"Jesus makes it pretty clear that he gives priority to the family of God over his biological family. Luke records it with even harsher language." John flicked forward a few pages in his Bible. "'If anyone comes to Me, and does not hate his own father and mother and wife and children and brothers and sisters, yes, and even his own life, he cannot be My disciple.'"[14]

"Wow," said Steve. "That's harsh."

"Absolutely," responded John. "Although that last phrase 'and even his own life' takes some of the sting out of his statement. I think Jesus is stating as clearly as possible that following him means letting go of everything and everyone who might make a claim on your life—including your parents. *And yourself.*"

"But isn't Jesus just pulling the God card, as you put it earlier, and telling people they don't need to take care of their parents if they're his disciples?"

"I'm not sure that's what he's saying. I think he's establishing the disciples' number one priority: following him." John paused. "However, it definitely creates tension that I've seen played out in the lives of church members."

Sam scratched his head. "Well, I don't know what I think about all that, but I still reckon Jesus kept the commandment to provide for his mother."

"By giving her some of his wages?" asked Ellie. "He was a carpenter, right?"

"Maybe that was the case when he lived with her, Ellie. But I'm thinking about when he was dying on the cross. Nails holding his beaten-up body in place and carrying the weight of our sin on his shoulders." Sam leaned forward. "I think I'd have been a little self-focused. But not Jesus. He looks down and sees his mother standing there, no doubt weeping. Her husband dead, her firstborn being crucified by the Romans, and the Pharisees and scribes no doubt looking on with grim satisfaction."

Sam looked around the table. "Do you know just about the last thing Jesus said before he died? I'll tell you. His disciple John is standing beside Mary, Jesus' mother. And Jesus says to her, 'Woman, behold, your son!' Then he says to John, 'Behold, your mother!' And from that time on, John took Mary into his own household."[15]

Sam leaned forward and pointed his finger at John. "Jesus, about to die, makes sure his mother is going to be taken care of." He sat back. "So, I reckon he kept the commandment. I reckon he honored his mother."

"Indeed he did, Sam. Indeed he did.

"And that's really helpful, because it gets to what I believe Jesus was doing. I think this is the final stage of the trajectory of the Fifth Word. Because Jesus is joining the natural family to the family of God. So the church becomes a kind of extended family. Followers of Jesus now extend the same honor to fathers and mothers who are not their own, but need the care that the commandment expects from children. We see in the book of Acts the disciples serving meals to the widows of the community on a daily basis. Whole households—parents, children, servants—become followers of Jesus together. Yet Jesus never lost sight of his obligation to his own mother, and neither should we."

He stretched and looked at his watch. "Wow, this is all good stuff! Very helpful, once again." He turned to Jenny. "I hope it's been helpful for you too."

"I guess we'll have to wait and see." She turned to the whole group. "But I do want to thank you for making me feel safe enough to be honest with you. It's a huge gift, one I'm slowly learning to accept."

"I hope so, Jenny," said John. "So, to wrap up our time together, any thoughts on what practices would help us keep this Word?"

Sarah said, "Well, I think I know what it means for me." She looked at Rick. "No matter what I think about how I see my mother deteriorating, I need to treat her with respect. To see that what looks like an easy decision for her to make is a lot weightier than I've allowed. So, working out from there, I guess a practice would be to treat all the aging people I'm around with that kind of understanding and respect."

Rick said, "I think it means rejecting anything that smells of ageism. To reject the temptation to see someone as worthless because of what they can no longer do."

Sam said, "Well, my pension and Social Security provide me with a comfortable retirement. But I know that is certainly not true for everyone my age—even among fellow members of my church." He turned to John. "Maybe I'll have a little chat with my pastor about that," he said with a grin.

John said, "That's great—plenty to think about there. And plenty to do! Next week we'll talk about the Fourth Word—'Remember the sabbath day, to keep it holy.'"

"Before we go our separate ways," said Will, "I'd like to read one more text from the Bible." He quickly found the place he wanted. "These are the last words of the Hebrew Bible. They seem to me to contain a word of hope for our conversation this morning. The prophet Malachi talks of one who will come before the day of the Lord, another Elijah, the person we know as John the Baptizer. Of that one, Malachi says this, 'He will restore the hearts of the fathers to their children and the hearts of the children to their fathers.'"[16]

No one looked at Jenny, although they all wanted to. After a long moment of silence, she turned to Will.

"Well, that book is full of miracles, right? Because I can tell you, that's what it would take."

"I know it would, Jenny. I know it would."

Will's statement seemed to signal the end of their time together, and as one they rose, leaving only Sarah and Jenny seated.

Sarah pulled Jenny in for a side hug. "Well, like I told you, I believe you keep coming back and wait for the miracle. At least that's how it worked for me."

"Can I borrow your faith, then? Because I don't think I have any of my own for this."

"That's how it works, Jenny. Now, how about another cup of coffee?"

7

From Striving to Rest

The Fourth Word

> *When your hands are full of thorns,*
> *but you can't quit groping for the rose . . .*
> *Lie down. Take a rest with me.*
>
> BRUCE COCKBURN,
> "SOUTHLAND OF THE HEART"

> *Remember the sabbath day to keep it holy.*
> *Six days you shall labor and do all your work,*
> *but the seventh day is a sabbath of the LORD your God;*
> *in it you shall not do any work, you or your son or your daughter,*
> *your male or your female servant or your cattle or your sojourner*
> *who stays with you. For in six days the LORD made the heavens*
> *and the earth, the sea and all that is in them, and rested*
> *on the seventh day; therefore the LORD blessed*
> *the sabbath day and made it holy.*
>
> EXODUS 20:8-11

Steve walked in, rain dripping off the end of his nose. He caught Sam's eye at the bar, paid for his coffee and walked over. "Morning, Sam."

"And a wet one it is. Still, we need it bad, so I'm not complaining. You reckon John will ride his bike over in this?"

"We'll know soon enough," replied Steve, cupping his ear.

Sam turned his cup in his hands. "How do you think Jenny's doing? I've been thinking about her a lot this week."

"Yeah, me too. Gotta be tough knowing your dad's dying. Even if he did . . ."

"Yeah, I know. People can do some pretty evil things."

Steve picked up his cup and took a sip. "You know, Sam, it's funny, but whenever I read the paper now it's like I'm looking for which one of the commandments got broken in every story. I never thought I'd say this, but maybe those council members were onto something."

Sam looked puzzled. Steve said, "Don't tell me you've forgotten how these Monday morning sessions got started?"

"Oh, right. The court case."

"Exactly. I still think it was a criminal waste of time and money, but it seems like these Ten Words do point out just how messed up we are as a society."

"Watch out, or next thing you know you'll be in the front pew of John's church!"

Steve laughed. "Don't hold your breath, Sam."

They looked up as Ellie's cell phone's piercing ringtone heralded hers and Yasmina's arrival, with Rick and Carlos just behind them.

Steve's smile faded. "But I tell you something. If everyone just started keeping the Words we've already talked about, well, that wouldn't be so bad, now would it?"

"You'll hear no argument from me about that," as the teenagers walked over and flopped down. With an innocent look Sam asked Steve, "By the way, has your neighbor got a new car yet?"

Steve punched him on the shoulder, and grinned broadly again. "OK, OK. I get it. I'm part of 'everyone.' It's not just 'those people' in the paper."

At the sound of a loud rumble from outside Steve said, "Well, now we know John's not just a fair-weather biker." A couple of minutes later, John appeared, his rain suit draped over one arm. The rest of the group followed on his heels, and soon everyone was seated and greeting each other.

"Well," said John, "this morning we get to the Word that I think is the most widely ignored of all the commandments, at least in our culture. Let's start by reading it." He opened his Bible and passed it to Yasmina. "Would you read for us this morning?" She took the Bible and read.

> *Remember the sabbath day, to keep it holy. Six days you shall labor and do all your work, but the seventh day is a sabbath of the* LORD *your God; in it you shall not do any work, you or your son or your daughter, your male or your female servant or your cattle or your sojourner who stays with you. For in six days the* LORD *made the heavens and the earth, the sea and all that is in them, and rested on the seventh day; therefore the* LORD *blessed the sabbath day and made it holy.*[1]

Yasmina passed the Bible across the table. "Wow, that's a long one."

"The longest Word by far. If the Ten Words were an apple pie, I'd ask for the Fourth Word, because I'd be getting about a third of that pie! And it's also the most common of the Ten Words throughout the Bible. The word *sabbath* is mentioned 172 times in the King James Version. *Idolatry* gets 131. *Adultery* 69, *murder* 43, *stealing* 28 and *covet* a mere 23. Yet like I said, it's the most widely ignored of the Ten Words, even among Christians."

He looked around the table. "OK, let me start with this question: when you ask people, 'How are you doing?' how many people's response includes some form of 'I'm tired'?"

With an exaggerated yawn, Carlos said, "That would be me."

"And me," said Ellie.

"Guilty," said Sarah. "Everyone's just rushing from one thing to the next. Is it just me, or do people shopping in the stores seem constantly hot and bothered? I mean, it used to be just Thanksgiving and Christmas when people were rushing around. But now it seems it's like that year round." People nodded in agreement. "And has anyone else noticed people cussing at the self-checkout machine? And," she said, looking at Carlos, "before you tell me it's because people don't know how to work them, I *do* know how to operate the scanner, but if it takes more than a split second to read the barcode, it makes me feel like the universe is conspiring to keep me from getting where I need to be."

Steve said, "That's why I do all my shopping on Sunday mornings. All the good Christian folk are in church, and if I need help finding anything, there're always plenty of employees hanging around. And," he said with a grin, "there's no one to hear me when *I* cuss out the U-Scan machine."

"Except for," said Sam, "the 'good Christian folk' who have to work the Sunday shift or lose their job. It may be convenient for you, Steve, but I miss the days when everything was closed on Sundays. It was like the whole country just stopped for a day. I certainly miss the peace and quiet of Sunday mornings—no traffic in the neighborhood, no kids yelling in the street."

"And," said Jenny, "nowhere for single parents to buy the stuff they needed 'cause they had to work the other six days of the week."

Sam sighed. "I know, Jenny. But somehow people back then still managed to buy groceries. And, I might add, go to church."

John said with a smile, "Although, of course, for some of us who go to church, Sunday is a work day."

"Yeah," said Steve, "but you get the rest of the week off, right?"

Steve ducked as the wadded-up napkin John threw at him sailed over his head. "What, preacher, are you telling me you don't just spend the week praying and preparing your sermon for Sunday?"

"Absolutely, Steve. But don't forget, I also manage to squeeze in pastoral visits to the coffee shop, to offer support to reprobates like you. But all joking aside, I do think it's increasingly hard to keep this Word. Gone are the days when I left my work at the church office and went home. Now, thanks to email, text messages and laptops, my office comes home with me, like so many of you, I bet."

Jenny picked up her phone. "Yup. Here's mine." She looked around the table. "How many of us have ever said, 'I wish there were a few more hours in the day'?" A show of hands. "I had a 'moment of clarity'—as Sarah calls it—the other day. I realized that if my wish was actually granted, that would just mean I had a few more hectic hours to live through each day. And I bet my mental to-do list wouldn't shrink one iota."

Sam spoke up, "That makes me think of something. My first trip out of state was a school trip to the 1964 World's Fair in New York." He smiled wistfully at the memory. "We ran from one display to the next, mouths wide open, looking at all those futuristic robots and time-saving devices, talking about what life will be like in the year 2000. I never did get my personal jet-pack.

"It was a long drive home, but the time seemed to fly by as we talked about all the amazing things that were going to be invented and what we'd be able to do. I remember our teacher wondering aloud how people would cope with a three-day work week. 'Whatever will we do with all that time?' she said." He laughed. "I guess we got the devices," pointing at Jenny's phone, "but we certainly didn't get the time."

Steve chimed in, "And then there are vacations. 'Time away from work, to relax and forget about everything back home.' Except you have to work twice as hard to leave things in good shape before you depart, so you're exhausted when you start the vacation, and just about the time you finally begin to feel relaxed, it's time to pack up the car and come home. Back to a pile of work on your desk."

Rick said, "Perhaps those Europeans are onto something. Two-hour siestas in the afternoon. Three-week-long summer vacations. Two weeks off at Christmas."

Steve said, "And their economy's in the toilet. I'm not convinced those two things aren't linked."

"That reminds me of a story I read once," said Yasmina. "Let me think for a moment here . . ." She leaned back in her chair for a few seconds and then leaned forward again. "OK, picture this scene. A corporate executive-type on vacation is walking across a tropical beach, yelling into his cell phone at someone. He hangs up with a snarl, and then waits for a return call. He sees a local fisherman, dozing in the shade of his boat pulled up on the beach. The fisherman wakes up, and the executive decides to have a crosscultural exchange.

"'Why aren't you out fishing?' he asks the fisherman. 'It's a beautiful day, there's plenty to catch—why are you just lying around?' The fisherman replies, 'Because I caught enough this morning.' 'But,' says the executive, 'if you went back out this afternoon a couple of times, you'd have three times as many fish to sell. Don't you see what that would mean?' The fisherman shook his head, puzzled.

"'Well,' said the executive, rubbing his hands together, 'for a start you could take the extra money and eventually buy a motorboat. Then you wouldn't have to rely on the wind or your muscles. Then, after a couple of years, you could buy another one. Start building up your own fishing fleet. Maybe you could build your own processing plant right over there,' pointing up the shore, 'and you could start an export business. Maybe buy some trucks and ship directly to the capital, and then . . .'

"'And then?' asked the fisherman.

"'And then,' the executive concluded triumphantly, 'after you've built your business up, you could retire, and spend your days looking at your beautiful ocean and dozing in the sun!'

"As the executive's phone rang, the fisherman said, 'What do you think I'm doing now?'"[2]

Sarah clapped her hands in delight. "I love it!"

"That's a great story, Yasmina," said John, making notes. He looked up. "You keep coming through for me!" He turned to the group.

"Why is it that we just don't seem to know how to do what that fisherman does? According to one study, 65 percent of working Americans had unused vacation days at the end of 2011. Nearly one-third of the respondents said they didn't use their allotted time because their to-do lists kept them tethered to their desks. Others feared that if they took all their vacation, their employer would believe they weren't needed."[3] John sighed heavily.

"So, we're all agreed that most of us work too-long hours, take our work home with us, even if it's just in our head, and have all kinds of other demands on our time. It's like our lives are one long run-on sentence. And how many of us secretly wonder what it's all worth anyway—our lives seem to have no real meaning beyond working and accumulating stuff. And yet," he leaned forward, "have you ever heard a Christian—or even a pastor—say, 'Hey, I think there's a commandment about that'?" He leaned back again. "I certainly haven't."

No one spoke for a moment, until Ellie said, "It's like music." When no one responded to her statement, she said, "You know, music."

"Yes," said Yasmina, "we know. Music."

Ellie frowned. "What I mean is, it's like what John said about our lives being run-on sentences. My teacher played a tune once that was just one note after the other—it sounded vaguely familiar, but really was just annoying. Then she played the same notes again, but this time as the composer had written the music—with the rests between the notes. Then we all recognized the piece. She said something like, 'It's not the notes that give the music meaning, but the rests between the notes that do.'

"So," she continued, looking at Yasmina, "it's like music. Maybe if we took rests between our work, it would help give our work meaning."[4]

There was a stunned silence for a moment before Yasmina said, "Wow, Ellie, that's really good."

"Yeah, it is, isn't it."

"Thanks, Ellie," said John, making another note, "I'm totally stealing that for Sunday."

"Wouldn't that be breaking the Eighth Word, preacher?" said Steve, which elicited a loud groan from John.

"Thank you, Steve. So, if this Word is about rest, what do we need rest from?"

"Ah, list time," said Steve, stepping up to the chalkboard and beginning to write.

"Homework," said Ellie, without hesitation.

"Unrealistic deadlines," offered Rick.

"Unpaid overtime," Carlos said.

"The speed of change," contributed Sam.

"Staring at a computer screen," Jenny observed.

"From being hurt," said Sarah. "And shopping, needless to say."

"Information overload," said Will.

"The endless nature of my work," said John. "How do I know when I've done enough?" He paused. "So, we're all tired, maybe overwhelmed, and all these gadgets and devices we buy that are supposed to make our lives easier fail to do so. Either because they make us constantly available to others or because of what it takes to maintain, clean, fix, replace and research which model to buy. It's endless, right? So, God gives us the Fourth Word to set us free from the tyranny of 24/7 life—one day in seven we are to rest."

"OK. So, what day *is* the sabbath?" asked Ellie.

Will spoke up, "The people receiving this Word would, in time, come to celebrate the sabbath from sundown on what we call Friday till nightfall on Saturday, because that was the order of creation—'there was evening and morning.' This is still the practice of observant Jews today.

"The church came to celebrate the sabbath on what we call Sunday, which was the first day of the week, the day that Jesus was raised from the dead. They saw it as a continuation of the sabbath practice, as prescribed in the form of the Ten Words we find in Deuteronomy." He grabbed John's Bible, and while he was turning to the text said, "Now, the reason given in Exodus for keeping the sabbath is because God rested on the seventh day of creation, blessing it and making it holy. But in Deuteronomy, this is the reason given for keeping the sabbath: 'You shall remember that you were a slave in the land of Egypt, and the LORD your God brought you out of there by a mighty hand and by an outstretched arm; therefore the LORD your God commanded you to observe the sabbath day.'[5]

"So part of what it means to keep the sabbath day is to remember what God has done for us in delivering us from slavery: not only slavery in Egypt, but now also slavery to sin and guilt. The community gathers to remember God's redemptive work, and so Sunday became the day when the church gathered for corporate worship and to celebrate the Eucharist or the Lord's Supper."

"Well," said Carlos, "church people must have very short memories." The attention shifted to him. "How many of you have ever waited tables?" Jenny, Sarah, John and Yasmina raised their hands. "And what was your least favorite shift?"

Almost together they answered, "Sunday lunch." They looked at each other and laughed.

"Yasmina, how much do you make an hour?"

"$2.13 plus tips."

"Right. Minimum wage is $7.25, unless you work for tips, then it's $2.13. And has been for, what, thirty years, I think? Which pretty much covers your taxes. So, everyone knows waiters and waitresses rely on tips for their livelihood. Everyone, apparently, except the church crowd."

He turned to Will. "So all those people pour out of their churches, having gathered 'to remember that God sets people free from slavery,' and then they race to beat the other church down the street to the restaurant. And it's not like they're rude or demanding—although sometimes they are—they just leave pitiful tips. Pretty much treating us like their slaves.

"Like I said," Carlos continued, leaning back, "short memories."

Jenny said, "Do you ever get one of those little pamphlet things instead of a tip?"

"Don't even get me started on that!"

John said, "I wish I could say you're exaggerating, Carlos, but from experience I know you're probably more right than wrong. But rest assured, if I dine out, I leave a big tip on Sundays. And I encourage my congregation to do the same. But you raise an important point about the sabbath. Because there is a huge economical component to it that most of us never come to understand. I want to come back to that later."

"So what does it mean to keep the sabbath day holy?" asked Sarah. "Because it says that in both places, I think."

"Well, the text tells us pretty clearly what we are *not* to do—our regular work—which is what the word *sabbath* means literally: to cease working. But it is not clear at all what we *are* to do instead. How *do* we sanctify—keep holy—this day of rest? The answer to that, I believe, unfolds throughout the whole of Scripture, as we have seen with the other Words."

Sam piped up, "Well, when I was growing up it was very clear how you kept Sunday special, or holy, if you like. You went to church in the morning. Came home and ate a big meal. Then played really quietly while Dad took a long nap. Back to church in the evening, then early to bed."

"Could you watch TV?" asked Ellie.

Sam snorted. "TV? We didn't even own one. We did have a radio, mind you, but that was strictly off limits on Sundays. No, Sunday was a day of peace and quiet and church attendance. I wish it still was."

Steve said, "So you only watch *Monday Night Football*, then, Sam?"

"Well, I confess my Sunday afternoon nap is sometimes taken in front of the TV, beginning about the third quarter, usually."

Will spoke up, "Whatever it may mean for us to keep the sabbath holy, this is serious stuff. The sabbath was a sign to God's people of the covenant they had made with God at Sinai." He picked up John's Bible.

> *You shall surely observe My sabbaths; for this is a sign between Me and you throughout your generations, that you may know that I am the LORD who sanctifies you. Therefore you are to observe the sabbath, for it is holy to you. Everyone who profanes it shall surely be put to death. . . . For six days work may be done, but on the seventh day there is a sabbath of complete rest, holy to the LORD. . . . So the sons of Israel shall observe the sabbath, to celebrate the sabbath throughout their generations as a perpetual covenant.*[6]

"Whoa," said Carlos. "They *killed* people for working on the sabbath? That's a little harsh."

"It certainly sounds that way, Carlos," said Will. "But then again, as we read the Torah, the penalty outlined in the law for breaking any of the Ten Words is death, as we've already seen."

"Yeah. But I can understand capital punishment for murder. I don't get it for working on the sabbath. After all, I often work on Sundays. Should the church crowd bring stones with them as well as their tracts?"

John interjected, "I think this is a good time to be reminded that the Ten Words are not commandments but instruction. There are no punishments prescribed when the Words were given—that followed later."

"OK, so it followed later. But they still stoned people to death for working on the sabbath, right?"

"Well, there's at least one story I can remember from the Torah where that happened.[7] But here's what I think: People back then may have thought that working on the sabbath was no big deal—certainly they had not been given a day of rest when they were slaves in Egypt. But this day set apart for God is not just a rule—it is a practice, and more than a practice, as Will read for us, it is a sign of the covenant they had made with God. I think that's why the death penalty is prescribed later for breaking the Ten Words: because no matter how insignificant it may seem to, for example, talk back to your parents, that would be to break covenant with God. If nothing else, for those of us who want to claim the Ten Words for ourselves or society, this should give us very serious pause before we treat the Fourth Word so cavalierly. Because I don't think just 'going to church on Sunday' is what the Word is calling us to.

"Getting back to Sarah's question, I think keeping the sabbath holy means doing what Exodus and Deuteronomy tell us to do: rest from our regular work. But it also means intentionally setting aside time to remember God's creative and redemptive acts, to celebrate them and express our gratitude for them. And then not forgetting them the other six days of the week as we go about our daily work!"

"OK," said Jenny, "so I can understand why this should be a big deal for church folk. And I can certainly see why taking a day to rest every week would be beneficial for anyone. But," she said, turning to Sam, "as much as you might wish otherwise, society has moved on. We're stuck in this 24/7 culture, for better or for worse. I just don't think people are ever going to take this Word seriously."

"But we should!" said John, leaning in. "Oh, that doesn't mean I think everyone should go to church on Sundays. Or laze around the house doing nothing one day a week—although that might not be so bad for starters. No, this goes back to the story of those ex-slaves in the wilderness."

He leaned back. "I know I keep harping on about the fact that these Words were given to a bunch of slaves, but that's because I think that's why they're so important for us. If nothing else, the fact that this particular Word is unique among the ancient Near Eastern cultures should make us pay special attention to it. All the other cultures had some kind of laws about killing, stealing and many of the other Words we've already discussed. But none of them have anything like the sabbath in their law codes.

"Here's why I'm so passionate about this Word. It defines for us the neighbor who we are to love in the ways outlined in the last six Words. And who is my neighbor?" He grabbed his Bible again. "'You shall not do any work, you or your son or your daughter or your male servant or your female servant or your ox or your donkey or any of your cattle or your sojourner who stays with you, so that your male servant and your female servant may rest as well as you.'[8]

"God's people were to seek the welfare of their neighbors, who are defined as their servants, their slaves. We are introduced to the neighbor first in the face of the *slave*. Because all of these Words are grounded in the fact that they are given to a bunch of freed slaves. By repeating those words it's almost like God is saying, 'In case you missed it the first time, give your slaves a day of rest too.' This is one of the clearest examples, I think, of what some have called 'God's preferential option for the poor, for the powerless.'"

"So," said Yasmina, "let me see if I get what you're saying. To be able to have servants means you're probably pretty wealthy. So you can take a day off if you choose—others are already doing most of your work for you anyway. And if they're slaves, then they have no say in their lives. But in this Word, God tells slave owners to give their slaves a day off—they couldn't just keep working them while they took their own day of rest. Is that kinda what you're getting at?"

"Exactly! Everyone—masters, their families, servants, slaves and, note, their livestock too—everyone gets to take sabbath rest. And again, this is rooted in the story of those ex-slaves. When Moses went to Pharaoh and said, 'Let my people go,' he wasn't *asking* Pharaoh to release them from slavery. Right, Sam?"

Sam scratched his head for a moment. "Right. Moses just asked Pharaoh to release them from their work so they could go off to worship the Lord." He chuckled. "Although I bet they weren't planning on coming back afterwards!"

"Maybe. So what does Pharaoh do in response to the request?" queried John.

"He makes them work even harder."

"So, the service of God is refused, and instead more exploitation takes place. By giving them the sabbath, God tells God's people, 'Don't become pharaohs. Don't do to people what was done to you. Remember, you were slaves in Egypt, and I set you free.'" John turned to the group. "So on the sabbath day, the whole of society was to rest together. The sabbath is the great social leveler." He turned to Carlos. "So, no church crowd to stiff you, because you wouldn't have to work that day. And, hopefully, because of what some people call 'sabbath economics,' you wouldn't be working for tips, because your work would be valued and rewarded accordingly."

"So," said Steve, "I'm also thinking that by making them take a day of rest every week, and making a point of remembering their liberation from slavery, God is hoping to get this stuff engrained in them?"

"Precisely," observed John. "This isn't just about giving people a day off once a week and feeling good about ourselves. This is about God shaping a people who would constantly be aware of anything that was keeping them and others enslaved, oppressed or in bondage of any kind. So that, as a community, they made sure that their common life meant *everyone* could flourish."

John leaned forward again. "The sabbath also holds in check one of our greatest idolatries, one of our greatest challenges: the fact that we make an idol of our work by drawing our identity from it, making it the center of meaning and value for our lives. Which, I might add, can hold just as true for preachers as it does for anyone else."

"I think I know a thing or two about that particular idol," said Steve. "And that form of slavery. Some of us put the shackles on ourselves."

Ellie interjected, "So, like, are you saying work is a bad thing?"

"No!" said John. "Work is a good thing. Or at least it's supposed to be. Adam and Eve didn't lie around in the Garden of Eden doing nothing. Their work was to tend the Garden, to care for the creatures, to work with God to ensure that all of God's creation flourished. And to rest one day in seven, to sabbath, just as God did. But once we decided we wanted life on our terms and not God's, then work quickly became something else. Until we ended up with most people doing endless, meaningless work for a few pharaohs, building monuments to their glory, while being reduced to mere cogs in an enslaving system."

Will spoke up, "On that note, I wonder if the sabbath is the primary basis for all that follows in the law in terms of seeking justice and having compassion for our neighbors, particularly the neighbor who is powerless or poor."

Jenny leaned forward. "It kind of sounds that way to me. It's like you said earlier. By commanding the people to take one day in seven to rest, and to give their servants or slaves that day to rest as well, it means everyone shares in the opportunity to relax, to get their batteries recharged, not just those who have the power to do so."

"Right. The sabbath is not given just because people get tired but because people are *human* and ought not be worked to death, which God's people had seen happen in Egypt. And yet, apparently, God saw that they might forget that and one day become pharaohs themselves. So, even if they did acquire servants and slaves, one day in seven, everything stopped. And those masters could not order their slaves to do anything on that day. They were free."

"But only for that one day," said Sarah. "Then it was back to slavery on Monday. Or whatever day it was. Why didn't God just tell them not to have slaves?"

"Perhaps God did," said Will. "I wonder if this is another of God's ways of making concessions to our tendency to make self-serving choices. God keeps telling them to remember that they were slaves in Egypt, and that God set them free. Maybe God does that because God knows how quickly we forget. And once we've forgotten that we were slaves, well, if you have the chance to acquire some slaves for yourself, why not? So God carves this Word in stone to instruct them how to treat their slaves—their neighbors."

He turned toward Jenny. "In the hope that through this shared practice of masters and slaves taking the same day to rest, the people would come to question the whole idea of having slaves."

"Well, apparently it took us a few thousand years to cotton on to that idea."

"Indeed. But I believe the end of slavery is already written throughout the law. Because the sabbath is about much more than just taking one day in seven to rest."

"Like what?" asked Rick.

"For one thing, it's not just about people."

"Yeah," said Carlos, "it says animals get to rest as well, right?"

"Right. But there's also a sabbath *year*, when the *land* gets to rest." He reached for the Bible lying open on the table. Flicking through a few pages, he found the text.

> *You shall sow your land for six years and gather in its yield, but on the seventh year you shall let it rest and lie fallow, so that the needy of your people may eat; and whatever they leave, the beast of the field may eat. You are to do the same with your vineyard and your olive grove.*[9]

"Every seventh year the land was to lie fallow. They weren't to till the ground or sow crops. This practice is rooted in the order of creation, the natural rhythm God has created whereby all life can flourish sustainably. For people and animals, one day in seven we cease from our work and rest. For the earth, one year in seven is set aside for rest. A year of lying fallow would give the land a chance to replenish nutrients—an important farming practice."

"And one we've pretty much done away with," said Jenny. "Following centuries of crop rotation to control pests, replenish nutrients and rest the soil, along came the green revolution, and thanks to fertilizers and pesticides we can force the earth to grow corn or soybeans or cotton in the same ground year after year after year. We don't naturally replenish the soil, we just use it up and then keep it producing artificially. And yes, I know that that corn has fed the world, but for how much longer? And don't even get me started on genetically modified seeds that are sterile and can't reproduce. I swear, the human race seems to be suicidal."

John spoke up, "I was struck by the fact that while the land rests, the poor are allowed to eat whatever grows voluntarily in the fields—presumably other people's fields." He picked up a book. "This is what John Holbert has to say about that:

> *We rest and the land rests in order that the poor and the wild creatures may eat! The implication is that constant labor without rest will exclude the poor and the wild creatures from the proceeds of that unceasing work. This connection . . . has important implications for a culture like ours, which works more and more with the statistical result that a few get richer while the many get poorer."*[10]

"I'll say amen to that," said Jenny.

"There are so many economic implications for this Word. It's not just about taking a day off work once a week. It really does challenge so many of our assumptions about 'the way things are.' Perhaps the ultimate expression of that is the Year of Jubilee. I wish I had time to go into that with you," he said, glancing at his watch, "but our time is nearly up. But in a nutshell there was a sabbath of sabbath years, the Year of Jubilee, which was supposed to take place every fifty years. They were to let the land rest for a second year running, and all debts were canceled."

"I'd be in favor of that, given how much I still owe on that diploma hanging on my wall," said Jenny.

"Not only debt, but land and houses were to be returned to their original owners. So, if you had sold your land for some reason, at the Year of Jubilee you got it back. If you had to sell *yourself*—as a hired hand of someone else—you were freed from any remaining debt or obligation."[11]

"Wow," said Steve, "that's some crazy economics. Did they actually do it?"

John laughed, "What do you think? There's no evidence that they ever kept the Year of Jubilee. Or, for that matter, that they ever gave their land a sabbath year of rest. In fact, the people of Israel spent seventy years in exile in Babylon, which Israel's historians noted was to give the land the sabbath rest they had never provided.[12] When they returned from exile, Nehemiah pledged to reinstate the practice of resting the land *and* canceling all debts."[13]

"And I bet that didn't happen either," said Steve.

John shook his head. "No." he turned to Jenny. "I guess working the soil to death isn't just a twentieth-century innovation."

"All right," said Sarah, "how are you going to take all this and condense it into a sermon on Sunday?"

"I know," said John, running his fingers through his hair, "where do I start? Still, when in doubt, start with Jesus, eh Sam?"

"I reckon. Especially since Jesus was always running into trouble on the sabbath."

"My thoughts exactly." He turned to the group. "In many ways the sabbath is crucial to understanding what Jesus was up to, at least as far as the authors of the four Gospels seem to be concerned. Jesus' ministry of teaching and healing begins on the sabbath in

Mark's and Luke's Gospels. In Luke's account Jesus is in his hometown synagogue on the sabbath and announces what he has come to do:

> *The Spirit of the Lord is upon Me,*
> *Because He anointed Me to preach the gospel to the poor.*
> *He has sent Me to proclaim release to the captives,*
> *And recovery of sight to the blind,*
> *To set free those who are oppressed,*
> *To proclaim the favorable year of the Lord.*[14]

"If I can be my theological nerd self for a moment, Jesus is quoting the prophet Isaiah here, but from two different places in that prophet's book. Why these two texts and not others? I don't know, but one word appears in both texts—*aphesis*—the 'release' and 'set free' that Jesus says he came to do. *Aphesis* is the Greek translation of the Hebrew word for the release from debt of the sabbath year, which we talked about earlier.[15] Jesus tells the crowd in the synagogue on the sabbath that, 'Today, this Scripture has been fulfilled in your hearing.' In other words, the kind of release that the Lord's sabbath was intended to bring was going to be embodied in Jesus' work." He leaned forward.

"Now, *aphesis* can also be translated as another form of release, that of forgiveness, freedom from the bondage of sin and guilt.[16] In the two versions of the first beatitude from the Sermon on the Mount, we read, 'Blessed are the poor,' in Matthew, and 'Blessed are the poor in spirit,' in Luke. I think this gets to the very heart of Jesus' life, death and resurrection. What began with the Fourth Word is ultimately expressed in Jesus: freedom from all that keeps human beings in bondage, whether that be poverty, debt, illness, sin or shame."

"But," Sam said, "not everyone was happy when Jesus set people free on the sabbath."

"No, they weren't," responded John. "And Jesus got pretty mad with people when they complained about him embodying the sabbath principle of release on the sabbath itself. On one occasion he healed a woman who had been crippled for eighteen years. The leader of the synagogue was incensed, telling the crowd that if they want to be healed they should see Jesus on the other six days of the week, but not on the sabbath."

"Wow," said Jenny.

"Yeah. Jesus called him out and said, 'You hypocrites! Don't you untie your donkey on the sabbath and lead him out to get water? Why shouldn't I then lead this woman out of the bondage she has been in for eighteen years!'[17] They missed the point. The sabbath is God's gift to us to meet human need and so sometimes to meet the human need we're presented with on the sabbath might mean doing something others might call inappropriate."

"Absolutely," said Sarah, "Like when Rick here came over one Sunday morning to fix a light switch in my house that was giving me a shock every time I touched it, missing church to do so."

"And yet *being* the church in doing so," said Will.

John smiled. "Right. In all four of the Gospels Jesus declares, 'The Son of Man is Lord of the Sabbath.' Mark adds this to those words: 'The Sabbath was made for humankind, and not humankind for the Sabbath.'"[18]

He turned to Sarah. "So, to go back to your question about what it means to keep the sabbath holy, I think Jesus' life and words tell us that it means not just to rest ourselves but to do what we can to give rest to others, to give life, to do good, to love our neighbors as ourselves."

"But not just on that one day a week," said Will. "By taking a day of rest and reflecting on why we do that, that sends us out into the world to be sabbath people, those who work to set people free from whatever keeps them in bondage."

John said, "The rabbis taught that it was not so much that the Jews kept the sabbath but that the sabbath kept the Jews. So no matter what oppression they suffered, no matter what ghettos they were forced into, the sabbath kept them as a people, even as they kept the sabbath. The sabbath gave them—and us—a glimpse of the world to come. A world where all oppression was ended."

There was a moment of silence, broken when Ellie said, "So it's not just a day off, then."

"No, it's not just a day off."

"So," said Sarah, "what kind of practices do you have in mind for keeping this Word?"

"Well, I think it begins by actually taking a day of rest. One twenty-four-hour period a week where we lay aside our work. Which for most of us means laying aside our phones, laptops, PCs and such. I know people who have a sabbath basket for those things—at the beginning of the sabbath, all their devices go into the basket to take a rest themselves. And to make sure their owners do as well."

Yasmina piped up. "I have a Jewish friend whose family takes their sabbath very seriously. They make sure their house is clean and tidy long before Friday evening arrives, so their home feels like a place of rest. They light candles, say some special prayers, eat a wonderful meal together. I really enjoy it when she invites me to join them. It almost feels like Christmas or something—you know, like a holiday."

"A holy day," said John. "One practice my family has is to make sure that what we do on the sabbath brings us joy—even though it may look like work to someone else. So we often spend time tending our garden on the sabbath. If the weather is nice, we'll often take a lengthy hike together to reconnect with nature and get out of the concrete jungle. If it's wet or cold, we play board games together as a family—something we usually do not have time for during the week. We avoid anything that even smells like work. My staff know they can't call me on that day unless it's an emergency, and that I won't be checking emails. I've learned to guard my rest."

Jenny spoke up, "What about families who have different days off? How do they share a common day of rest?"

"That's difficult. Perhaps they set aside one evening that works for everyone to be together. Enjoy a leisurely meal, spend time talking or playing a game—again, whatever feels restful for everyone."

"What about the sabbath economics stuff?" asked Rick.

"Yeah," said Carlos. "How do we do that?"

"That," said John, "is something we could talk about for another hour and still only be scratching the surface. But it's a conversation we desperately need to have as a church—and as a society."[19]

Ellie glanced down at her phone and then leaped up, grabbing Yasmina's arm. "Oh my God, look at the time. We're going to be late."

As she grabbed her backpack, John said, "And that's a nice segue way to the Third Word, which we'll be talking about next week."

Ellie drained her cup quickly. "What? How so?"

John smiled. "Look it up when you get home."

8

From Blasphemy to Reverence

The Third Word

> *Worshiping the devil in the name of God.*
> NEW MODEL ARMY, "CHRISTIAN MILITIA"

> *You shall not take the name of the*
> *LORD your God in vain, for the LORD*
> *will not leave him unpunished*
> *who takes His name in vain.*
>
> EXODUS 20:7

Sam looked up from his paper as the owner of the coffee shop handed him a steaming cup of coffee. "There you go, Sam. Sorry for the wait."

"Don't be silly. If I show up before you open, I can hardly expect you to have the coffee brewed already, can I?" He took a sip and smacked his lips with relish. "Thanks for letting me in early."

"Of course." She leaned on the bar. "I've been meaning to ask you something for weeks now. I can't help but notice your little group on Mondays. I'm so busy with the morning rush I don't have time to listen in on what always looks like a very interesting conversation. Not least because of who's sitting around the table—I think you must make up the most diverse group of any of my regulars. So, what do you talk about?"

As Sam explained how the group came together, the two morning baristas arrived, greeted the owner and Sam, and then went into the back of the shop. "So," said Sam, wrapping up his explanation, "that's what we're getting up to on Mondays."

"Sounds fascinating. Which commandment are you talking about this morning?"

"Taking the Lord's name in vain." As the owner began to say something in response, the loud sound of breaking crockery came from the backroom, followed by a string of profanity-laced expletives. She pushed back from the bar with a sigh. "That sounds like an expensive start to the work week." As she walked toward the backroom, she said over her shoulder, "And it sounds like someone who's not overly concerned about your topic this morning."

As she walked through the swing doors, Sam took another sip of coffee and thought, *I'm not so sure any more that's what this Word is really about.*

As Sarah took her seat, John said, "All right, looks like the gang's all here. Let's get right down to it, shall we?" He passed his Bible across the table. "Sarah, would you do us the honors this morning, please?"

"Delighted to." She read, "You shall not take the name of the LORD your God in vain, for the LORD will not leave him unpunished who takes His name in vain."[1]

She handed the Bible back to John. He looked around the table. "So, what do we think it means to take God's name in vain?"

Carlos kicked things off. "Well, I suppose the obvious answer is cussing, right? Saying, 'Goddamn' or 'Jesus Christ' when some idiot pulls out in front of you in traffic. For instance."

"What about the fact that every other text I get from friends begins with OMG?" asked Yasmina.

"And," said Ellie, "that you have a friend who says it out loud all the time." She looked at John. "See, I did go home and look up this Word last week."

John chuckled. "I'm glad you're taking my homework seriously, Ellie." He turned to the group. "There's a cartoon strip I love called *Coffee with Jesus*.[2] I remember a while back one of the characters asked Jesus what he thought about her using OMG in texts. Jesus replied with something like, 'How about we start by leaving the 'F' out of it?"

Jenny snorted. "Now that's funny. I'll have to check out that strip."

"I don't get it," said Sam.

Jenny leaned across and patted him on the arm. "I love that you don't get it, Sam."

With Sam still looking bemused, Carlos said, "Well, if it *is* about cursing and swearing, I guess I've done my fair share of that." He looked at Rick. "Including in AA meetings. I thought it showed people how angry or how powerful I was. That I didn't care what people thought of me." He shook his head. "All it really showed people was how out of control I was."

"Exactly," said Rick. "And how limited your vocabulary was."

"I know, I know. And, as you pointed out more than once, it revealed my lack of imagination."

"But, as I also told you more than once, I didn't think you were consciously committing anything like blasphemy, despite what a couple of the guys said to you. I think using the names of God and Jesus lightly is commonplace because people don't seem to respect authority figures of any kind."

Sam piped up. "Now *that* I do get. And agree with."

"So," said John, "we've started with swearing and using God's name to express anger or frustration. What else do we think this Word is about?"

Jenny leaned forward. "I'll tell you what came to mind when I read this Word. Or, rather, *who*. The Westboro Baptist Church. Every time I see a picture of them protesting a funeral and read their disgusting signs, it makes me sick. 'God hates fags'? 'Thank God for dead soldiers'? Now *that* is taking God's name in vain. There's something profoundly wrong with those people."

John shook his head sadly. "I couldn't agree more with you, Jenny." He picked up a book. "Joan Chittister says this about the kind of despicable stuff people like the Westboro group does: 'When we use the name of God to demean or diminish any other human being, it is not they whose merits we measure. It is ourselves. And in public. How embarrassing.'"[3]

"Those people aren't real Baptists anyway," said Sam vehemently. "They just call themselves that. Have they no shame, picketing dead soldiers' funerals? I saw one of their signs that said, 'God hates you.' As far as I'm concerned that is about as bad as it gets when it comes to taking God's name in vain."

"Amen to that," said Sarah. She turned to John. "What about name-dropping with God? Because that's what I thought about this week."

"What do you mean?" asked Ellie.

"You know," Sarah replied, "when people say or do stuff that suggests that God likes them better than others. Like they have an extra-special relationship with Jesus or something. The way some of us use God to support or justify our own behavior or positions on certain issues. Sometimes I think we invoke God's name confidently when what we really have is just a belief or hope or even a hunch."

"Like what?" asked Yasmina.

Sarah thought for a moment and then smiled. "Well now, I went to a small Christian college, and by the time I graduated I came to the conclusion that God's intention for marriage was polygamy."

"What? Why was that?"

"Because of the number of earnest young men who informed me with great confidence that God had told them I was going to marry them."

Yasmina almost spit. "Really? They actually said that to you?"

Sarah cocked her head to one side. "Is it *that* surprising that someone wanted to marry me?"

Color rose in Yasmina's cheeks. "That's not what I meant."

"I know. Sorry, honey. I couldn't resist teasing you just a little. But yes, several of my fellow students did name-drop God as part of their attempts to woo me. A strategy that pretty much ensured their failure to secure the object of their desire—lil ol' hot mama me."

John laughed. "That's great, Sarah. And it captures what I've been thinking about this Word. As I've thought and read about it over the last few days, I'm increasingly convinced that this Word is more the sin of the pious than it is that of the sinner. As Carlos pointed out, most people probably think of swearing when they see this Word." He turned to Sam. "Back in your day people took that pretty seriously, right?"

"You betcha. One of my buddies from school was over at my house one afternoon and he said," and here Sam lowered his voice, "'He said 'damn it' in the presence of my father, who gave him a good clip around the ear."

"So *you* never said that, Sam?"

"Never. Well, not unless I was sorely provoked."

"But you might have said something like 'Dagnabbit,' right?"

Sam laughed. "Yeah, probably said that, instead. Or something like it."

"Right. You avoided saying 'God' in any way that was less than reverent."

"Absolutely. But that was a long time ago. Seems like I can't turn the TV on without someone saying, 'G-damn it.' Or worse."

"But is that really such a big deal?" asked Ellie. "I don't even really notice stuff like that. And compared to the other Words, like killing someone . . ."

Will picked up John's Bible, and while he flicked through the pages he said to Ellie, "I can see why it might seem strange for cursing to appear to be in the same moral league as killing or stealing. Yet there it is, all the same. And, interestingly . . ." he turned a couple more pages. "Well, rather than me just telling you, listen again to how this commandment is worded—which is the same in Deuteronomy and Exodus—and tell me if you notice anything different from the other Words we've read before. 'You shall not take the name of the LORD your God in vain, for the LORD will not leave him unpunished who takes His name in vain.'"[4]

Ellie chewed her lower lip for a moment before saying triumphantly, "Ah! It says God will punish the person who takes his name in vain. I don't remember hearing anything about punishment before."

"Exactly. And you're absolutely right—this is the only one of the Ten Words that has a very direct sanction: God says he will punish a person for failing to keep it."

"Wow," said Ellie.

"And," said Jenny, "it also says it twice."

"Yes," said Will, "It's almost like God is underlining this Word. And that repetition is unique among the Ten Words as well. So," turning to Ellie, "apparently taking the name of the Lord your God in vain *is* quite a big deal."

"OK, if it *is* such a big deal, then what does it mean to take God's name in vain? *Is* it just swearing?" She turned to John. "You said you thought it was more something that . . ." she hesitated for a moment, searching for the word, "something that the *pious* did more than sinners. What did you mean by that?"

"The answer to your question lies in what I think this commandment is really about. How *do* we take God's name in vain? There's been a lot of genuine debate about that. So there are several different English translations of this Word. Is it, 'to take God's name in vain'? Or 'to use God's name carelessly'? Or 'to misuse God's name'? Or even 'to idly utter the name of God'?"

"Well," said Ellie, crossing her arms, "that sounds like a really boring debate, 'cause I don't hear that much difference between those versions."

John laughed. "I think to answer your question it would be helpful to identify the name we are not to take in vain or misuse or idly utter." He picked up the Bible from in front of Will and opened it to a bookmarked page. "Whose name?" He read, "'The name of the LORD your God,' just as we heard at the beginning of the Ten Words, where God says this: 'I am the LORD your God, who brought you out of the land of Egypt, out of the house of slavery.'[5]

"The name is not the word *God*. It is the Hebrew word translated as 'the LORD,' which in Hebrew is YHWH, usually pronounced in English as Yahweh or sometimes Jehovah. It is the name God revealed to Moses from the burning bush." He flicked back a few pages.

> Then Moses said to God, "Behold, I am going to the sons of Israel, and I will say to them, 'The God of your fathers has sent me to you.' Now they may say to me, 'What is His name?' What shall I say to them?" God said to Moses, "I AM WHO I AM"; and He said, "Thus you shall say to the sons of Israel, '[YHWH] has sent me to you.'"[6]

"This is the name God revealed to Moses, a name that is found close to seven thousand times in the Hebrew Bible. But it's not just the name that's important, it's how God chooses to self-identify to the crowd gathered there at Mount Sinai. As 'YHWH your God, who brought you out of Egypt, out of the house of slavery.' Throughout the Hebrew Bible this is both how God continues to say who God is and how the leaders and prophets of Israel refer to God. As the one who brought them out of slavery in Egypt. The exodus event is the defining moment for Israel's identity and for their understanding of who their God is—the one who delivers people from bondage."

"So," said Jenny, "it seems like taking the name of the Lord in vain must have something to do with that, then. If people who claim the name of the Lord do things that somehow take freedom away from others or, worse, actually oppress them, then that would be to take the name of the Lord in vain, right?"

"Absolutely. I think that's at the heart of this Word. And *that's* why I think this Word is the sin of the pious more than of the non-believer. Because to take the name of the Lord your God in vain is presumably only possible if the Lord *is* your God. So, to answer Ellie's question, I wonder if taking the name of the Lord in vain is to talk about God or do things in God's name that are contrary to how God has revealed Godself in the Bible."

John pulled out a document from his bag. "This is how Rabbi Lynn Gottlieb expresses it in poetic form."

Levi Yitzhak from Berdichev
declared all the matzah
made in the town factory
traif/unsuitable for Passover use.
"Do you not see the young girls
who work for pennies
forced to bake

from dusk to dawn
so you can feast
while they go hungry
never mind the lonely dark miles to and from home.
Not Kosher!"
The women still repeat his single line of prayer:
"Ribbono Shel Olum, give a power
to everyone exhausted."[7]

"That's great," said Jenny. She sat back in her chair. "And it makes me wonder how many good Christian people are caught up in stuff like that—knowingly or not." She leaned forward and looked John directly in the eye. "So, pastor, does your church serve fair- or direct-trade coffee on Sunday mornings?"

John put his hands up in mock defense. "Not guilty, your honor. I'm pleased to be able to report, Jenny, that we have served—and sold—only fair-trade coffee for a decade or more. And, on a much larger scale, my denomination's pension plan divested from any company that we could document was engaged in exploitative business practices."

"Wow. That's pretty impressive."

"Maybe. But as my wife often declares, 'Ignorance is bliss.' Once you start taking justice issues seriously you realize just how complicit you are in all kinds of activity that's out of sync with God's intentions for people—and the world God made and loves. Now our church is looking at environmental issues."

"How'd you get onto that?"

"Through hymn singing," answered John.

Jenny raised an eyebrow.

"One of our favorite hymns is 'This Is My Father's World.'[8] One day after a worship service several months ago, one of the oldest members of the church stopped me and said something like, 'You know pastor, when we got to that line in the hymn that says, "the birds their carols raise," it suddenly struck me that I don't hear many songbirds anymore. While you were preaching I kept reading and rereading that hymn. "Of rocks and trees, of skies and seas; His hands the wonders wrought." And I got to thinking of how we're removing mountaintops, cutting down forests, polluting the air with our smokestacks and cars, and spilling oil in the seas. If my kids treated my place like that, I'd be pretty angry. So pastor, if this *is* our Father's world, what are we going to do about all that?'"

Jenny slapped the table. "I'd like to meet that old lady. She's my kind of people." She grinned. "And I never knew hymn singing was so subversive."

"Only if you pay attention to the words, Jenny, only if you pay attention to the words."

"So what did you do about it?"

"What do you think we did? We formed a committee."

"Ha! And how's that going?"

"Slowly. But I'll tell you something. There are a lot of big American sedans in our parking lot with bumper stickers you'd normally expect to see on Subarus."

"Mmm, mmm," said Sarah. "You got to watch those little old ladies. They sure can get feisty sometimes."

Sam said, "It's not just big corporations that oppress people, you know."

The table quieted down. "I reckon it goes on in families all the time." The group became still. "Least it did in mine." He looked down at his hands, rubbing his calluses. "The worst a corporation can do is fire you if you don't comply with the rules, right? Well if you didn't comply with the rules in my house, you got threatened with God. As in 'God punishes little boys who . . .' Or 'God doesn't like little boys who . . .' If a corporation makes good on its threat, I guess you can go to an industrial tribunal. At least in this country. But where do you go once you've been threatened with God?" He looked down again. "I can tell you where you go. Into a whole lot of guilt and fear. Which only got reinforced in church. Which, I know, may not come as a huge surprise to some of you."

He sighed heavily. "Now guilt and fear go a long way toward getting the kind of obedience my parents and pastor were looking for. At least for a while. But I'm not sure that mere *compliance* is what God is looking for." He turned to John. "That's what you've been trying to get at all these weeks, isn't it? This is all about freedom. These Ten Words are supposed to lead to freedom. The people of Israel had been set free from slavery, and now God invites them to freely choose another way of life, so they could stay free.

"Well, that's not what I heard growing up. These Ten Commandments were just that: commandments. And if you broke one, well, God will get you for that. God will also get you for a whole bunch of other things too, by the way. I don't recall hearing a whole lot about freedom. Just the promise of heaven for good little boys. Although even then, before you could enter Paradise you had to stand in front of a screen and watch a replay of all the sins you'd ever done in your life. And worst of all—your mother would be there, watching."

At this, Sarah laughed out loud before quickly stifling her outburst. She held her hand over her mouth, emitting little squeaks as the laughter threatened to burst forth again. She caught Jenny's eye, who was also visibly holding in her own laughter. They both exploded at the same moment, and within seconds the whole table had joined in. Even Sam himself started to chuckle.

As the laughter subsided, Sarah said, "I'm sorry, Sam."

"That's all right, dear. It *is* kind of a ridiculous scenario, ain't it? Still, I confess I was more afraid of my mother finding out my secrets than I was of Jesus seeing them on that screen."

He turned back to John. "As I thought about the Third Word this week, I got to thinking along the same lines as you. I reckon there were times when my father broke the Third Word while trying to get me to keep another of them. Oh yes, I think there were times when my father took God's name in vain. And that's hard to admit. Because even though I vowed I wouldn't do that to my kids . . ." His voice trailed off. "Maybe that's why God says he will visit the sins of the fathers on the sons to the third and fourth generations. Because it seems some of us can't help but do what was done to us."

He picked up his cup and took a swig of coffee. "I know I have been harping on about getting back to the good old days here on Monday mornings, but I got to thinking this week that maybe they weren't always as good as I like to think."

Yasmina tentatively reached out her hand to pat Sam's. He looked into her face. "Oh, don't worry about me. I'm all right. After all," pointing at John's Bible, "that Book tells me that as far as the east is from the west, so far has God removed our transgressions from us.[9] So if there is a screen up there, I reckon it'll be blank. All right, I could use a laugh about now." He squeezed Yasmina's hand. "Got one of your funny stories for this Word?"

Yasmina squeezed his hand back before letting go and turned to the group. "Well, there was this one story that came to mind. The Sufi tell the story of a teacher who sent his disciples to have a new shirt made for the upcoming feast day. 'This is a very busy week and so the shirt is still in process. But come back in a week,' the tailor said, 'and God willing, your shirt will be ready.' But it was not. 'Come back next week,' the tailor said the second time, 'and if God shines on us, your new shirt will be finished.' But it was not. 'Come back again tomorrow,' the tailor said, 'and if God blesses us, your new shirt will be waiting for you.' When the disciples explained to their master the tale of the unfinished shirt, the master said, 'Go back to the tailor and ask him how long it will take to finish the shirt if he leaves God out of it.'"[10]

A chorus of laughter rang out. John scribbled some notes down. "Yasmina comes through for me yet again." He chewed the end of his pen. "I wonder how often people use God as an excuse for their own shortcomings or in an attempt to spiritualize their circumstances."

"What do you mean?" asked Sam.

"Well, how often have you heard people say something like, 'Well, I guess God didn't want me to get that job' or 'The Lord must have other plans for that relationship'?"

"Sure," responded Sam. "While I'm usually thinking to myself that God might be able to do something for the person if he or she gave God a little more to work with. Like showing up for the job interview on time. Or bathing regularly."

"Exactly. Although I confess I'm not above doing that myself, on occasion. Like when a parishioner makes a suggestion for the church that is completely off the wall, and I say, 'Well, I'll pray about that,' when I have no intention of doing so. But by bringing God into it, then that makes it easier for me to say no later on. Like I said—this is the sin of the pious. Including myself."

"I want to talk some more about what it means for people to claim that God is on their side," said Jenny. "Even if they're doing evil things, like the Westboro family."

"I wonder," said Will, "if it's *always* dangerous to invoke God's name for our cause even if it seems like an obviously righteous one. Remember: in one of the blackest times in our nation's history, the Civil War—when brother took up arms against brother—both the North and the South claimed God's support. I'm reminded of a story about President Lincoln after the fall of Atlanta to Union forces. A woman reportedly said to the president at a White House function, 'Mr. President, I feel certain that God is on our side, don't you?' To which President Lincoln replied, 'I am more concerned, madam, that we should be on God's side.'"

"But," said Yasmina, "if you take the name 'Christian' for yourself, it seems like whatever you do, you're doing it in God's name. So if you call yourself a Christian and then act in ways that are unloving or hateful or mean or cruel, you're taking God's—Christ's—name in vain, right?"

"Sounds about right to me," said Sam.

"And in a similar vein," said Sarah, "I've said it before and I'll say it again: *Christian* may be a helpful noun, but it's a lousy adjective. Yet it's one we in the church are all too quick to add to our political platforms or social agendas or pet moral issues. We don't baptize *issues*—we baptize people."

"Amen to that," said Jenny.

"Not long after September 11," said John, "Elie Wiesel was on a panel discussing religious extremism and violence. At one point he asked the other members of the panel to name the unhappiest character in the Bible. Most people answered Job, because of the suffering he endured. A few named other people. Wiesel said that he believed the correct answer was God, because of the pain God must surely feel in seeing us fight, kill and abuse each other in his name."

John turned to Steve. "You're quiet this week, Steve. What's on your mind?"

"I'm not sure you really want to know."

"Try us."

"Well, after reading this Word last week, it seemed like I couldn't open the paper or open Facebook or walk through my neighborhood without seeing something that got my goose along the same lines as Jenny expressed earlier."

"Go on."

"OK, here's a for-instance. I was walking for exercise on the university campus and came across some kind of preacher in the free speech area who was yelling at a crowd of students. He was calling the girls 'whores' for wearing what I would just consider fashionable clothing, and calling the guys 'whoremongers' for looking at them. He told them they were all going to hell unless they repented. There were some students who were obviously from one of the campus ministries trying to reason with the guy, but he just shouted them down, machine-gunning Bible verses from the hip."

He turned to Sam. "You're not the only one who grew up with the threat of hell hanging over your every misdeed. My dad was all about using God's name to exert power over others, not least of all his children.

"Yeah," he continued, his voice rising in volume, "let's talk about prayer, shall we? Let's talk about Christians using God's name to manipulate God. You ask God to be on your side in some issue, to do *your* will, and, yes, to hurt the people you want to hurt but daren't because of the pious image you like to project. Let's talk about using God's name to avoid acknowledging your own failures. Let's talk about asking God to do for you what you ought to be doing yourselves—feeding the starving millions, providing adequate housing for people, paying people a living wage, ending wars. All prayed from the comfort of air-conditioned theater seating after dropping a wad of cash into the offering plate to pay the utility bills of the church."

As Steve spoke even more earnestly, people in line turned to listen.

"Let's talk about Christians quoting Scripture *at* people as if that somehow ends the discussion, point made, God has spoken and he agrees with me. Let's talk about using God's name to assure yourself of your moral superiority, while conveniently ignoring the hard questions of life that simply *cannot* be answered with bumper-sticker theology like 'God said it. I believe it. That settles it.'"

He sat back in his chair and ran his fingers through his hair. "How about that for taking God's name in vain, preacher?"

There was a stunned silence around the table. John cocked his head to one side as he looked at Steve. "Do you want to come and preach for me on Sunday, Steve?"

Steve looked at John, unsure if he was making fun of him, then smiled, somewhat sheepishly. "I guess I did go on a bit, didn't I?"

"And good stuff it was, my friend. So, what do you say we do a pulpit exchange on Sunday? I'll hold forth here at the coffee shop, and you can have a go with my congregation." He paused. "Of course, I'll be sure to turn off the A/C in honor of your visit."

Steve roared with laughter and was soon joined by the rest of the group. "I'm not sure if I'm ready for the big-time just yet, preacher, so I'll pass, if it's all the same to you." He paused, and then said, soberly, "Besides, doesn't it say something about hypocrites in that big Book of yours? Because I know that even as I point my finger at Christians who don't seem to be doing anything for anyone else, I'm pointing three back at myself."

"And," Carlos said, tilting his head toward Rick, "as my sponsor here is always telling me, when we judge others, we're also pointing one finger up at God." He looked down at his hand. "Well, a thumb, I guess." He shook his head. "I know John said this is a sin for the pious, but I reckon I've done plenty of this, and I've never really thought of myself as anything close to pious.

"I'm still pretty new to this God stuff, and I certainly wouldn't call myself a Christian yet. But I think I've broken this Word pretty consistently. I can't tell you the number of times I've tried to make deals with God. Y'know, like, 'If you just get me out of trouble this one last time, I swear I'll quit.' Or begged him to take away a skull-splitting hangover—self-inflicted, needless to say. I treated God—the Creator of the universe—as someone to call on only in emergencies. Yeah, I think I know a thing or two about taking God's name in vain."

John said, "I think you've hit on an important part of this, Carlos, in terms of the fact that some of us only find God's name on our lips when we need something. Or, as Sarah mentioned, when we try to add God's name to our words in order to give them more weight. Either way, we're *using* God rather than treating God's name with the reverence this Word requires. It's not that long ago that people giving testimony in court were required to place their hand on the Bible and make an oath that they would tell the truth, 'so help me, God.'"

"And," said Sam, "there were plenty who took that oath what didn't tell the truth. Which I guess is to make a liar out of God as well as yourself."

Will said, "The Jewish philosopher Philo wrote quite a bit about oath taking. He argued that in most cases there was no need to swear to anything. If we are telling the truth, then swearing is not necessary. And if we are lying, swearing what we are saying is true only makes the lie worse. Most grievous of all, we dishonor the name of God, who is all being and all truth, by calling on divine truth to bear witness to a lie."

"Let your yes be yes," said Sam, "and your no, no."

"Indeed," said John. "I think that's how Jesus upped the ante on oath taking.[11] Speak the truth, and don't drag God down with you when you fail to keep your word."

Yasmina spoke up, "I have a friend at school whose family is Jewish. We were working on a history project once and I noticed that she spelled 'God' like this." She opened her notebook and wrote "G_d" in large letters, which she held up for the group to see. "I thought that was kind of odd, so I asked her about it. She said that God's name is so holy that you don't even say it out loud. And if you have to write the name, you do so like that to avoid any possibility of failing to keep this commandment."

"Seems to me," said Jenny, "that's something the Westboro folk could stand to learn. They're making God responsible for the people they hate, which makes God part of their sick behavior. They ought to just redo their signs to say, 'We hate people.' But I'm not going to hold my breath waiting on that one."

"What they're doing," said Sarah, "is no better than saying 'God damn you.' And maybe that is what they're saying under all the other stuff. I think saying 'God damn you' is truly taking God's name in vain—not because it's cussing but because it implies that God will damn the people we think ought to be damned."

"OK," said Steve, "here's another question for you, John. How come there are so many people out there like the Westboro folk? What about all those TV preachers who attribute every natural disaster to God—claiming it's God's judgment on sinners, or it happened because we took prayer out of schools, or some such nonsense?"

"Like after Hurricane Katrina hit new Orleans?" asked Carlos.

"Exactly. Or when the earthquake leveled Port-au-Prince in Haiti—killing hundreds of thousands of people—and that guy on TV said God did that because some Haitians had made a pact with the devil two hundred years earlier. Like it took God two hundred years to get around to hitting the smite button!"

"Or," said Sarah, "how about attributing 9/11 to God, as his punishment of people living alternative lifestyles? Rather than the work of terrorists? I'm not sure what's the worse breaking of this Word— the people who flew the planes into the Twin Towers with God's name on their lips or TV preachers damning people they don't like in the name of God."

John stroked his chin. "How would *you* answer your question, Steve? I'm not sure there *are* hordes of people out there saying this stuff—more like a few folk with a big audience."

"But that's my point exactly. There may only be a few people *saying* it, but there are a ton of people *watching* them say it—and sending them money to enable them to *keep* saying it. If they didn't agree with them, then how come those guys are still on the air?"

John shook his head. "Maybe because the rest of the content on their stations offsets the odd, crazy statement? I don't know. I admit, it baffles me too. But you're right, Steve. Any one of those kinds of definitive proclamations ought to make people switch off and stop sending checks. But then again, when these guys' lavish lifestyles started becoming known—air-conditioned dog kennels!—it didn't stop people sending them money."

"I tell you what would have been more helpful," said Sam. "If those TV preachers had discovered God's vengeance was coming *before* it happened and warned people to repent. Or at least get out of town. Some prophets they are."

"And there you have it," said Will. "Isn't this exactly what we've been talking about all these weeks? My guess is plenty of the people writing checks to these guys know the Ten Commandments, have them hanging on the walls of their church buildings and homes, and yet don't have a clue as to how they actually call us to live." He turned to Sam. "So their favorite TV preacher can make some outrageous claim about what God is doing in the world that utterly contradicts the portrait of God the Scriptures paint for us—which seems to me to clearly be taking God's name in vain—and their viewers seem to be unable to join the dots between the Third Word and what the preacher said."

"But don't you think," said Yasmina, "that TV preacher is just saying what his audience wants to hear? Isn't that what everyone with an audience does? Look at all the political rallies going on. Seems like each candidate has a different message about what he stands for depending on who's in front of him. And it seems like all everyone is really interested in doing is dividing the world into 'them and us'—and we need to be afraid of 'them' because of what will happen to 'us,' because of what they're doing, or want to do. Whether it's the economy tanking because of *their* policies or people dying for lack of health care because *they're* heartless."

"And that's what's crazy about what those TV preachers say," said Steve. "Because not everyone who died in Haiti was into voodoo, right? My parents' church sent a mission team to their sister church in Haiti, which was leveled and lost half their members. I'm sure God was all torn up about having to kill his people so he could take vengeance on the 'sinners.' Talk about collateral damage."

"And," said John, "therein lies the rub when it comes to saying things like that. Especially before you've really thought things through. When you're trying to capitalize on a breaking news story to reinforce your own way of viewing the world or maybe seize the moment to do some fundraising, you end up leaving people outside your audience shaking their heads at the inanity of your words."

"But," said Sam, "they're not the ones writing the checks, so what does he care, right?"

Yasmina nodded. "As long as the audience keeps hearing what they want to hear: that they're right, that they're on God's side, and those people—whoever *those* people are—are wrong or sinners or infidels or whatever, then they'll keep listening and keep writing checks, whether it's to a ministry or a political campaign. We believe lies because we *want* to believe them. Because they reinforce our opinions. Because being *right* is more important than the truth."

"Wow," said John. "Steve has turned me down, but would *you* like to come preach for me instead?"

Ellie punched Yasmina's shoulder. "I would totally get up early for that."

Yasmina's cheeks colored slightly. "He's joking, Ellie."

"I suspect," said John, "that some of your words will find their way into the sermon anyway." John turned back to the group, "Well, this morning has been immensely helpful—and more than a little convicting. As a preacher, I recognize that every time I get up to speak I'm running the risk of taking God's name in vain in so many ways. Not least of which is the fact that so often my life does not match my words. At least not to the extent I might hope for. You've all given me a lot to think about in preparation for this Sunday."

"Do you have a particular Scripture in mind?" asked Sam.

"And," asked Sarah, "what practices do you have in mind for keeping this Word?"

"Pretty much doing the opposite of everything we have discussed this morning would be a good start! And as far as a text goes, I was thinking of the beginning of the Lord's Prayer. If the Third Word says we are not to take God's name in vain, it seems to me that Jesus' prayer begins with the positive way of saying that, 'Hallowed be thy name.' I wonder if the way we hallow God's name is by embodying the words that follow: 'Thy kingdom come, thy will be done, on earth as it is in heaven.'

"Because when we read the Gospels, these four accounts of Jesus' life and the kingdom of God that he proclaimed, it was the *pious* who failed to see God's presence in their midst. It was the 'sinners' who saw and loved him. The pious blamed the presence of the occupying Roman army on the sinners, while Jesus ate dinner in the sinners' homes. And when the religious elite challenged his authority and his claim to be doing the will of the Father, Jesus said this to them, 'Truly I tell you, the tax collectors and prostitutes are entering the kingdom of God ahead of you.'[12]

"So, Steve, I think those of us who are quick to call the other a 'sinner' are more in danger of taking God's name in vain than the ones we're pointing the finger at. Because the reason Jesus gives for the prostitutes entering the kingdom ahead of the pious is because the prostitutes *knew* they were sinners: it was the pious who failed to see themselves that way."

Sam spoke up, "Love the sinner, hate your *own* sin."

"Amen to that," said Sarah.

"Well," said John, "thanks again, everybody, for coming and helping me think through this Word. You've given me a lot of great stuff to work with for this Sunday." He paused. "I was thinking about telling a story that I think illustrates this Word really well."

"From the Bible?" asked Ellie.

"No. From my family. I have a brother who started following the way of Jesus a few years back. He's a diamond in the rough for sure, but there is no question that he has met 'the LORD your God, who brought you out of slavery.' His passion is antiques—he's a wheeler-dealer. He loves estate sales because every now and then he'll find a real bargain. He has a bunch of friends who do the same, and they're always boasting about how little they paid for something that they turned around and sold on eBay for a huge markup.

"A while back he went to the estate sale of an old lady who was moving into an assisted living facility and was selling off most of her home. My brother went and bid on a bunch of furniture, including one particular piece he thought might be really valuable. He outbid his mates, and then when he sold it later, he got some ridiculous price for it—something like fifty times what he gave for it."

He looked at Steve. "You know what my brother did? Instead of boasting to his mates about the deal he got, he took half the money he made and gave it to the woman he'd bought the piece from. You can imagine her surprise and delight. Somehow his friends found out and could not believe what he did. They told him he was a fool. That he didn't owe that woman anything. They told him becoming a Christian had made him soft."

"What did he say back?" asked Ellie.

"Nothing. When he told me the story, I asked him what made him do it. He cocked his head to one side as if to say, 'why are you even asking?' Then he said, 'Because it was the right thing to do.' I reckon that's keeping the Third Word. That's hallowing God's name. That's God's kingdom coming on earth as it is in heaven."

"Even I'll say amen to that," offered Steve.

Ellie said, "We gotta go, Yasmina." She looked at John with a grin. "Before I break the Third Word again." She pushed back from the table, grabbed her backpack and stood up. "What Word are we going to talk about next week?"

"It's hard to believe," said John, "but we only have two more to go. Next week it's the Second Word: 'No idols.'"

Ellie gave him a mock pout. "But that's my favorite show!"

"OK, Ellie. How about as well as thinking about the idols we might have in our own lives, we think about this question: What's the biggest 'American idol'?"

"Now *that*," said Sarah, "should be a really interesting conversation."

"Like every week!" said Yasmina, as she stood up.

As the rest of the group began to stand, John grabbed Steve's elbow and drew him back down. "Seems to me that we pushed a bunch of your buttons this morning—want to talk about that?" Steve looked John in the eye before saying with a smile, "I've got a lot of buttons to push." Then his face took on a serious mien. "But yeah, perhaps it's time I told you how I came by some of those buttons. Which will require some more caffeine." He pointed at John's cup. "Want a refill?"

"I never turn down a good cup of coffee."

"Now that sounds suspiciously like a little idolatry," said Steve, grinning, as he took their two cups and stood up.

9

From Idolatry to Worship

The Second Word

When all around you seems like hell,
just one sip will make you well.
BIG AUDIO DYNAMITE, "MEDICINE SHOW"

You shall have no other gods before Me.
You shall not make for yourself an idol, or any likeness
of what is in heaven above or on the earth beneath or in the water
under the earth. You shall not worship them or serve them; for I,
the LORD your God, am a jealous God, visiting the iniquity
of the fathers on the children, on the third and fourth
generations of those who hate Me, but showing
lovingkindness to thousands, to those who
love Me and keep My commandments.
EXODUS 20:3-6

Yasmina's mother looked at Ellie in the rearview mirror. "I must say, I'm really impressed that you girls have made the effort to come to your group every week. It's the one day of the week I don't have to drag Yasmina out of bed."

"That's not true, Mother," said Yasmina. "Or funny."

Ellie looked up from her phone to respond while continuing to type a text. "Well, I guess I'm just addicted to lattes."

"I don't think it's that," said Yasmina's mother, glancing at Yasmina in the mirror. "At least not for my Yasmina. I think you must be having really interesting discussions. Not that I would know— Yasmina doesn't really tell me much about what you talk about. And she's made it very clear that she doesn't want me to come in and sit in on the group."

Ellie stopped typing. "Yeah, I don't think I'd want my mom to come either." Seeing the expression on Yasmina's mother's face, she quickly added, "Oh, not because we're, like, talking about you or anything. It's just that, I don't know, it's nice to be with other adults and talk about interesting stuff. And for people to, you know, actually want to hear what we have to say."

Yasmina's mother made eye contact with her daughter again. "*I* want to hear what you have to say."

Yasmina turned to look out the window.

Her mother sighed. "So what are you talking about this morning?"

"Idols."

"Idols? What, like those carved figures we saw at the museum on the field trip last week?"

"Yeah, I guess. Some of them were really creepy, weren't they?"

Yasmina's mother laughed. "Absolutely. Although I thought that one with the big beak kind of looked like your math teacher."

"Mother!" said Yasmina.

"Oh, so you *are* listening." She glanced back at Ellie. "So, you're talking about ancient gods and stuff?"

"Maybe. I mean, that's what I would think." She glanced down at her phone and typed a few characters quickly. Then she looked up. "Although I guess we always end up talking about stuff I never would have thought of at the start of the discussion." She chewed a fingernail for a moment. "I guess I don't just come for the latte."

"So why do you go?"

"Because this stuff is, I don't know, it's like, real. It's not just ideas or beliefs. We always end up talking about our lives." She looked at Yasmina. "It's pretty amazing, the stories people tell on themselves." Her cell phone vibrated with an incoming text, but Ellie ignored it. "It's certainly not what I expected from a Bible study thing."

As the car pulled into the parking lot, Yasmina's mother said, "It sounds really great. I'm glad you girls have a group like that to be part of. I guess you'll be sad when it ends, huh?"

Ellie looked up sharply. "What?"

"Well, it's been nine Mondays now, and if you're talking about the Ten Commandments, I guess that only leaves you one more week after this one, right?"

"I guess so." She turned to Yasmina. "I hadn't really thought about that. Had you? Do you think we'll really stop meeting after next week? That would be a total bummer."

But Yasmina had already climbed out of the SUV.

Lattes in hand, the two teenagers joined the rest of the group. John smiled at them before turning to the group. "Good to see you all this morning. And what a big morning it is! Because this week we get to the Word that seems to define the rest of the story of Israel. Sure, there are plenty of stories of killing and theft and adultery in the Hebrew Bible, but open the book in any random place and chances are you're going to find idolatry. Either someone doing it or a prophet railing against it or, on a few rare occasions, someone rejecting it. It was the sin that plagued God's people from the very beginning—as we'll hear in a minute—and the one that was the greatest hindrance to them living in the freedom God intended for them. So, let's listen to the Second Word. Sam, would you mind?"

Sam picked up the open Bible.

You shall have no other gods before Me.

You shall not make for yourself an idol, or any likeness of what is in heaven above or on the earth beneath or in the water under the earth. You shall not worship them or serve them; for I, the LORD *your God, am a jealous God, visiting the iniquity of the fathers on the children, on the third and fourth generations of those who hate Me, but showing lovingkindness to thousands, to those who love Me and keep My commandments.[1]*

Sam laid the Bible back down. "That's a long one."

"It is," agreed John. "Although for us Protestants, this is actually the first and second commandments combined."

"And," said Will, "for Roman Catholics, this is the first commandment."

"So why are you calling this the Second Word?" asked Carlos.

"Because that's the way the Jewish tradition has numbered them. The First Word for the Jews is considered to be the prologue to the Ten Commandments by the church. I think the Jewish understanding grasps something that we've missed."

"What's that?" asked Ellie. "What's the First Word?"

John picked up the Bible. "I am the LORD your God, who brought you out of the land of Egypt, out of the house of slavery."[2]

"But that's not a commandment. That's, like, a statement."

"And that's why the church has tended to view it as the prologue or the introduction to the Ten Commandments. But in doing so I wonder if we've somehow missed the importance of God's declaration, the importance of God's First Word to these newly freed slaves, and missed the identity-shaping power it was supposed to have for God's people. Because what follows this Word, as we've seen, is the way of life, the practices that God gave to Israel to ensure they'd continue to live in the freedom God had just given them, and so that they wouldn't become like Egypt themselves."

John took a sip of coffee. "One of the challenges of reading the Bible—or any historical account, for that matter—is that because we know what happens later on we sometimes miss what was happening at the time."

"Uh, I don't get what you're saying," said Ellie.

"OK. Let me see if I can give you an example. Hmm, well, it's not exactly history, but how about this. A couple of weeks ago my wife and I decided our kids were old enough to watch the *Star Wars* movies without being scared. We were excited to watch the movies with them for the first time—thinking somehow that their experience would be just like ours had been. The first time Princess Leia kissed Luke Skywalker, our daughter went 'Eww! She's kissing her brother.' I said, 'How do you know that's her brother? We don't find that out till the third movie.' She just rolled her eyes. 'Oh, Dad. Everyone knows that.'"

Ellie laughed. "OK, I think I see what you're saying now."

"When we talk about God we tend to think of one Supreme Being, the Creator of the universe, that kind of thing. Judaism is one of the three major monotheistic faiths, along with Christianity and Islam. But that was all in the future for those ex-slaves at the foot of Mount Sinai. For them there wasn't just *one* God, there were *many* gods. All the gods they'd known in Egypt and a few others from surrounding cultures. They'd seen the images of these gods in homes, in temples, in roadside shrines, and carved into the walls of the buildings they were forced to build for the Egyptians as slave labor."

"We saw some of those in the museum last week," said Ellie. "Lots of people with animal or bird's heads."

"Exactly. But now they've seen all those gods unmasked as powerless before this God who has brought them out of slavery, the one who revealed himself with the name YHWH. God delivers them from slavery in Egypt and brings them into the wilderness to offer them a covenantal relationship with him. Moses and Aaron go onto the mountain and God speaks these Ten Words to Moses and then gives him a long list of laws, which explain what keeping the Ten Words will look like. Then Moses goes back down to the people. This is what happens next." He picked up his Bible. "'Then Moses came and recounted all the words of the LORD and all the ordinances; and all the people answered with one voice and said, "All the words which the LORD has spoken we will do!" Moses wrote down all the words of the LORD.'[3]

"Next, Moses builds an altar, and some of the young men offer bulls as sacrifices to the Lord. Moses takes some of the shed blood, and then gathers the people together again."

Then he took the book of the covenant and read it in the hearing of the people; and they said, "All that the LORD has spoken we will do, and we will be obedient!" So Moses took the blood and sprinkled it on the people, and said, "Behold the blood of the covenant, which the LORD has made with you in accordance with all these words."[4]

John laid his Bible back down on the table. "If you remember, I talked about this covenant between the Lord and Israel being something like a marriage. In a sense, God, through Moses, just got down on one knee and proposed to the people. They said yes, and now they're engaged to be married."

Yasmina's brow wrinkled. John said, "I know, it sounds strange, but in many ways that is what was happening. Now, it's not like our engagement, where you still have time to back out before the wedding day. For all intents and purposes they're now married. But they still need the rings, if you like. So Moses heads back up the mountain to get the rings—the two stone tablets upon which God will write the Ten Words. Moses was on the mountain with God for forty days."

"And while the cat's away," said Sam, "the mice will play."

"Well, that's one way of putting it."

"What happened?" asked Ellie.

"The golden calf," said Sam. "That's what happened."

"That sounds vaguely familiar," said Ellie.

"We saw one in the museum last week," said Yasmina.

"Right! The little one, with the circle on its head."

"The bull god, Apis," said Will, "with the sun disk of his mother, Hathor, on his head. It was used as a symbol for the Pharaohs in their funeral processions."

Ellie looked confused. "So the people had brought a whatsit, an Apis, with them from Egypt?"

"No," said Sam. "They made one for themselves."

"Why would they do that?"

"That," said John, "is the question at the heart of this Word. Why are we humans so enamored with making idols to worship?"

Ellie turned her cup in her hands. "But surely we don't do that anymore. I mean—all those idols in the museum. They're there because they're *old*, right? I haven't got a little bull thing in my bedroom, with candles round it and stuff." She pointed at the Bible. "That was thousands of years ago. It's all, like, superstition."

Yasmina turned toward Ellie. "So, you think we don't have idols today? We modern people are above all that old superstition?"

Ellie shrugged. "Yeah. No. I don't know. Are we?"

"You've probably done some traveling, Ellie, haven't you?" asked Will.

"Sure."

"Ever sat in row thirteen on a plane? Or stayed on the thirteenth floor of a hotel?"

"No. Because, duh, I know they go from twelve to fourteen. But I haven't carved a little bird-headed man out of wood and bowed down on the floor in front of it either."

"But what *have* you bowed down to?" asked Yasmina.

"Nothing!" Seeing the look on Yasmina's face, she said, "Have I?" She shook her head. "I'm so confused." She turned to John. "OK, what is an idol? Like, today."

"I think an idol can be whatever we turn to when we're in pain. Or when we feel powerless. When we're afraid. When we're lonely. When we feel 'less than.' An idol is whatever we turn to when we're looking for security, for identity, for meaning in life. An idol is whatever we turn to that is not the God who freed those people from slavery in Egypt."

"And," said Sarah, "because it is not God, it always fails to do what we want it to. What we *need* it to. Even if our idol seems to serve us well for a while, eventually we end up serving *it*."

"That," said Will, "is the danger of any idol. I think that part of the attraction of idols is that we know they are *not* God. So we come up with something we are willing to give ourselves to as a means to deal with the pain, insecurity and fear that we live with, *but* which we think we can still control."

"Like alcohol," said Rick. He turned to Ellie. "Let me tell you about an idol I used to have. Oh, I didn't call it that, but that's what it was. I started drinking when I was about your age as a way to cope with the pain I felt because of some things that happened when I was a kid. Alcohol kept me comfortably numb and got me through high school and college. Then when I began to succeed in business, I built an altar to that idol—a little home for him—a really nice wet bar. And I worshiped at that altar every night. I became willing to make sacrifices to and for that idol—as long as it dealt with my pain, I was willing to give up anything for it. Alcohol became more important to me than friendships, family, employment, even my health. Like Will said, I thought I could control my little god, but eventually it took control of me."

"Cunning, baffling, powerful," said Carlos.

"Yes. And that's not only true for alcohol. I suspect all idols fit that description. Like Sarah said, we think they serve us, but eventually we end up serving them. Until we finally get honest about our powerlessness—not just over our idols but over life itself. But if we're fortunate, someone will introduce us to a Power greater than ourselves who can restore us to sanity." He turned to John. "The kind of Power that frees slaves from bondage, and," turning back to Ellie, "not just slavery in ancient Egypt."

John nodded. "The kind who gives us a spiritual awakening so that we need never serve another idol again. Instead we learn to serve God and our neighbor who is still suffering, right?"

"Right," said Rick.

John turned to the group. "There's no question that alcohol can become a god that demands everything from us. But clearly some people can drink alcohol without that happening. Many people can enjoy a couple of beers watching the game or a glass of wine with dinner, without alcohol having any power over them."

John leaned forward. "It's when we ask alcohol to do for us what only God can do—deal with our pain, provide life with meaning, give us our identity—that it becomes an idol. And that's true for all manner of things that are good, but which can become twisted when we ask them to do for us what only God can."

"Like what?" asked Ellie.

"You name it. Possessions. Wealth. Careers. Sport. Beauty. Family. Music. Country. Any good thing that we draw our identity from, or trust in for security, or that calms our fears, or dulls and masks our pain, can become an idol. And, clearly, people are willing to make great sacrifices for any of the things I just listed."

"How about children?" asked Yasmina. The group's attention shifted to her. "Or living vicariously through your children?" She put her hands around her coffee cup and stared into the foam for a moment. "I love my mom, and I know she only wants the best for me." She looked up at Ellie. "But it's always *her* definition of *best*. The best pre-K, the best kindergarten, the best middle school, and now, the best high school. And because I've had nothing but the best—which I know my parents *have* made sacrifices for—they expect the best from me in return. The best grades, participation in the best clubs and—of course—applications to the best universities. All so my mom can boast to her friends about having 'the best daughter a mother could ever have.' I really think that's how she sees herself—mother of the best girl in the world."

"Don't you think that's a bit harsh?" asked Ellie.

Yasmina's shoulders slumped. "Probably. But you have no idea how much pressure she puts on me to succeed. And what if I don't *want* to go to an Ivy League school next? What if I want to join the Peace Corps, try and do some good in the world first? What if what I really want is to be a writer, not a businesswoman? Or what if I want to start a nonprofit—like Jenny—and not be a high-flying lawyer?" She paused for breath. "It doesn't matter what I want, because none of those options fit her definition of what is best for the daughter she idolizes."

"That's a heavy load you're carrying for such young shoulders," said Sam.

Yasmina offered him a weak smile. "Oh, it's not all bad. I'm sure there're any number of kids who would trade places with me in a heartbeat. I guess the load is always being aware that my mother's happiness—maybe even her identity—is so deeply dependent on my performance."

Ellie grabbed Yasmina's hand and gave it a squeeze. "So what idol do you think I've bowed down to?"

"Honestly?"

"Of course, honestly! Remember what I told your mom? I like that we're keeping it real."

"OK." She reached for Ellie's other hand and turned to look at straight in the eyes. "I think your idol is your body. Or, rather, the body you think you ought to have."

Ellie held Yasmina's gaze for a long moment. "Maybe not *that* real." She blinked back the tears that had suddenly filled her eyes.

"Ellie, you're beautiful, and you have a body most of the other girls at school would kill for. But it's not good enough for you, is it?"

Ellie started to protest, but Yasmina cut her off.

"No, it's not." She pointed at Ellie's backpack. "If we pulled any one of those magazines out that you're always reading, you would look at just about every model in them and tell me why you don't measure up to her. Even though you *know* that's not even their real body, that those images are airbrushed and photoshopped and whatever else they do to them to make them look perfect. You're not competing with the rest of the girls at school—you're competing with the impossible image of beauty those magazines push on us. And no amount of exercise and restricting your diet will get you there." Yasmina let go of Ellie's hand to brush the tears that now fell from her own eyes. "Nor will whatever else I'm afraid you might be doing to control your weight."

Ellie, ignoring the tears that now fell freely down her face, pulled Yasmina into a fierce hug. Yasmina spoke softly into Ellie's ear, causing the rest of the group to strain to hear. "If idols *are* what we look to for identity and meaning, and to deal with pain, then I think you bow down to yours every time you look in the mirror. And then you do something to try to change what you think you see there."

Ellie pushed back from Yasmina. "I think I liked it better when we were talking about ancient history." She brushed the back of her hand across her eyes, looked at Yasmina for a moment and then leaned back to kiss her on the cheek. "Thanks," she whispered. Then she turned to John. "So, getting back to the golden calf thingy, what happened?"

John held Ellie's gaze. "Are you OK?"

"No. But I don't want to talk about it."

Jenny touched Ellie's arm. "Maybe you and I can talk about it later."

Ellie's face softened. "Maybe." She turned back to John. "Golden calf. Go."

"OK. So, the people started getting worried when Moses had been gone up the mountain for quite some time—several weeks in fact. Perhaps they felt abandoned. They were running out of food, feeling lost, insecure, alone, afraid. What's next? What if the Egyptians figure out where their workforce is hiding and raise another army to drag them back to slavery? There's no Moses to raise his staff this time.

"So they went to Aaron and did what so many of us do when we're scared—they looked for something tangible to make them feel secure. They asked Aaron to make them some gods—graven images, something they could see and touch—to take the place of Moses and his God, who, after all, they had never seen themselves."

"But," said Rick, "they *had* seen what God did for them."

"Absolutely. But they were used to gods they could see, and it's all too easy to forget what God has done for you in the past when you're afraid in the present. So they wanted something tangible to have with them."

"What did Aaron do?" asked Yasmina.

"Aaron asked them to give him their gold earrings, and he took these and crafted a single golden calf from them. When the people saw them, they cried out, 'This is your god, O Israel, who brought you up out of Egypt.'"[5]

"But why would they look at this idol and say that *it* brought them out of Egypt? They had just seen Aaron make the thing!"

"That's another thing about idols," said Will. "They *represent* your god, but clearly are *not* your god. However, they can get so closely identified with your god that you begin to act as if they are God."

Steve laughed out loud, startling Ellie, who let out a little squeak. "What? What's so funny?"

Steve looked around the table. "Doesn't anyone else see the irony here?" Blank looks greeted Steve's question. "Come on—think about it!"

No response.

Steve shook his head. "OK, let me spell it out for you. An idol is a graven image, right—something carved in stone, which represents God. Something we bow down before and, presumably, want other people to as well. Something we are willing to make great sacrifices for. *Costly* sacrifices. And an attack on our idol is an attack on our God. *And* an attack on *us*, his faithful followers." He held out his arms. "Well?"

"Ah," said Carlos. "I get it. The Ten Commandments. You're talking about the Ten Commandments, right?"

Steve leaned back in his chair with a satisfied grin on his face. "Exactly, Carlos. How did we all end up meeting together, after all? Because some Christians over in Eastern Kentucky wanted to display a carved stone image representing their God in a building. Not their own house of worship, mind you, but a courthouse, presumably in the hopes that all those heathen criminals who darkened its doors would bow down before it and see the error of their ways. And they were so convinced of the power of their idol that they were willing to make a costly sacrifice to it. Half a million dollars, if you recall. Although, I'm not sure if it's much of a sacrifice when it's not your money."

"That's a little harsh, Steve," said Sarah. "But I guess not as far off the mark as I might like to hope."

"And," said Jenny, "I think it touches on the Word we talked about last week. If you're going to post a symbol of the God who liberates people from bondage in a courthouse, then you better be sure that the justice being done in that courthouse doesn't take the name of the Lord your God in vain, right? That it doesn't perpetuate unjust bondage in the form of imprisonment. And, as we've talked about over and over again with these Words, if God is concerned with the most vulnerable, the powerless in society, then if we're going to post his symbols in our courthouses we better make sure our criminal justice system reflects that."

"Which," said Steve, "I imagine you would argue it does not."

"Well, does it? We like to think that justice is blind in this country, but I think she just looks the other way while what passes for justice gets done.[6]

Ellie leaned forward. "OK. So Aaron makes this golden calf—which breaks the Second Word about making graven images, right? And then the people break the First Word by saying this calf represents the God who brought them out of Egypt. What happens next? Does God go postal on them? I mean—it's like they're totally cheating on him with this idol thing."

"It was something like that all right," said Sam. Ellie raised an eyebrow. Sam turned to John with a wry smile. "So, what *does* happen next?"

John shook his head. "Thanks, Sam." He turned to Ellie. "You're absolutely right, Ellie. Aaron broke the Second Word when he made the calf, but when he heard what the people said in response to it, he tried to redeem the situation."

"How?"

"By trying to identify the calf not with some vague god but with YHWH. When he heard them say, 'This is your god who brought you out of Egypt,' he declared to the people, 'Tomorrow shall be a feast day to YHWH.' He built an altar before the idol, and the next day they made burnt offerings to the Lord on it."

"And then?" asked Sam.

"You're really hoping to see me squirm aren't you, Sam?"

"Yup!"

"So, Ellie, what Sam is waiting to hear me explain is this." He picked up his Bible.

"And the people sat down to eat and drink, and rose up to play."[7]

"What's so awkward about that?" asked Ellie.

"It's what 'rose up to play' means."

"Which is?"

"Basically, it means their feast devolved into a drunken orgy."

"OK. Awkward."

Will spoke up, "And this incident sets the tone for much of what follows in Israel's history. Idolatry was usually linked with immorality. It was the abomination that Israel continually fell into. The assumption being that idolatry always leads to other sinful behavior." He turned to Rick. "I'm sure that Rick did not *intend* to neglect his family or any of the other harmful behaviors he alluded to earlier, but that was where alcohol—his idol—ultimately led him."

"At least," said Rick, "I'd like to think I wouldn't have done those things."

Sam said, "It was the orgy that led God to—how did you put it, Ellie?—'go postal' on them."

"Well," said John, "more accurately, we can say that God told Moses he was *going* to destroy the people."

"Sure," said Sam.

"And did he?" asked Ellie. "Kill them all, I mean?"

"No. Moses talked God out of it.[8] But Moses took the two stone tablets that God had written the Ten Words on—the covenant they had made together—and returned to the people. When he saw the drunken mess laid out before him, he smashed the tablets and stormed into the camp."

"Why did he do that?" asked Carlos.

"Perhaps to symbolize that they had broken covenant with God. Or," nodding toward Steve, "because he thought they might make the tablets into an idol as well. Whatever the case, Moses strode into the camp, took the golden calf, melted it down and ground it into powder. He threw this into their watering hole, and made the people drink it to taste the bitterness of their betrayal."

"What did he say to Aaron?" asked Yasmina. "After all, Moses left him in charge."

John's face broke into a broad smile. "That is possibly my favorite verse in the whole of the Bible. But only because it reminds me of myself. And because it offers a moment of comic relief in the midst of a tragic story."

"Well?"

"So, naturally Moses asked Aaron to explain himself. Which he began to do, ending by saying this to Moses." John picked up his Bible. "'And I said to them, "Whoever has any gold, let them tear it off." So they gave it to me, and I threw it into the fire, and out came this calf.'"[9]

John looked at the group expectantly. Their lack of response clearly disappointed him. "Don't you think that's hilarious?"

"Because?" Yasmina asked.

John shook his head. "Come on! Picture it. Aaron's trying to defend his actions to Moses, and instead of saying, 'I took the gold and made an Egyptian idol,' he says, 'I threw the gold into the fire . . . and . . . and . . . and out came this calf.'"

"OK," said Yasmina. "Now I get it. That *is* pretty funny."

"But, of course *you've* never said anything like that."

"Well . . . maybe once or twice."

"Well, *I* certainly have," said Rick. "Many was the morning I promised my wife I'd be home for dinner, then roll in after midnight. She'd ask me what happened, and I'd say something like, 'I don't know. I was on my way home from work, and next thing I knew I was sitting at the bar.' And the sad thing was, I meant it. I really *didn't* know how I ended up there."

"And out came this calf," said John.

"And out came this calf," agreed Rick.

"A calf which may serve us well to begin with, but, as Sarah said, an idol which *we* always eventually come to serve. And," he said, reaching down for a book, "the language of the First and Second Words make this clear." He flipped to the page he wanted. "Listen to what John Holbert says on that point:

> YHWH in the first commandment was shown to be most centrally the 'God who brings us out of Egypt.' But the house of Egypt is more specifically 'the house of slavery.' The word translated 'slavery' in the first commandment is the noun from the verb used now in the second commandment, here translated 'serve.' To

*serve an idol or other gods is to once again become a slave.
YHWH did not free us from captivity in order that we fall again
into slavery, into bondage to a false god."*[10]

"Maybe Bob Dylan had it right," said Steve. "You gotta serve
somebody."

"So choose wisely," said Sarah.

"Amen to that," said Sam.

Rick scratched his head. "I wonder if all these idols aren't really
the problem." The group turned toward him. "Well, I'm thinking
on the fly here, but what if our idols still mask our biggest idol?"

"And what's that?" asked Ellie.

Rick pointed to his chest. "Me. I wonder if all our idolatry is
ultimately about self-worship. About my need to try to control
my life. About my needs taking priority over everything—and
everyone—else. Sure, I have my idols, but I turn to them because
of *my* fears, *my* insecurity, *my* need for identity. They're all about
me. Of my need to be in control—or, at least, my need to convince
myself that I am."

Carlos piped up, "It's what you keep telling me. 'Selfishness—
self-centeredness! That, we think, is the root of our troubles.'"[11]

"Exactly. And, as it says a bit further on in the Big Book, 'The alcoholic is an extreme example of self-will run riot, though he
usually doesn't think so. Above everything, we alcoholics must be
rid of this selfishness. We must, or it kills us!'"[12]

Sam added, "That sounds a bit like Jesus. 'If any man will come
after me, let him deny himself, and take up his cross, and follow
me. For whosoever will save his life shall lose it: and whosoever
will lose his life for my sake shall find it.'"[13]

Steve laughed. "'Denying yourself' as the way to life? That's just
crazy talk! I mean, what would happen to the economy if we didn't
give in to all those ads that tell us 'You deserve this.' 'It's all about
you.' 'Spoil yourself.'"

"I know your tongue is firmly in cheek, Steve," said Jenny, "but I think the economy is the biggest American idol. No matter what issue we talk about in politics, what does it all come back to? 'How will that affect the economy?' Economic growth seems to be an absolutely unquestioned good—it trumps everything else. We just disagree on how to achieve it. And what does this idol promise us? What myth does it represent? That the goal in life is to become rich. And the American version of that myth is that *anyone* can become rich if they're just willing to work hard enough."

She pointed out the window. "But how many people in this neighborhood work really hard and are barely making it—let alone becoming rich? How many are holding down two or three part-time jobs rather than one job with a livable wage?" She turned to Steve. "I know you've always done right by your employees, but I'd say you're the exception rather than the rule." She turned to John. "So if what you're saying is right—that idols promise to give us what we need but fail to deliver on that promise, *and* that we end up serving them, then I think that just strengthens my case for economic growth being our biggest idol. Because clearly we're willing to sacrifice our children—and our world—on that altar."

"And that's all right there in this story," said Will. "What do they carve the calf out of? Some driftwood lying around? Some sandstone out of a hillside? No, they give up their wealth—their *gold*—to make this idol. In the Bible, idol making is closely associated with gold and silver, with wealth. As Moses begins to elaborate on the Ten Words, the first thing he says is this." He picked up the Bible. "'You shall not make other gods besides Me; gods of silver or gods of gold, you shall not make for yourselves.'[14]

"This idol, and so many others, were icons of excessive wealth."

Sam chimed in again. "'You cannot serve God and mammon.'"[15]

"And why do you think that is, Sam?" asked Will.

"Because Jesus said we can't."

"Absolutely. But *why* did Jesus say that? Because there were people who *did* serve two masters in the ancient Near East."

"I don't know. I guess I've never really thought about it." He laughed self-deprecatingly. "Just quoted it."

"I wonder," said Yasmina, "if it's because people are willing to do just about anything to become wealthy. To have the kind of life we see in all those magazines in the racks by the checkout lanes at the grocery store. The lifestyle of the rich and famous."

"Thou shalt not covet thy neighbor's wealth?" said Sarah.

"But we do!" exclaimed Yasmina. "And not just at my private school." She turned to Jenny. "The kids you work with. I'm not blind. I see the Escalades cruising the blocks behind the school. That's the symbol of success for your kids, right? The idol they're willing to run drugs for? Maybe shoot each other for? Because that's the only way they're ever going to have access to the American Dream. Am I wrong?"

Jenny shook her head. "I only wish you were, Yasmina."

Yasmina turned back to the group. "So we'll try and get on reality TV shows and parade all our character defects for millions to see just to get our fifteen minutes of fame—and the riches we hope will come with it. Or we'll gamble with people's life savings to make a killing on the stock market—and still get a big bonus if we buy the wrong stock and wipe out other people's meager wealth. All with a clean conscience, it seems, if the brokers I've seen interviewed are anything to go by."

"It's not just the traders," said Jenny. "It's our whole system. Why do we need to have whistleblower legislation? Because people get *punished* for exposing illegal business practices, not thanked. People get rewarded for making a profit for their company—regardless of how they do it. So we see that and come to believe that in order to succeed we have to distort our own sense of right and wrong if we're going to get ahead."

John picked up a book.

Why do we let this happen to us? Because we are afraid—afraid of failing to impress our "superiors," afraid of wrecking our chances for a comfortable life, afraid of losing our jobs, and with them our sense of self-worth and our financial security. The same fear that gripped the ancient farmers who prayed to the rain gods for their sustenance grips us as well.[16]

"Maybe, Sam," said Sarah, "that's why you can't serve God and wealth." She laughed, and reached into her purse. She took out a dollar bill and waved it. "Which makes it a bit ironic that our money says, 'In God We Trust.'"

"Maybe," said Jenny, "it's just a typo. Maybe what the Treasury Department meant to print was, 'In *Gold* We Trust.'"

"But," said Steve, "it's not just the corporate world that is based on that, is it?" He turned to John. "Isn't that how the story you tell every weekend ends? With people in heaven, where the streets are paved with gold? And what about the preachers I stumble across when I'm channel-surfing who tell their flocks that God wants them to be rich, just like he is? And how did they get rich? By fleecing the flock. And look at their sanctuaries. Some of them are nicer than any of the theaters in this town. I've seen plenty of mammon in the church."

"So have I," said John. "And I've judged the people who roll up to worship in their high-end cars and whose houses have more bathrooms than my family has bedrooms." He leaned forward. "But I've also seen how generous some of those people are. How quick they are to respond to need when they see it. And not just in the church, either. I've had parishioners whose wealth has not been an idol—it's been a means for them to serve God."

"How many people are we talking about here?" asked Steve.

John leaned back with a sigh. "Not as many as you and I might hope, I suppose. But people doing an awful lot of good for an awful lot of others. People whose wealth has no hold over them, nor for whom does it provide their identity." He picked up his Bible, then turned back to Steve. "But as for 'streets paved with gold,' that's just *one* of the images the Bible has for how the story of God ends. Let me read you another one." He thumbed through the pages.

> *And it will come about in the last days*
> *That the mountain of the house of the* LORD
> *Will be established as the chief of the mountains. . . .*
> *[And] nations will come and say,*
> *"Come and let us go up to the mountain of the* LORD *. . .*
> *That He may teach us about His ways*
> *And that we may walk in His paths. . . ."*
> *Then they will hammer their swords into plowshares*
> *And their spears into pruning hooks;*
> *Nation will not lift up sword against nation,*
> *And never again will they train for war.*
> *Each of them will sit under his vine*
> *And under his fig tree,*
> *with no one to make them afraid.*[17]

John laid the Bible back down on the table. "I love the prophet Micah's vision of the future. How much conflict going on right now in the world is because of our desire for security? How much is because the wealthy nations have the power to protect their way of life? How much damage are we doing to the world that God loves so we can have the life we want, consequences—and our children's future—be damned?"

He leaned forward. "But that's not Micah's vision of the coming kingdom of God. It's not a place of vast orchards and vineyards. No. It's a vision of a world where everyone has enough—*one* vine, *one* fig tree. No one will be rich. But everyone will have enough. But economic growth is not about 'enough'—it's always about 'more,' by sheer definition. And we appear to be willing to endure all kinds of human suffering and environmental destruction so a few of us can have 'more.'"

"Now you're preachin'!" said Jenny, with a broad grin.

"Maybe, Jenny. Maybe."

Sam piped up, "I've been thinking about the question you left us with last week, John. What are 'American idols'? Now, Jenny here says it's the economy. I reckon there's another one that's just as big."

"What's that?" asked Jenny.

"Personal freedom. My rights."

"Radical individualism," added Jenny.

"Sure. It's like Rick was saying, it's all about 'me.'" Sam turned to John. "You keep talking about what the purpose of these Words was—to form a people, to shape their identity. Not a collection of individuals but a people. And a people whose purpose was to make sure that everyone in society had a good life. 'Blessed to be a blessing' and all that. Well, I guess that's slowly gotten through my thick skull. All these things we've been talking about—envy, lying, theft, adultery, killing, honoring your parents—I reckon the reason we don't do what the Words tell us is because we're not thinking about others. Just ourselves."

He shifted his weight on the stool. "Whenever we talk about what's wrong with our country or what we're going to do about some social issue, we always seem to end up talking about our personal rights, no matter what our politics are. So, someone shoots up a movie theater or an elementary school, and before the victims have even been buried, half of my friends are ranting about their right to carry a gun for protection. Bring up abortion when you're running for office and people will tell you they have a right to do what they want with their body. Talk about marriage and divorce, and people will say they have a right to be happy or sexually fulfilled or whatever. Talk about health care and people will say the government's taking away their right to choose. No one's asking, What's best for our country? What's best for everyone? What about the common good? Oh, we may dress it up with that kind of talk, but what it boils down to is *me. My* rights. *My* personal freedom. Everyone else be damned."

He leaned forward. "*That* is the American idol. And where has all that personal freedom gotten us, huh? I'll sit over here claiming mine, you'll sit over there claiming yours, and we'll all go to hell in a handbasket together."

Sam sat back, and smoothed his hair back into place. "I'm sorry I cussed."

"Wow, Sam," said John, "How'd *you* like to come and preach this Sunday?"

"Yeah," said Steve. "I might even come for some more of that."

Sam picked up his coffee cup and gulped the dregs down. "Well, as much as I'd love to get you to church, Steve, I don't think so. Besides, I don't want to blow my perfect Sunday school attendance."

John laughed. "Well, the invitation's always open, Sam. And what you said gets to the heart of the paradox of freedom. Those ex-slaves out in the desert weren't a free people. They were a *freed* people. They would still have to choose where to give their allegiance, whom they would serve. The invitation there at Mount Sinai was to choose the God who had set them free—and would help them live into the freedom they had been given. But they continually gave themselves to other gods, to idols, who took them back into bondage of all kinds."

"OK, John," said Steve, "let me ask you a question. Do *you* have any idols?"

"Well now, Steve, if Sam were preaching, you're definitely meddling."

"That *is* my self-appointed role in life. Meddler-in-chief."

John stroked his chin. "As a pastor I've encountered a bunch of idols in church. For sure not graven images. But we certainly have a bunch of sacred cows. If idols are anything we turn to for identity, assurance and security other than God, or even just *more* than God, then we have a bunch of idols in the church."

"Like what?" asked Yasmina.

"In my first church it was the organ. Don't laugh! You'd think I'd committed blasphemy when I suggested we could have some of the youth lead worship on their guitars once in a while. But over the years I've seen churches that idolize great preaching or 'pure' doctrine or their music program. Because that's where they draw their identity from. 'Oh, we're the church with the great choir. We're the church that always has great preachers.' Rarely, 'Oh, we're the church that is doing our best to love God and our neighbors as ourselves.'"

"You're ducking my question," persisted Steve. "Do *you* have any idols?"

"Well, Steve, the idol I'm most often tempted to bow before is my understanding of who God is. And, I suppose, alongside that, what I think God approves and disapproves of. Theology is always a dicey game, and we're always running the risk of falling into idolatry when we play it."

"I don't get it," said Ellie. "How can God be an idol?"

"Not *God*. Who I *think* God is."

Will said, "*Si Dieu nous a faits à son image, nous le lui avons bien rendu.* Voltaire. 'If God has made us in his image, we have returned him the favor.'"

Ellie shook her head. "You really are something, Will!"

"And he's absolutely right," said John. "I'm always in danger of thinking my very limited understanding of who God is, is actually who God is. And like the Big Book of AA says, if selfishness and self-centeredness is the root of all our troubles, how can that *not* color my perception of God?" He reached down for another book in the pile on the table. "Here, this guy says it a lot better than I can.

> *Thus theologians and clergy may be especially susceptible to idolatry by developing images, theological systems, and construc-tions of God that objectify the transcendent and make us deceive ourselves into thinking that we can see God theologically, with our concepts if not our eyes and hands.*[18]

"As one of my friends often reminds me, the opposite of faith is not doubt but certainty. The minute I think I understand God completely, I have created an idol."

"But," said Sarah, "how can you *ever* have faith in God if you can never say for certain who God is?"

"Speaking only for myself," John replied, "my faith is in the God I believe is revealed in the Bible, and I try to live my life as consistently and faithfully as I can to my understanding of what the Scriptures reveal about who God is. *But* I also try to have enough humility to recognize that I always have so much more to learn, especially from people who aren't like me. That's why conversations like the ones we've been having these past Mondays are so helpful for me. They encourage me to reexamine what I already believe, and through them God often widens, or deepens, my understanding of who God is, and what God is up to in the world.

"I spent many years convinced I knew the whole truth of God, and I'm afraid my arrogance hurt the very people I was trying to serve. I felt threatened by people who asked questions I thought had already been answered, or—on those rare occasions when I was honest with myself—who asked the questions I didn't dare ask myself. But I finally got to the place where my ideas about who God was could not answer those questions. And so I borrowed a prayer from the Christian mystic Meister Eckhart: 'God, rid me of God.'"

Seeing Ellie's wrinkled brow, John continued, "Oh, it's not that I stopped believing in God. Or that I stopped reading the Bible or even being a pastor. I just got honest with myself about all the cultural, family and personal baggage I brought to who I thought God was. So when I opened the Bible, I would pray that prayer, and then try to find the God who is actually revealed in Scripture, not come with my own ideas of who God is and then look for Bible verses to back that up, if that makes sense."

"Kind of," said Ellie.

Will said, "I find it's always dangerous when I think that God agrees with me on everything."

"Amen to that," said John.

"So who *is* the God you find when you read the Bible?" asked Ellie.

John smiled and looked at his watch. "That's a great segue to next week, Ellie, when we finally get to the First Word—God." He looked around the table. "I *so* look forward to Monday mornings with you all. This is so life-giving for me. Not just in terms of all the ways you help me think through things before I preach. But in the ways you share your stories with me, with each other. I confess I'm not looking forward to our last discussion next week."

"Me neither!" exclaimed Ellie. "Don't you have another sermon series you need help with?"

"I'd like to think I planned that far ahead, Ellie. But maybe we can figure something else out."

"I hope so." A chorus of "Me too's" echoed her sentiment.

As the group began to leave, Jenny took Ellie's arm and gently pulled her aside. "My offer was serious, Ellie. If you ever want to talk, I'd love to listen." She glanced across at Sarah. "It's good to have someone who listens."

"Thanks, Jenny. You're really kind. I'll think about it."

10

God

The First Word

Love—it will not betray,
dismay or enslave you,
It will set you free.

MUMFORD & SONS,
"SIGH NO MORE"

Then God spoke all these words,
saying: "I am the LORD your God,
who brought you out of the land of
Egypt, out of the house of slavery."

EXODUS 20:1-2

Steve sat down heavily in a chair, splashing coffee out of his mug in the process. He grabbed a napkin. "Sorry I'm late, everyone. Battery died. And guess who had to walk out of his house just as I was cussing out my car?" He laughed. "Mister Jag, of course. He didn't say a word as he hooked up the jumper cables. But I just know he was laughing on the inside." He looked around the table. "Hey, where's John?"

"I was just telling the others," said Will. "He may not make it this morning. A member of his church was taken to the hospital yesterday, and he's over there with her before she goes into surgery. He sends his apologies."

"But he can't miss the last week," cried Ellie. "That's not right!"

"Yeah," said Jenny. "It's kinda weird without him." She laughed. "*Now* what do we talk about?"

"Same stuff, I reckon," said Sam. He looked Jenny in the eye. "I get the feeling us getting together wasn't just so John could preach a better sermon."

Jenny held his gaze. "Maybe not, Sam, maybe not. But speaking of which," turning to the group, "I've been wondering. Did any of you ever go to hear him preach? Besides you guys, of course." She gestured towards Rick, Sarah and Carlos.

"I did," said Yasmina.

"What?" said Ellie. "You never told me. Or asked me to come with you!"

"I didn't want to go with you, Ellie." Before Ellie could respond she added, "What I mean is, I wanted to go with someone else."

"Who?!" Ellie spluttered.

"My mom."

Ellie's mouth formed a silent "O."

"When I got home last week I thought about what I said about my mom. And then I thought about what we said about honoring our parents a few weeks back. I kinda felt bad and thought maybe I should do something with her. I knew she really wanted to come here, but I'm not up for that. So I figured the next best thing might be for us to go hear John preach. So we went yesterday."

"And how was that?" asked Jenny.

"Good, yeah. He's a pretty good speaker."

"No," Jenny said, leaning forward, "How was it with your mom?"

"Y'know, it was really nice. Different. Not just her taking me somewhere I needed to be, and giving me the pep talk on the way. It was just going somewhere together. We even had a good conversation over lunch." She swirled a finger in the foam of her latte. "Probably because I didn't have to perform. Just be with her."

"Are you going to go to church again?" asked Sam.

She looked up. "Hadn't really thought about it. But we did talk about going out for dinner next weekend. Just the two of us. That'll be good. I think."

Sam turned to Steve. "How about you, Steve? Next week's your last chance to go hear what John's been doing with our conversations. Tell you what—I'll even skip Sunday school to come with you. Whaddya say?"

"Oh, I don't think so, Sam. Besides, I'd hate for you to ruin your Sunday school attendance record on account of me."

"It'd be worth it," Sam said with a grin. He jabbed a finger in Steve's direction. "After all, you did get this whole thing started. Are you up for finishing it out? There's just one word left. The biggie: God." He raised a questioning eyebrow.

Steve leaned back in his chair and looked at Sam for a long moment. Then he leaned forward and picked up his newspaper from the table. "I believe this whole conversation began because of the headlines in the paper a couple of months ago. How about we take a look at the headlines today, and then I'll answer your question." He began to flick through the paper and read out the headlines.[1]

> Newtown Mourns; School Resumes
> Stores Distance Themselves from AR-15 Rifles
> Woman Says Police Officer Raped Her

2 Indicted in Shooting

More Young Adults Are Homeless

Exxon Mobile Oil Deal Triggers Dispute Between Southern
    Iraq, Kurdistan Region

He threw the paper back on the table. He ran his fingers through
his hair and sighed heavily. "I may be agnostic when it comes to
God, but not when it comes to people. We are utterly and completely screwed up, and I don't think *anyone* knows what to do
about any of those headlines." He leaned forward. "I was telling Joe
a while back that our conversation about these Words has made me
read the paper differently. Every story I read, I find myself trying to
figure out which of the Ten Words got broken in it. I usually can,
and it's often more than one.

"Then there's all of us," Steve continued. "We've freely and honestly admitted the ways we've not done what these Words tell us to
do—regardless of what we might think about them. And we've been
hearing about all those folk in the Bible who totally blew them. And
finally there's Jesus, who didn't just teach the Ten Words but actually upped the ante on what they tell us to do."

He leaned back again. "So, I reckon all the Ten Words do is
remind us that we don't—and can't—live the life that book,"
pointing at Will's Bible on the table, "tells us to live. No matter how
many copies of the Ten Commandments are put on display. John
keeps telling us the Ten Words were designed to make a people
who'll look out for each other, but I think most of us'll just keep on
looking out for ourselves. The common good? Ha! That's just
wishful thinking."

"I don't believe that," said Yasmina.

"Me neither," agreed Ellie.

"Not yet," said Steve. "But you will." He shook his head. "Ah, but
don't listen to me. I'm just cynical. Getting old, I guess."

"Well," said Sam, "I've got you beat there, Steve. And I tend to agree with you." He pointed at the paper. "I don't think I'm going to read about too many of my fellow church members in there, but these past weeks have got me thinking. I wonder if most of us Baptists don't break those Words on a regular basis, and we don't even know it. I can quote chapter and verse about 'loving my neighbor as myself,' but I'm beginning to think I haven't got a clue what that actually means."

"I don't think that's limited to the Baptists," said Sarah.

"Probably not, Sarah."

"Or to church members," said Jenny. "It's not like the rest of us are doing any better."

"Well, this is depressing," said Ellie. "I thought we'd be ending on a high note." She added hastily, "Not that I'm ready for this to end."

Yasmina turned to Sam. "So, forgetting about us for a minute, did *anyone* in there," pointing at the Bible on the table, "keep the Ten Words? Or *is* this really just wishful thinking?"

"Besides Jesus, you mean?"

"Yeah. Besides someone who was God. Someone like us."

"But that's just it," interjected Will. "Jesus *was* like us."

"But if you believe he's *God*, then he's *not* like us, is he?"

Will reached for his Bible. "Let me read you something."

Have this attitude in yourselves which was also in Christ Jesus, who, although He existed in the form of God, did not regard equality with God a thing to be grasped, but emptied Himself, taking the form of a bond-servant, and being made in the likeness of [humanity]. Being found in appearance as a man, He humbled Himself by becoming obedient to the point of death, even death on a cross.[2]

Ellie's brow wrinkled. "What does that mean?"

"It depends on who you ask, Ellie. There's a lot of discussion about what 'he emptied himself' means."

"But," said Yasmina, "you obviously read it for a reason. So what do *you* think it means?"

"I think it means that when the Word became flesh, as the Gospel of John puts it, God the Son laid aside his divine attributes." Seeing Sam about to object, Will raised his hands. "I know! We could talk about what that means all morning. But whatever it means, I think the end result was that when things got tough, Jesus chose not to play the 'God card'—whether we think he had it to play or not. He chose to live life on the same terms you and I do. Either trying to muddle through life best he could on his own or choosing to obey God the Father, and trusting the Holy Spirit to help him do it."

Carlos spoke up. "Praying only for knowledge of God's will for us and the power to carry that out."

"That's a good way of putting it, Carlos."

"It's not original to me," grinned Carlos. "It's the Eleventh Step."

Ellie looked stressed. "This is all a bit heavy for me."

"You're not alone in that, Ellie, I can assure you," said Will. "All I'm trying to say is that, contrary to most of the paintings you might have seen, Jesus didn't float a couple of feet above the ground in pristine white robes, keeping the law perfectly, simply because he was God. No, he got home at the end of the day tired out, with smelly, dirty feet, having faced the same temptations you and I do."

"Yet without sin!" interjected Sam.

"Yes, Sam, without sin.[3] He showed us what it means to love God and to love our neighbor as ourselves. He fulfilled the law. And we nailed him to a cross for it."

"Still pretty heavy," observed Ellie.

"But," Will turned to Sam, "there *was* one person other than Jesus who kept the Ten Words. Or, at least, he *thought* he did, right Sam?"

Sam scratched his chin. "Riiight. The rich young ruler. Hmm."

Sarah chimed in, "That's the guy my momma always said I should keep an eye out for. Someone who kept the command-ments." She laughed. "And it wouldn't hurt if he happened to be rich too."

"So, this guy kept all the commandments?" asked Carlos.

Sam responded, "Like Will said, he thought he did. And maybe he did as far as he knew." He offered a wry smile. "Much like I might have thought *I* did till we started this group."

Jenny spoke up. "For those of us who don't know the story . . ."[4]

"Sorry," said Sam. "OK, so this young feller comes to Jesus and says, 'What do I need to do to inherit eternal life?' And Jesus says, 'You know the commandments: "You shall not commit adultery, you shall not murder, you shall not steal, you shall not give false testimony, honor your father and mother."' And the young guy said, 'I've kept them all since I was little.'"

"Impressive," said Carlos.

"Or he's a big, fat liar," said Ellie.

Sam laughed. "No, I don't think he was lying, Ellie. Because it says Jesus looked at him and loved him."

"Why?"

"Well, from what I understand, people back then believed that keeping the commandments was what got you eternal life. Yet here's this guy who's kept them all asking Jesus what else he needed to do. Seems like he knew that wasn't enough somehow. I think that's why Jesus looked at him with love—'cause he admitted there was something missing. But then Jesus upped the ante again."

"How?" asked Yasmina.

"Jesus said, 'Well, there's one thing left for you to do. Sell all you have, give the money to the poor and come follow me.'"

"Because it's wrong to be rich?" said Ellie.

Will chimed in again, "Not because he was rich. Jesus had rich friends—some of them were women who supported him and his disciples.[5] No, this man's problem wasn't his wealth. It was what his wealth meant to him."

"Which was?"

"His identity. His status. His scorecard, if you like. It's like having all A's on your grade card. Good for getting into the right university, good for getting the right career, good for living the American

Dream. Good for keeping score against everyone else. Really impressive for climbing up the ladder of life. Until you discover your ladder has been leaning against the wrong wall. This guy did everything right and had missed the whole point. He thought his wealth was there to enable him to live the good, pious life. To be someone everyone looked up to. But underneath all that, he had this sneaking suspicion that it wasn't enough."

"So Jesus asked him to give up his wealth," said Sam. "And not just give it up. Give it away to the poor. Which would make him poor himself, I guess."

"Exactly," said Will, "And if he did follow Jesus, that'd mean he'd need the support of those wealthy women himself. Quite the comedown for someone used to being the person other people came to for help. But that's what it means to follow Jesus! Jesus, 'who although he was equal with God, humbled himself, becoming a bond-servant,' as I read just now. Seems like this young man was only willing to humble himself by admitting he was missing something. Maybe he thought he just needed to tweak his life a little. But Jesus wasn't interested in tweaking his life. He wanted him to be transformed. I don't think he's just asking him to give up his old life. He's asking him to embrace a whole new way of living. A way of living that would turn his life upside down."

Sarah cocked her head to one side. "Isn't that what the Ten Words were? I mean, originally. Weren't they a whole new way of living—something that would transform slaves into human beings, like John keeps saying? What if Jesus *isn't* upping the ante? What if all this *isn't* just about following a bunch of rules? What if this has always been about changing us from the inside out?"

"Sounds good to me, Sarah," said Rick. He looked around the table. "You know, for the longest time, I thought the goal of becoming a member of Alcoholics Anonymous was for me to stop drinking."

"Uh," said Ellie, "that isn't the goal?"

"No, Ellie. Oh, the desire to stop drinking was what got me in the rooms, but I discovered that me stopping drinking was just a means to an end. It wasn't the end in itself."

"So what *is* the goal?"

"To have a spiritual awakening. That's what the Twelfth Step tells me. 'Having had a spiritual awakening as the result of these steps, we tried to carry this message to alcoholics, and to practice these principles in all our affairs.' It's not about me *not* doing something. It's not about me *not* drinking. I quit drinking hundreds of times, after all! But whenever I did, I was just a dry drunk. And some people will tell you they preferred me when I *was* drinking. A sober life is so much more than just not drinking. It's a whole new life. It's about becoming less selfish and self-centered, and learning to become of service to alcoholics who're still suffering. It's about admitting when I'm wrong and asking for forgiveness. It's about making amends to the people I've hurt in my drinking. *And* in my sobriety. It's about asking God to remove my defects of character, so I stop doing the things I don't want to do. But, of course, for that to happen I had to stop drinking first. But *not* drinking is not the goal. The goal is to have a spiritual awakening. Like Sarah said, it's about being changed from the inside out."

He picked up Will's Bible. "And so I think these Ten Words we've been talking about, they have to be more than just *not* doing those things, right? I mean, if all they can write on my tombstone when I'm dead is 'Did not kill anyone,' 'did not steal,' 'did not beat his wife' or whatever, then that's hardly a eulogy to be proud of, is it?"

He turned to Sam. "I think that's what would have been written on that rich kid's tombstone, right? But even he knew that wasn't enough. That *that* wasn't supposed to be the sum total of his life. But I wonder if he couldn't get there until he gave up his wealth. His power. The first step of AA is to admit our powerlessness and our need for a Power greater than ourselves. Maybe he would never take that step till he gave up his wealth. So Jesus invites him to do just that. And then to follow him, to become part of the fellowship of the disciples. To live all this stuff out with them.'"

Carlos put his hand on Rick's shoulder and looked around the group. "I remember the meeting when I decided I wanted Rick to be my sponsor." He turned to Rick. "You were chairing the meeting, and when you shared, you said something like, 'On any given day I could control my behavior. I could avoid taking a drink for twenty-four hours. Take care of business at work. Be kind to my wife. But I just couldn't string many of those days together. Because on *no* given day could I transform my heart. And my drinking was not the problem. It was my heart.'"

Rick nodded. "Only a Power greater than myself could do that. And as I turned my will and my life over to the care of God through working the Steps, I discovered God doing for me what I could not do for myself. I began to experience the promises. And I was freed from the compulsion to drink." He reached for the Bible.

"'I am the LORD your God who brought you out of the land of Egypt, out of the house of slavery.'"

"Out of the bondage of addiction." He placed the Bible back on the table. "I stopped trying to control my life, control my behaviors, and surrendered to God. And I haven't had a drink since."

Seeing a look approaching awe on Ellie's face, he said, "Oh, I've still got a long way to go! Remember—not drinking is only the beginning. I still have plenty of character defects left for God to remove. But God is doing that—in his own time. God is doing for me what I cannot do for myself."

"It's no longer I who live," said Sam, "but Christ lives in me."[6]

The roar of a motorcycle downshifting sharply reached their ears from the street. "Well," said Steve, "sounds like John hasn't missed the party after all." He stood up. "Anyone need a refill before he comes in?"

John pulled up a chair and took the mug of coffee Steve held out for him. "Thanks, Steve. I'm still a bit groggy. Early start."

"How's your parishioner?" asked Will.

"She was in good spirits before they came to prep her for surgery. I think she's going to be OK. The doctor sounded confident it would end up being fairly routine."

"I guess it's routine if you're the one holding the scalpel," said Sam. "Doesn't feel too routine when you're on the sharp end."

"No doubt, Sam! Well, what have I missed? Have you been talking about the First Word?" He looked at Steve. "Or did you find something other than God to talk about?"

"I'll have you know, preacher, that your little flock here is quite capable of talking about God with or without you."

"Never doubted it, my friend. But I thought we were *your* flock?"

John ducked as Steve tried to swat him with the paper. "OK, OK, I surrender."

Steve sat back and smoothed out his paper. "Funnily enough, Rick was just talking about that." He spent a few minutes summarizing their conversation for John. He looked around the table. "Did I miss anything?"

"Sounded good to me," said Jenny. She turned to John. "So now it's your turn. What have you been thinking about the First Word?"

"All kinds of things. Some of which it sounds like you've already discussed. Mostly I've been thinking about the question Ellie left me with last week."

"Which was . . ." said Ellie.

"Who is the God you find in the Bible?"

"Oh yeah, right. Got the answer?"

"Well, I don't know about *the* answer! I started with this Word. When God speaks to those slaves, how did God identify himself?"

"As the God who brought them out of slavery," said Ellie.

"Right. But why that? Why not, 'I am the Creator of all that there is'? Or 'I am the Lord of heaven and earth'? Or even, 'I am the God of your ancestors Abraham, Isaac and Jacob'? Why, 'I am the LORD your God, who brought you out of the house of slavery'?"

"Er, because that's what he just did?" asked Ellie.

"But God is also the Creator. *And* the God of their ancestors. Yet God chooses *this* way to identify himself. Why?"

"Because," said Yasmina, slowly drawing out the words, "that was how God *wanted* to be remembered? As the God who frees slaves?"

"Yes! At least that's what I think. Because all the Words that follow—the Words we've spent the last nine weeks discussing—flow out of that First Word. This God was a freer of slaves. Now, that may not seem like a big deal to us today, but to make that claim in this country even just two hundred years ago would have been scandalous! We were still using the Bible to *justify* slavery back then. The institution that fueled our economy. An institution that had been an accepted part of life throughout the world for thousands of years."

Will spoke up, "But once a year, on the Feast of Passover, the descendants of those slaves in Egypt reminded each other that their God was a freer of slaves. One people kept those words alive in a world where slavery was the norm for thousands of years."

"Exactly," said John. "And the God who freed those particular slaves gave them the other Nine Words to structure their common life, so that they could be a witness to a completely different way of living that *didn't* oppress the weak and powerless, that ensured that everyone's needs were met. To become a society where everyone flourished. And not just people—but also the land, and all other living creatures. To be a people who sought the common good in all that they did. To offer a very different story than the one other societies told—that the gods ordained the few at the top with the power and the wealth to subject everyone else to their will, putting them in chains if necessary."

"That's all well and good," said Steve, "but they never did it, right? And as you just reminded us, two hundred years ago there were plenty of churches in the South preaching about how God had ordained certain kinds of people to be slaves. Seems like there haven't been too many people living out this alternative story of yours. They've just been supporting the status quo."

John shook his head. "I'm sad to say you're right, Steve."

"Maybe," said Sarah, "that's why God told them to celebrate the Passover every year. So at least once a year they'd be reminded about what God had done for them—and what they ought to do for others."

"Yeah," pressed Steve, "but don't you Christians do something like that every week when you take communion? And yet most church folk I know don't live too much different than the rest of us." He threw up his hands. "So what's the point? Isn't this all just a nice story that no one takes seriously, or finds it impossible to actually live out? I can't even live up to my own standards—let alone these Ten Words!"

"I think your cynical side is peeking out again, Steve," said Sarah.

"I know, I know." He turned to John. "Didn't you say something about 'ignorance is bliss' a while back? Well, I kinda wish I'd never started this whole conversation." He laughed bitterly. "I think I preferred it when I could just critique *other* people."

John grabbed a book out of his backpack. "Let me read you something, Steve. Because I'm not sure you have to be a cynical person to think it's impossible to keep these Ten Words." John thumbed through the pages and then read.

So if I can't be trusted to figure out what is best for myself and then do it, it becomes obvious that God's command is necessary.

But I need something more! For if I know the law but still can't keep it, and if the power of sin within me keeps sabotaging my best intentions, I obviously need help! I realize that I don't have what it takes. I can will it, but I can't do it. I decide to do good, but I don't really do it; I decide not to do bad, but then I do it

anyway. My decisions, such as they are, don't result in actions.
Something has gone wrong deep within me and gets the better of
me every time.

It happens so regularly that it's predictable. The moment I
decide to do good, sin is there to trip me up. I truly delight in
God's commands, but it's pretty obvious that not all of me joins in
that delight. Parts of me covertly rebel, and just when I least
expect it, they take charge.

I've tried everything and nothing helps. I'm at the end of my
rope. Is there no one who can do anything for me? Isn't that the
real question?[7]

"Who's that, then?" asked Steve. "Another one of your saints with
clay feet? I certainly get what he's saying, but I don't think I'd call
the problem sin. I think my problem is me. Anyway, who said that?"

"The apostle Paul. Who wrote an awful lot about the law in his
letters in the New Testament. And, as you just heard, said that even
though he loved the law, he couldn't keep it. Someone who reached
the end of his rope. Or," turning to Carlos, "hit bottom, as you'd
say. Someone who admitted he was powerless to live the life he
wanted to live."

"So, does he answer his own question?" said Steve. "I'm assuming
he does, as you preachers seem to be pretty good at doing that."

"Ouch." John plunged an imaginary knife into his chest, with a
mock grimace. Then his expression turned serious. "Yes, Paul answers his question. But it's not just Paul's question. It's my question.
It's your question, Steve. My guess is," he swept his arm around the
table, "it's all of our question. It's the problem of the gap."

"The gap?" said Ellie.

"The gap between the person I want to be and the person I am.
The gap between the things I want to do and what I actually do. The
gap between my words and my life."

"Oh. *That* gap."

"The Ten Words are like a two-edged sword. They show us how we're supposed to live. We feel the first cut when we realize how far we are from living that way. We feel the second cut when we try to actually keep the Words—to live that life—only to find that we can't. Those slaves had been set free from the brutal tyranny of the Pharaohs—from a life of slavery. That's the story of the exodus. But they needed a second exodus—to be set free from the tyranny of sin, from the bondage of self, which would prevent them from keeping the Ten Words."

"So," turning to Steve, "Paul answers his own question by saying this." He picked up the Bible again. "It's a pretty long answer."

"I imagine it is," said Steve. "It's a pretty big question."

"Indeed it is," said John. Then he read,

Is there no one who can do anything for me? Isn't that the real question?

The answer, thank God, is that Jesus Christ can and does. He acted to set things right in this life of contradictions where I want to serve God with all my heart and mind, but am pulled by the influence of sin to do something totally different.

With the arrival of Jesus, the Messiah, that fateful dilemma is resolved. Those who enter into Christ's being-here-for-us no longer have to live under a continuous, low-lying black cloud. A new power is in operation. The Spirit of life in Christ, like a strong wind, has magnificently cleared the air, freeing you from a fated lifetime of brutal tyranny at the hands of sin and death.

John leaned forward as he kept reading.

God went for the jugular when he sent his own Son. He didn't deal with the problem as something remote and unimportant. In his Son, Jesus, he personally took on the human condition, entered the disordered mess of struggling humanity in order to set it right once and for all. The law code, weakened as it always was by fractured human nature, could never have done that.

The law always ended up being used as a Band-Aid on sin instead of a deep healing of it. And now what the law code asked for but we couldn't deliver is accomplished as we, instead of redoubling our own efforts, simply embrace what the Spirit is doing in us.

Those who think they can do it on their own end up obsessed with measuring their own moral muscle but never get around to exercising it in real life. Those who trust God's action in them find that God's Spirit is in them—living and breathing God! Obsession with self in these matters is a dead end; attention to God leads us into the open, into a spacious, free life. . . .

But if God himself has taken up residence in your life, you can hardly be thinking more of yourself than of him. . . . But for you who welcome [Christ], in whom he dwells—even though you still experience all the limitations of sin—you yourself experience life on God's terms. It stands to reason, doesn't it, that if the alive-and-present God who raised Jesus from the dead moves into your life, he'll do the same thing in you that he did in Jesus, bringing you alive to himself? When God lives and breathes in you (and he does, as surely as he did in Jesus), you are delivered from that dead life. With his Spirit living in you, your body will be as alive as Christ's!

So don't you see that we don't owe this old do-it-yourself life one red cent. There's nothing in it for us, nothing at all. The best thing to do is give it a decent burial and get on with your new life. God's Spirit beckons. There are things to do and places to go!

This resurrection life you received from God is not a timid, grave-tending life. It's adventurously expectant, greeting God with a childlike "What's next, Papa?"[8]

No one seemed willing to break the silence that greeted the end of John's reading. He put his Bible back down on the table and then looked at each person in turn before speaking again. "That last part literally says this: 'For you have not received a spirit of slavery leading to fear again, but you have received a spirit of adoption as children, by which we cry out, 'Abba!' 'Papa!'"[9] He reached for his mug and took a swig.

"When God freed those slaves from bondage in Egypt, I really *don't* think it was to give them a bunch of rules they had no way of keeping. That could only lead to fear of God—making God just like Pharaoh. I believe these Ten Words were given to form a people who could live free of fear. Not by keeping rules out of fear of punishment, but by adopting this new way of life out of gratitude for what God had done for them."

"But," said Jenny, "they *didn't* keep them! How could they? You've just read Paul admitting *he* couldn't do it. And we've all admitted we can't. So even if they're not rules, they're still impossible to live by. So what was the point of it all?"

John leaned forward. "I think the point is the words of Paul that I just read. The Ten Words show us how we're supposed to live, and then show us that we can't do it! Because even those of us who want to live that way discover that we can't. There's this power inside us—call it sin or selfishness or whatever you like—that keeps us from living up to our *own* standards, let alone God's, right? So we live with fear and insecurity and suspicion and pain, and we can't make enough money, or buy enough stuff, or do enough drugs, or drink enough booze, or have enough sex, or go to church enough, or whatever else we do to try and mask the reality of our lives. The reality that we are indeed powerless to live the life we want. *And* that one day no matter what we do, we will die. So even that rich young man who had everything recognized that wasn't enough." John ran his fingers through his hair. "I've said it before, and I know it sounds cheesy, but it wasn't enough to just get those slaves out of Egypt. God had to get Egypt out of them."

Will leaned forward. "A second exodus, like you said. The first from slavery in Egypt. The second from slavery to sin and death. That's what Paul was describing in the passage John read." He looked around the table. "This story we've been discussing for the past ten weeks is about God taking a bunch of slaves and giving them a new identity through relationship with him. And that story line unfolded over centuries, with each generation failing to live into that identity. Until the story reached its climax in Jesus, when God became one of us, showing us the kind of life that the Ten Words were supposed to produce in us. A way of living that was so threatening to those invested in other stories—stories of power, whether it be political, economic or religious, the stories of Egypt, of Rome, even of Israel under King Solomon—that those powers conspired to kill Jesus. Because the ultimate power of those other stories is the power to kill." Will paused. "But when God raised Jesus from death, the bonds of sin and death were finally and deci- sively broken. The last weapon of the tyrant—death—was defeated."

"And," said Sam, "when the Holy Spirit came, we got the power to do what Jesus told us to do. Which was to love God and love our neighbors. To keep the Ten Words." His shoulders slumped. "So why do I find it so hard to do that?"

Jenny leaned her head on his shoulder. "Oh, I don't know about that, Sam. You've done a pretty good job of loving me." With her head still resting on Sam's shoulder, she looked around the table. "You all have." A tear ran down her cheek. "If you'd have told me a couple of months ago that I would have told my darkest secrets to a bunch of strangers at some kind of Bible study, I'd have laughed in your face. But that's what's happened. And some of that weight that's been pressing on my chest for so long has lifted. I don't ex- actly know why, but this has become a safe place for me. *You've* become a safe place for me. And that's something I've been looking for, for a long time."

She turned toward John. "You've consistently told us that these Ten Words are supposed to set us free. Free from all the stuff that keeps us bound up—inside and out. Well that's happened for me in this group. All that shame and anger and resentment I've been carrying around? It doesn't feel so heavy on me all the time like it has for years." She reached for Sarah's hand. "You've been so kind and helped me so much. You all have." She eased off of Sam's shoulder, sat up and turned back to John. "But I don't know about all this Jesus stuff. I really liked what you read—it made sense. Well, most of it! I guess I just don't believe it. So here's my question for you. If Jesus is the one who does the setting free, but I don't believe he, you know, is still around, how come I feel some of that freedom?"

John stroked his beard. "That's a *great* question, Jenny." He turned to Rick. "I imagine a bunch of your friends in AA could ask the same question, right?"

"Absolutely. I have friends who don't believe in any kind of personal God, and who have years of sobriety. The group is their Higher Power."

"So," asked Jenny, "is that my experience, then? Our group here is like God for me?"

"I don't know about that," said Rick. "But I believe that God shows up whether we recognize him or not."

"'The kingdom of God is in your midst,'" said Sam. He turned to Jenny. "Here's what I think. If God chose to identify himself as the God who sets slaves free, then I reckon whenever people get set free from anything, God has a hand in it somehow. Whether he gets the credit for it or not. But what I reckon God wants most is for all of us to live with freedom all the time. Both in here," tapping his chest, "and out there," gesturing toward the window. "And all I know is that I can't do that on my own. I need God.

"And," Sam patted Jenny's hand gently, "I need you." He turned to the group. "I can only speak for myself, but I tell you, after nine weeks of thinking about all the ways I *don't* keep the Ten Words, to hear that there's a God who does it for us? Well, that's good news for this old Baptist."

He turned to Steve. "I reckon you're right after all. There's not much point carving them in stone and hanging them in courthouses. Or getting them tattooed on our foreheads, as I think I said a while back. No, I reckon they have to be written in here," tapping his chest again, "if we're going to have the life I think we were made for. All of us, together."

Will reached for a Bible. "That's what the prophet Jeremiah said, Sam."

> *"This is the covenant which I will make with the house of Israel after those days," declares the* Lord, *"I will put My law within them and on their heart I will write it; and I will be their God, and they shall be My people."10*

"Amen to that," said Sam.

"Amen, indeed," said John. He looked at his watch. "Well, as much as I hate to bring this to an end, it's about that time. I can't thank you all enough for these past ten weeks. As helpful as it's been for my sermon preparation, the real gift has been getting to know you. To hear just a little bit of your stories." His voice cracked. "It's been really beautiful. You're all beautiful." He threw an arm around Steve and planted a kiss on the top of his head. "Even you, Steve."

"Amen to that!" Sarah hollered out, and the group burst into grateful laughter. As it subsided, Ellie spoke up. "So is this it? Are we done? 'Cause I don't want to be done."

"I don't know, Ellie," said John. "I do finish up the series on Sunday."

"But this hasn't just been about your sermons, right? Or my lattes. This has been about, I don't know, about *us*. And I don't want *us* to be over."

John looked around the table. "Well, I'm usually in here on Mondays anyway, so if anyone does want to come back next week . . ."

"I'm in!" said Ellie. She linked an arm through Yasmina's. "I mean, we're in, right?"

"Sure. Although if I ask my mom to keep bringing us, she'll want to come in. Maybe that'll be OK."

Rick put an arm around Carlos's shoulders. "We'll be here."

Sarah looked at Jenny. "I'm in."

"Me too," said Jenny.

"I've got nothing but time," said Sam. "I'll be here."

"As will I," said Will.

John turned to Steve and raised a questioning eyebrow. "Oh, you know me," Steve responded. "I'm always here. Me and my paper!"

"All right," said John, with a broad smile. "I guess I'll see you all next week!"

Carlos leaned forward. "Before we go, could we, I don't know, pray or something. I feel like I've still got a long way to go when it comes to this freedom stuff."

John hesitated, casting a quick glance at Steve.

Steve grabbed Carlos's hand. "Don't you say a prayer at the end of your AA meetings?"

"Yeah. We do." As the group leaned forward and reached for their neighbor's hands, Carlos bowed his head. "Whose father? Our Father, who art in heaven, hallowed be Thy name . . ."

For Discussion

1. What role, if any, have the Ten Commandments played in your life? Why?

2. Why is talking about matters of religion so tricky?

3. What's the most diverse group of people you've had a significant discussion with? How did you come to be part of that group?

4. Which character in the book did you identify with the most? Why?

5. Which character did you identify with the least? Why?

6. Which chapter grabbed you the most? Why?

7. Which chapter was the hardest for you to read? Why?

8. Which of the Ten Words would you feel least comfortable discussing in a group like the one in the book? Why?

9. Which Word do you think would have the greatest impact on our society if people began to keep it? Why?

10. Which Word do you think people are most resistant to keeping? Why?

11. Which practice mentioned in the book would you be most likely to take on? Why?

12. Which practice would you be least likely to take on? Why?

13. After reading this book, has the way you view the Ten Commandments changed? If so, how?

Notes

THE TEN COMMANDMENTS—WHO CARES?

[1]Bill Estep, "Ten Commandments Fight Is Costly for Kentucky Counties," *Lexington Herald-Leader*, May 19, 2011, www.mcclatchydc.com/2011/05 /19/114428/ten-commandments-battle-is-costly.html#.UYgQGKLCaSo.

[2]See "Better Know a District," *Colbert Report*, June 14, 2006, www.colbert nation.com/the-colbert-report-videos/70809/june-14-2006/exclusive ---georgia-s-8th.

[3]Steve Turner, "Wait," *Up to Date* (London: Hodder & Stoughton, 1983), p. 119.

[4]I think I heard N. T. Wright use this analogy.

[5]John 1:17 NIV.

[6]Matthew 5:17-20 *The Message*.

[7]Exodus 19:4-6 *The Message*.

[8]Exodus 3:7-8 *The Message*.

[9]Herbert McCabe, cited in Stanley M. Hauerwas and William H. Willimon, *The Truth About God* (Nashville: Abingdon Press,1999), p. 118.

[10]Exodus 34:28.

[11]Mark 12:28-31.

[12]Exodus 20:2 *The Message*.

[13]An approach taken by J. John, *Ten: Living the Commandments in the 21st Century* (Eastbourne, UK: Kingsway, 2000).

CHAPTER 1: FROM ENVY TO CONTENTMENT

[1]Exodus 20:17 *The Message*.

[2]*Alcoholics Anonymous*, 4th ed. (New York: Alcoholics Anonymous, 2001), p. 64.

[3]J. Ellsworth Kalas, *The Ten Commandments from the Back Side* (Nashville: Abingdon Press, 1998), p. 105.

[4]Genesis 3:6. The words for "delight" (*ta'awa*) and "desire" (*nehmad*) in this verse are the only other place in Scripture where words from the two root words for desire in Deuteronomy 5:21 are to be found. (Patrick D. Miller, *The Ten Commandments* [Louisville, KY: John Knox Press, 2010], p. 400).

[5]Genesis 4:3-5.

[6]Genesis 4:7.

[7]Genesis 4:9.

[8]David Hazony, *The Ten Commandments* (New York: Scribner, 2010), p. 245.

[9]C. S. Lewis, *Mere Christianity* (London: Fontana, 1955), p. 107.

[10]Zygmunt Bauman, "The London Riots—On Consumerism Coming Home to Roost," *Social Europe Journal*, September 8, 2011, www.social-europe .eu/2011/08/the-london-riots-on-consumerism-coming-home-to-roost.

[11]Kalas, *Ten Commandments*, p. 104.

[12]*Alcoholics Anonymous*, p. 62.

[13]Attributed to Carrie Fisher.

[14]See Clive Hamilton, *Growth Fetish* (Crow's Nest, Australia: Allen & Unwin, 2003).

[15]Paraphrase of Miller, *Ten Commandments*, pp. 413-14.

[16]James 4:1-2 NRSV.

CHAPTER 2: FROM DECEPTION TO TRUTH TELLING

[1]Exodus 20:16 *The Message*.

[2]*The Week*, February 25, 2011.

[3]If you're interested in learning more about agribusiness, a good place to start is the 2008 documentary "Food, Inc.," directed by Robert Kenner, Magnolia Pictures.

[4]Earl Wilson, quoted in J. John, *Ten: Living the Ten Commandments in the 21st Century* (Eastbourne, UK: Kingsway, 2000), p. 65.

[5]This definition of gossip may help explain why about 25 percent of Americans still believe that President Obama is not a natural-born citizen of the United States. And why many of my Facebook friends were so quick to repost the claim that Pat Robertson told a man to divorce his wife who was suffering with Alzheimer's disease and marry another woman, without taking the time to watch the entire segment of the show, which

casts his comments in a very different light than does the brief version that went viral.

[6]J. Ellsworth Kalas, *The Ten Commandments from the Back Side* (Nashville: Abingdon Press, 1998), p. 92.

[7]David Hazony, *The Ten Commandments* (New York: Scribner, 2010), p. 214.

[8]Ibid., p. 216.

[9]John, *Ten*, p. 65.

[10]Patrick D. Miller, *The Ten Commandments* (Louisville, KY: John Knox Press, 2010), p. 345.

[11]New York Times/CBS News poll, *New York Times*, October 26, 2011.

[12]Genesis 3:1.

[13]Revelation 12:9.

[14]Genesis 3:10.

[15]Genesis 3:11.

[16]Joan Chittister, *The Ten Commandments: Laws of the Heart* (Maryknoll, NY: Orbis Books, 2006), p. 102.

[17]Abraham Lincoln, quoted in John, *Ten*, p. 64.

[18]John 1:1 NIV, John 1:14 *The Message*.

[19]Chittister, *Ten Commandments*, p. 109.

[20]*Alcoholics Anonymous*, 4th ed. (New York: Alcoholics Anonymous, 2001), p. 58.

[21]Ibid., p. 60.

[22]Peter Rollins, *How (Not) to Speak of God* (Brewster, MA: Paraclete Press, 2006).

[23]Mark 3:1-6.

CHAPTER 3: FROM THEFT TO GENEROSITY

[1]Exodus 20:15 *The Message*.

[2]"CPG Sec. 510.500 Green Coffee Beans—Adulteration with Insects; Mold," U.S. Food and Drug Administration, www.fda.gov/ICECI/ComplianceManuals/CompliancePolicyGuidanceManual/ucm074432.htm.

[3]Rudyard Kipling, quoted in Stanley Hauerwas and William Willimon, *The Truth About God* (Nashville: Abingdon Press, 1999), p. 109.

[4]Matthew 6:24; Luke 16:13.

[5]Psalm 24:1.

[6]Deuteronomy 14:22-29. The preacher is Tony Campolo, and you can find this story in his book *The Kingdom of God Is a Party* (Dallas: Word, 1990), pp. 25-28.

[7]Basil the Great, quoted in J. Ellsworth Kalas, *The Ten Commandments from the Back Side* (Nashville: Abingdon Press, 1998), p. 84.

[8]This story is based on something that happened at Mercy Street, the church I copastored in Houston, Texas.

[9]Ephesians 4:28.

[10]On April 24, 2013, a garment factory in Dhaka, Bangladesh, collapsed, leaving more than 1,100 people dead.

[11]Visit the Slavery Footprint website at slaveryfootprint.org to get an idea of how many slaves you "own."

[12]David Hazony, *The Ten Commandments* (New York: Scribner, 2010), p. 198.

[13]See Patrick D. Miller, *The Ten Commandments* (Louisville: John Knox Press, 2010), p. 327.

[14]Ibid., p. 319.

[15]Genesis 37:26-27.

[16]Exodus 22:1-15.

[17]For instance, Exodus 22:25-27 and Deuteronomy 24:10–25:4. See also James 5:1-6.

[18]"Health Care Fraud," http://www.veriskhealth.com/resources/blog/health-care-fraud-four-keys-addressing-400-billion-problem.

CHAPTER 4: FROM BETRAYAL TO FIDELITY

[1]David Hazony, *The Ten Commandments* (New York: Scribner, 2010), p. 166.

[2]1 Kings 11:3.

[3]2 Samuel 11.

[4]Patrick D. Miller, *The Ten Commandments* (Louisville, KY: Westminster John Knox Press, 2009), p. 274.

[5]Proverbs 7:17-19 NIV.

[6]Proverbs 30:20 NIV.

[7]Jonathan Wilson-Hartgrove addresses the challenges our mobile culture presents in *The Wisdom of Stability* (Brewster, MA: Paraclete Press, 2010).

[8]Elaine Storkey, quoted in J. John, *Ten: Living the Ten Commandments in the Twenty-First Century* (Eastbourne, UK: Kingsway, 2000), p. 108.

[9]See, for instance, the book of Hosea.

[10]Joan Chittister, *The Ten Commandments: Laws of the Heart* (Maryknoll, NY: Orbis Books, 2006), p. 80.

[11]J. Ellsworth Kalas, *The Ten Commandments from the Back Side* (Nashville: Abingdon Press, 1998), pp. 79-80.

[12]Matthew 5:27-28 NIV.

[13]John 8:1-11 NIV.

[14]Attributed to G. K. Chesterton.

[15]Chittister, *Ten Commandments*, pp. 83-84.

Chapter 5: From Violence to Peace

[1]Twelve people were shot dead and fifty-eight wounded by gunman James Holmes at the midnight premier of *The Dark Knight Rises* in a movie theatre in Aurora, Colorado, on Friday, July 20, 2012.

[2]Joan Chittister, *The Ten Commandments* (Maryknoll, NY: Orbis Books, 2006) p. 70.

[3]*Lexington Herald Leader*, July 23, 2012.

[4]Over 150 soldiers took their own lives in the first six months of 2012, compared with 120 military fatalities in Afghanistan (*The Week*, June 22, 2012).

[5]William P. Mahedy, quoted in Chris Hedges, *Losing Moses on the Freeway* (New York: Free Press, 2005), p. 110.

[6]Hedges, *Losing Moses*, p. 108.

[7]Patrick D. Miller, *The Ten Commandments* (Louisville, KY: Westminster John Knox Press, 2009), p. 261.

[8]Stanley M. Hauerwas and William H. Willimon, *The Truth About God* (Nashville: Abingdon Press, 1999), p. 80.

[9]Miller, *Ten Commandments*, p. 227.

[10]1 Kings 21.

[11]Matthew 5:21-22, adapted from NASB.

[12]Karl Barth, quoted in Miller, *Ten Commandments*, p. 250.

[13]Leviticus 19:17-18, adapted from NASB.

[14]Genesis 9:6.

[15]Genesis 6:13.

[16]Isaiah 65:25 NIV.

[17]Chittister, *Ten Commandments*, p. 68.

[18]Miller, *Ten Commandments*, p. 265.

[19]For more, see Barry Estabrook, *Tomatoland: How Modern Industrial Agriculture Destroyed Our Most Alluring Fruit* (Kansas City: Andrews McMeel, 2011).

[20]1 John 3:15-18, adapted from NASB.

[21]Matthew 5:43-45.

[22]Romans 12:20-21.

CHAPTER 6: FROM OBLIGATION TO RESPECT

[1]U2, "Sometimes You Can't Make It on Your Own," *How to Dismantle an Atomic Bomb*, 2004.

[2]*Lexington Herald Leader*, August 6, 2012.

[3]Exodus 20:12.

[4]Ephesians 6:1.

[5]Ezekiel 22:7-8.

[6]See Mark 7:1-13.

[7]Luke 11:46, my paraphrase.

[8]Ephesians 6:2-4.

[9]Exodus 21:15, 17 NRSV.

[10]Colossians 3:21.

[11]Matthew 4:21-22.

[12]Mark 3:21.

[13]Mark 3:33-35.

[14]Luke 14:26.

[15]John 19:26-27.

[16]Malachi 4:6.

CHAPTER 7: FROM STRIVING TO REST

[1]Exodus 20:8-11.

[2]See J. John, *Ten: Living the Ten Commandments in the Twenty-First Century* (Eastbourne, UK: Kingsway, 2000), pp. 186-87.

[3]"Every Day Is 'Labor' Day," *Lexington Herald-Leader*, September 3, 2012.

[4]See Matthew Sleeth, *24/6* (Carol Stream, IL: Tyndale House, 2012), p. 85.

[5]Deuteronomy 5:15.

[6]Exodus 31:13-16.

[7]See Numbers 15:32-36.

[8]Deuteronomy 5:14.

[9]Exodus 23:10-11.

[10]John C. Holbert, *The Great Texts: The Ten Commandments* (Nashville: Abingdon Press, 2002), p. 55.

[11]See Leviticus 25. For more on this see Ched Myers, *The Biblical Vision of Sabbath Economics* (Washington, DC: Tell the Word Press, 2001).

[12]2 Chronicles 36:21.

[13]Nehemiah 10:31.

[14]Luke 4:18-19.

[15]Deuteronomy 15:1.

[16]See, for instance, Luke 7:48.

[17]See Luke 13:10-17.

[18]Mark 2:27, author's paraphrase.

[19]Ched Myers is one of the leading proponents of sabbath economics. For more, see his website chedmyers.org, and also the Sabbath Economics Collaborative website, sabbatheconomics.org.

CHAPTER 8: FROM BLASPHEMY TO REVERENCE

[1]Exodus 20:7.

[2]Dave Wilkie, *Coffee with Jesus* (Downers Grove, IL: InterVarsity Press, 2013).

[3]Joan Chittister, *The Ten Commandments: Laws of the Heart* (Maryknoll, NY: Orbis Books, 2006), p. 34.

[4]Deuteronomy 5:11.

[5]Exodus 20:2.

[6]Exodus 3:13-14.

[7]Rabbi Lynn Gottlieb, in "Open the Gates of Justice," www.justiceathyatt .org/openthegates/openthegatesofjustice.pdf.

[8]Maltbie D. Babcock, "This Is My Father's World," 1901.

[9]Psalm 103:12.

[10]The story of the tailor is told in Chittister, *Ten Commandments*, p. 33.

[11]See Matthew 5:33-37. See also James 5:12.

[12]Matthew 21:31 NIV.

CHAPTER 9: FROM IDOLATRY TO WORSHIP

[1]Exodus 20:3-6.

[2]Exodus 20:2.

[3]Exodus 24:3-4.

[4]Exodus 24:7-8.

[5]Exodus 32:1-4.

[6]For more on this see Jeffrey Reiman and Paul Leighton, *The Rich Get Richer and the Poor Get Prison*, 9th ed. (Boston: Allyn & Bacon, 2010).

[7]Exodus 32:6.

[8]Exodus 32:11-14.

[9]Exodus 32:24.

[10]John C. Holbert, *The Great Texts: The Ten Commandments* (Nashville: Abingdon Press, 2002), p. 30.

[11]*Alcoholics Anonymous*, 4th ed. (New York: Alcoholics Anonymous, 2001), p. 62.

[12]Ibid.

[13]Matthew 16:24-25 KJV.

[14]Exodus 20:23.

[15]Matthew 6:24 NKJV.

[16]David Hazony, *Ten Commandments* (New York: Scribner, 2010), p. 58.

[17]Micah 4:1-4.

[18]Patrick D. Miller, *The Ten Commandments* (Louisville, KY: Westminster John Knox Press, 2010), p. 57.

CHAPTER 10: GOD

[1]These are taken from my local paper, the *Lexington Herald Leader*, on the day I began to write this last chapter, December 19, 2012.

[2]Philippians 2:5-8.

[3]Hebrews 4:15.

[4]See Luke 18:18-30.

[5]Luke 8:2-3.

[6]Galatians 2:20.

[7]Romans 7:16-24 *The Message*.

[8]Romans 7:24–8:6, 9-16 *The Message*.

[9]Romans 8:15, adapted from NASB.

[10]Jeremiah 31:33.

Bibliography

Chittister, Joan. *The Ten Commandments: Laws of the Heart.* Maryknoll, NY: Orbis Books, 2006.

Hauerwas, Stanley, and Will Willimon. *The Truth About God: The Ten Commandments in Christian Life.* Nashville: Abingdon Press, 1999.

Hazony, David. *The Ten Commandments: How Our Most Ancient Moral Text Can Renew Modern Life.* New York: Scribner, 2010.

Hedges, Christopher. *Losing Moses on the Freeway: The 10 Commandments in America.* New York: Free Press, 2005.

Holbert, John C. *The Great Texts: The Ten Commandments.* Nashville: Abingdon Press, 2002.

John, J. *Ten: Living the Ten Commandments in the 21st Century.* Eastbourne, UK: Kingsway, 2000.

Kalas, J. Ellsworth. *The Ten Commandments from the Back Side.* Nashville: Abingdon Press, 1998.

Miller, Patrick D. *The Ten Commandments.* Interpretation. Louisville, KY: John Knox Press, 2010.

Robertson, Anne. *God's Top 10: Blowing the Lid off the Commandments.* Harrisburg, PA: Morehouse, 2006.

About the Author

Originally hailing from Norwich, England, Sean Gladding has made his home in the United States for the last two decades, where he has served as a pastor with college students, in church plants and as part of the new monasticism. He enjoys growing food, friendships and facial hair.

THE STORY OF GOD, THE STORY OF US

Travel with Sean Gladding between the lines of the Scriptures to listen in on the conversations of people wrestling with the Story of God for the first time. Whether sitting around a campfire in Babylon, reclining at table in Asia Minor or huddled together by candlelight in Rome, you'll encounter a tale that is at once familiar and surprising.

THE STORY OF GOD, THE STORY OF US (VIDEO SERIES)

Six discussion-starting videos exploring major themes in the Bible, including the metanarrative of Scripture, creation, covenant, freedom, descent and reconciliation. Also includes a discussion guide, making these videos a powerful resource for group use.